WITCH & WIZARD

THE KISS

JAMES PATTERSON is one of the best-known and biggest-selling writers of all time. He is the author of the Maximum Ride, Witch & Wizard, Daniel X and Middle School novels. This is as well as writing three of the top detective series around – the Alex Cross, Women's Murder Club and Michael Bennett novels – and many other number one bestsellers including romance novels and stand-alone thrillers. He lives in Florida with his wife and son.

James was inspired by his son, who was a reluctant reader, to write books specifically for young readers. James is a founding partner of Booktrust's Children's Reading Fund in the UK. In 2010, James Patterson was voted Author of the Year at the Children's Choice Book Awards in New York.

WITCH & WIZARD
THE KISS

JAMES PATTERSON
AND JILL DEMBOWSKI

Published by Young Arrow, 2013

2 4 6 8 10 9 7 5 3 1

First published in Great Britain in 2013 by
Young Arrow
Random House, 20 Vauxhall Bridge Road,
London SW1V 2SA

www.randomhouse.co.uk

Addresses for companies within The Random House Group Limited can be found at:
www.randomhouse.co.uk/offices.htm

The Random House Group Limited Reg. No. 954009

A CIP catalogue record for this book
is available from the British Library

ISBN 9780099544166

The Random House Group Limited supports the Forest Stewardship Council® (FSC®), the leading international forest-certification organisation. Our books carrying the FSC label are printed on FSC®-certified paper. FSC is the only forest-certification scheme supported by the leading environmental organisations, including Greenpeace. Our paper procurement policy can be found at:
www.randomhouse.co.uk/environment

MIX
Paper from
responsible sources
FSC® C016897

Printed and bound in Great Britain by CPI (UK) Ltd, Croydon, CR0 4YY

For Adlai, with love and sparks
—J.D.

⚜ THE FIRST TRUTH ⚜

KNOW THE SELF.
ILLUSIONS TRICK THE EYES,
BUT NOT THE INNER EYE.

———

⚜ THE SECOND TRUTH ⚜

KNOW THE FAMILY.
TRUST IS NOT TRUTH;
IT IS BUT A FLICKERING FLAME.

———

⚜ THE THIRD TRUTH ⚜

KNOW LIGHT FROM DARK.
MAGIC IS NOT EQUAL TO RIGHTEOUSNESS.
A WIZARD MAY DESTROY OR SAVE.
A CITY HANGS IN THE BALANCE.

PROLOGUE

DESTINY'S RIDDLE

One

Wisty

I CAN'T BELIEVE what I'm witnessing.

You would think it was a riot if you saw us on TV.

Shouts cut through the crisp air. Bodies push and sway. Hands rip at flags and banners, and feet kick in surveillance screens. A great bonfire swallows up the splintered pieces of the destruction.

But no fists are raised, and this isn't a protest. I'm opening my lungs, but it's to join the ecstatic voices in *celebration*: The One Who Is The One, the Overworld's violent dictator, is dead, and the New Order regime has fallen.

We are free.

Free to listen to music—and it's pumping through the loudspeakers.

Free to read books. We're clutching them to our chests.

Free to believe what we want and to say what we feel. Even free to walk the streets without being arrested.

Excitement fizzes through my whole being, and every

3

nerve stands on end as the crowd moves as one toward a vast stage in the center of the capital's square for the ceremony marking the end of the New Order's totalitarian regime and the return to a peaceful democracy. I'm grinning in the middle of the sea of people, and I pull my tangled hair back from my face as I jostle for a view.

A man in a smart gray suit takes the stage and taps the microphone. He's doughy and stern-faced, with his white hair parted severely to the side, and I recognize him as General Matthias Bloom, one of the last holdouts against the New Order in the outer suburbs.

A hush falls as thousands upon thousands of eager eyes gaze up at him.

"My dear, dear friends, today is a new beginning, a beautiful beginning for all of us. And to mark that birth," his voice booms, "I introduce to you now...your new Council!"

I'm tingly all over, almost like the electricity I feel when my magic is strong, or the awesome rush of adrenaline when I'm performing onstage. It's like the air itself is buzzing with hope.

General Bloom starts to read off the names of seventeen men and women and seventeen kids our age: the group chosen to restore this place to the way it once was, to the City we loved before The One Who Is The One brutally enforced the madness of his New Order.

"Wisteria Rose Allgood," he reads, and I can't help it—

tears are streaming down my cheeks as I mount the stone steps, my name echoing through the loudspeakers.

My brother, Whit, is right by my side—and this is why I love him so much—Whit has tears in his eyes, too, and he's not ashamed. As divided as our City once was, with neighbor killing neighbor and only suspicion to feed us when food was scarce, it's incredible to be part of the leadership that will bring us back together for something else—something *good*.

As I stand on that stage, representing all these united voices, the rebel in me can't resist. I pull a scrap of a banner from my shoulder bag. I spread the crimson fabric open with two arms above my head, and the crowd starts to jeer and yell as the sign of the New Order billows in the wind.

Red means the New Order. Red means the Blood Plague. Red means death.

My brother elbows me—this whole ceremony has been planned out minute by minute, and I'm definitely straying way off script—but there's a method to my madness, and he knows it.

I concentrate on the buildup of heat in my chest, and flames lick out from my fingertips and climb up the banner, enveloping it in seconds.

The crowd is in a frenzy of cheers and shouts, and I'm up here grinning giddily. By seeing that shock of red blackening to ash, we know that even though we can never get back the things we lost, we have overcome so, so much. And with hands clasped, hearts pounding, and a few deep breaths, we can still do this—we can mold this society into something great.

I'm a part of it, and you're a part of it.

It's just the beginning.

TWO

Whit

DUSK IS FALLING, and we're singing. My heart seems to be lodged way up in my throat.

Having taken our vows, we thirty-four Council members stand side by side in a circle on the stage. We wear different badges of honor or war or age, but standing here together, we're equals.

We sing the old songs today, songs we learned from our parents. Songs I sang with the Neederman family last year on the Holiday, not knowing whether my sister would live or die from the plague. As our voices waver on the final note, General Bloom takes the stage again.

"Today, we sing for new beginnings." Applause echoes across the square. "But we sing to remember our history as well, and an older order!" He holds a hefty, yellowed tome above his head, and an audible gasp can be heard from the crowd.

I'm in awe, like everyone else. *The Book of Truths.* The

7

most sacred text in the Overworld. Destiny's riddle. The book that has defined our lives. We all grew up revering its words, but few of us have seen it, and actually touching its dusty pages seems unthinkable.

But because Matthias Bloom salvaged the book from the embers while so many great texts burned, he is its new Keeper.

At her cue, Janine strides to the podium. I'd be sweating bullets if I had to actually speak today, but she's poised and confident, and gives the crowd a long, measured look. She's in her standard combat boots. Her hair is as wild as ever, and she wears no makeup. But as usual, she's *luminous*.

"*The Book of Truths* prophesized that only a sister and a brother, a witch and a wizard, could defeat The One Who Is The One," Janine says into the microphone, her voice clear and strong. "It told of their power, of a sky filled with flames." At the mention of my sister's Gift of fire, the square erupts in cheers. "Among many things we celebrate today, we pay tribute to their strength and courage that led to The One's ultimate downfall."

Now the cheers crescendo, but Janine's not finished. "But never forget, we are all brothers and sisters. I know the fire of life, love, and leadership is burning not just in Wisty Allgood, but in each one of us."

No one cheers that line more than my sister. Wisty hoots her agreement, rebel-style, and I grin. Janine was just supposed to introduce Wisty and me, but give her a platform and some willing ears, and she'll tell you what's what every time. She's a great speaker—articulate, endearing, whip-smart—and the crowd is eating up her every word.

So am I.

"We all have equal power and responsibility to make this City great," Janine continues. "Because that fire inside us is hotter than any magic, stronger than any spell. It's the spark of change and the slow burn of new hope!" She looks out over the transfixed faces, satisfied. "And now, my friends, without further ado, I give you your heroes... Whit and Wisty Allgood!"

We step forward, and the crowd pulses and chants both of our names, but I know it's Wisty's fire they've come to see today.

She doesn't disappoint. First, sparks shoot from her hands again, but as the fire grows, my sister becomes a human torch, the flames on her head even redder than her hair. Her feet singe a black spot onto the platform, and even her gaze smolders.

Plenty of people have seen her flame out, though, so this time she takes it to the max. She swoops her hand across the sky dramatically, and a splash of light follows her arc, exploding in a million dots of color. Her hands dance inside their flames, the shower of fireworks becoming brighter as the choreography becomes more complex. It's the most beautiful show any of us has ever seen, but there's something deeper going on here, too.

Wisty's magic painted across the sky says what Bloom did not: We have the freedom to write our own story now.

I gaze out across the crowded square flickering with vivid color underneath the fireworks. I take in the many faces, old and young, magic-making or not, from near and far. Color dances in their eyes, and their faces glow with a joy we'd forgotten could exist.

Except...

There's a small group at the very edge of the crowd, apart from the rest. As I squint my eyes, trying to make out their dark clothes—street rags or shredded New Order Youth uniforms—the tallest one drags a finger slowly across his neck. My own throat goes dry.

He's looking straight at me.

I glance at my sister to see if she noticed the ragged group on the outskirts. Wisty's still eating up the attention, waving to the people and grinning at our parents, who are levitating above the crowd to show their support.

When I look back to the threatening figure, there's no one there.

It's not over yet....

Is it?

BOOK ONE

THE FIRST TRUTH: YOU CAN'T TRICK THE INNER EYE

Chapter 1

Wisty

THE INAUGURAL CEREMONY earlier was superemotional and important, but *this* is what I have been waiting for: music pumping through my veins. The spotlight bathing me in its beam. My hair flying around me as I shred my guitar.

It's not *quite* like when I played for thousands at the underground Stockwood Music Festival last year—I mean, I have to admit, it was pretty fun to break the law—but rocking the open-mic stage at the Art Is Alive Gala is pretty thrilling.

For one thing, the gala involves all the stuff we love that's been banned for so long. There are tons of new sculptures, films, and writing exhibited here, and looking out from the stage, it's incredible to see all the paintings The One confiscated now restored and lining the walls. You'd never guess this gallery used to be a New Order armory.

I wipe the sweat from my brow and shout into the

microphone, "We can't forget: art is alive...*because The One is dead!*" The crowd roars.

I strum the final chord and step off the small stage to rejoin my group of friends—mostly kids from the former Resistance. As the lights dim for the next act, Sasha hands me some strong-smelling punch.

"Cheers to the rock star," he says.

I take a sip...and spit it out as the astringent burn takes over my nostrils.

"Sorry. Maybe it's my strong aversion to the color red, but not for me."

Whit nods. "Trust me, she's already pretty spazzy as is without alcohol." I scoff, and Whit breaks into a smile. "Hey, spazzy is a good quality in an entertainer. You were awesome up there, by the way."

I beam at him. "So is this DJ," I say as a new act starts up.

"Yeah. That's my friend Ross Lilienfield," Sasha says. "We used to record mixes together in his basement when we were kids. This is definitely his best stuff."

I nod appreciatively and start to move with the music, the energy making its way down to my hips and feet.

Janine nudges me. "Looks like you've got a fan."

Now I sense the eyes on me. Through the darkness, I can see a boy. His eyes lock on mine, and something in me feels as explosive as the fireworks I created earlier.

Janine squeezes my arm and giggles, but I can't even brush it off.

As the boy starts walking over, my pulse thuds faster with each step.

But then Byron appears at my side, demanding attention. As usual, he's in wooing mode. "You're a virtuoso, Wisty," he says, eyes shining with sincerity.

He's overdressed, but he still looks dapper—almost handsome—in his crisp white shirt and black tie. I'm sure some other girl would find the anxious wrinkle in his brow endearing. Unfortunately, he doesn't want some other girl.

"Thanks, Byron," I murmur, eyes scanning the crowd for the gorgeous stranger in the shadows. *Where did he go?*

"I mean, you were completely *on fire* up there!" he presses, sensing my attention drifting. Gotta give the kid credit. He never gives up.

"On fire? Really?" I look at him wryly, and Byron chuckles.

"I can understand your friend's mistake," a voice says in a low, playful tone into my ear.

When I turn around, my stomach does a triple flip. It's the beautiful stranger. Up close, he seems to tower over me, and his features are chiseled, strong. I'm so flustered I spill my unwanted punch.

He smiles and leans in even closer. "That smoky voice…" I inhale the leathery smell from his jacket and his aftershave, and feel dizzy. "Your flaming red hair…Everything about you *smolders*."

Yet it's *his* eyes that seem to blaze, even in the dim light.

They're simultaneously intense and bemused. I can't seem to look away.

I also can't seem to speak.

It's the most forward thing anyone has ever said to me. Normally I'd give a guy some kind of sharp verbal slap for coming on like that, but there's something different about this one. It's like he knows I'd suck up anything that comes out of that perfect mouth.

"Did you really come over here just to give her a cheap line?" Whit butts in before I can think of an answer.

"Whit!" Janine elbows him and pulls him away, but I'm totally mortified.

"Sorry about my brother...." I mutter lamely.

"No, it's okay." The boy laughs and runs a hand through the jet-black hair that stands up wildly from his forehead. "Actually, I came over to say I enjoyed your performance. A little punk, a little blues, and the vibrato technique and tonal variations on the power chords were stellar." He smiles at me, all easy confidence. "Even if you did rip off Smash's shredding style a little bit."

"Every guitar player rips off Smash a little bit!" I protest, but relent as he shrugs, amused. "You seem to know a lot about music," I observe, impressed.

"I know a lot about a lot of things."

"Oh, yeah?" I smirk. "What else do you know?" I'm usually pretty skeptical with boys and don't get into a flirt, but the banter with this guy comes easily somehow.

He bends down a bit so his face is next to mine, his chin brushing against my hair. "I know...what you want." His voice is a whisper in my ear, and he says each word like he's tasting it, savoring it. For a fire girl, it's pretty weird to have goose bumps.

"What's that?" I ask when I finally find my voice.

"To dance. With me." He's extremely attractive—like, beyond—but it's his unwavering gaze that unhinges me— the kind of look that could conquer the world.

I eye all the people standing in clusters, talking. "But no one is dancing."

"You were. I saw you from across the room. Looking like you wanted to *move*. Like you wanted to break all the rules."

"That was only swaying," I say quickly, embarrassed by how plainly he can see the real me. "I meant no one *else* is dancing."

Hearing that, Janine grabs Whit's hand and drags him onto the dance floor. She gives me a wry look over her shoulder, and I glare daggers back.

The boy cocks an eyebrow, and the shadows play across his striking face. "So. How about that dance?"

It seems so easy to fall into the rhythm, to let our hips find the beat, to get closer....But I'm not sure I'm ready. He just seems a little too gorgeous, a little too tall, a little too mature, a little too confident. A little too much *man* for me right now.

I wait a second too long, and the guy sighs, turning. "I'm Heath. Call me when you get sick of standing still, and we'll move." He's walking away.

"I don't think you could keep up," I call after him.

"You really are a firecracker, aren't you?" Heath grins, and his electric gaze flickers back at me. "I hope I get the chance to prove you wrong."

Then he's gone, and I let out a slow, measured breath. Of all the times I've been on fire, I've never felt sparks quite like that.

"Who does that guy think he is?" Byron grumbles beside me.

"What?" I look at him, startled that the rest of the world hasn't fallen away.

"Interrupting our conversation, waltzing in here like he owns the place, and pestering you when you've made it clear that you're obviously not interested." He frowns. "He's way too old for you, anyway."

"Shut *up*, Byron," I huff. I snap my fingers to work a little magic, and suddenly Byron is no longer standing in front of me. In his place, there's a squeaking weasel. "I should just leave you like this—your true form."

But I can never stay mad at Byron for long. I clap my hands, and he's back.

"Feel better now that you've gotten that out of your system?" he snaps.

I nod, smiling. "Definitely."

My hips start to twitch again, swaying with the music.

On the dance floor, Whit and Janine are moving together under the lights. Around Whit, Janine's serious eyes sparkle, and her laughter peals across the room. Regardless of how many girls have batted their eyelashes at him, it's weird to think of my brother as some kind of ripped heartthrob. Janine seems to see Whit more deeply than that, though—she understands Whit the poet, and Whit the goofball.

He looks utterly smitten, too, and I have to admit, Janine is one awesome chick. I'm so glad he's found someone special again, after losing Celia.

I sigh. Maybe I shouldn't have been so quick to dismiss Heath....But there's time. Everything feels fresh tonight. I'm surrounded by friends, family, and amazing artwork, and there are no bombs.

Just beauty.

Chapter 2

Pearl

IF ANYONE COULD have used a new beginning, it was Pearl Marie Neederman.

All she had known in her young life was the thunder of gunfire, the stench of death in the streets, and the bitter taste of poverty. Since they didn't need to beg and steal anymore, Mama May had wanted her to stay closer to home, but Pearl had just laughed. She might've been only seven, but she knew the labyrinth of the capital's alleys better than anyone.

Besides, the danger was over now.

She brushed her mop of black hair out of her eyes as she squinted into the pile of trash, looking for the perfect sparkle, the just-right shape. She wanted to impress everyone tonight at the fancy art show, but first she needed to find something to contribute.

"Isn't it only for the rule makers?" she'd asked when Whit had invited her to the celebration.

"The *Council*. It's different now," he had said, smiling at her ignorance. If he were anyone else, she probably would've cut him for that, but the wizard held a special place in her heart. "Art Is Alive is for everyone. And the party is for all our friends."

Pearl had turned away, a little embarrassed, but beaming with pride: she was considered a friend to the great Whit Allgood.

As she scavenged, Pearl collected bits of broken glass that sparkled in the light and scraps of metal that twisted in the craziest ways. Perfect for creating her own piece of art for the gallery. Whit had told her that with the new Council, there wasn't going to be any garbage in the streets, but she knew that underneath a shiny new finish, there was always a layer of grime.

She was up to her arms in trash when a sudden, loud popping sound made her jump.

Pearl dropped to her knees in an instant. Silent as a shadow, she slipped behind the Dumpster among the rats, and listened. She'd been called a "gutter rat" as long as she could remember, but she never understood the insult. Rats survived, didn't they?

There wasn't a sound to be heard, but she saw a fizz of light coming from around the corner. Pearl stood up and let out a breath, grinning.

Had to be Razz and Eddie from down the block, who had taught Pearl to pickpocket long ago. They had seen the beautiful fireworks display this morning and had spent all day rigging up their own with fertilizer and charcoal. That explained the noise. They'd probably blown off a hand or something.

"You idiots!" Pearl yelled, walking over.

But before she could even round the corner, Pearl's gray eyes widened with shock as a rough hand clamped over her mouth.

The men suddenly surrounding her were huge, with grizzled faces and dark clothing. They carried heavy, crude weapons—one of them even had an ax. She saw they had Razz by the collar, but Eddie was nowhere in sight.

One of the brutes started lighting the fuses on the homemade fireworks, and Razz went nuts. "Those are mine!" he yelled belligerently. As a warning, Razz's captor dragged an edge of jagged glass across the boy's throat, drawing a thin line of blood, but Razz clenched his teeth, refusing to scream.

The man who'd grabbed Pearl spun her around to face him, holding her off the ground, his giant hands wrapped around her throat. She was transfixed by his stare, so cold and empty. One eye was as milky as snow.

Just as she started to see spots, the man threw her into the truck like a sack of garbage. Razz came hurling in after her, and he leaped up, clawing at the door. But the bolt had already closed, and the engine was rumbling.

Pearl scrambled against the side of the truck, coughing and trying to get her breath back.

"We didn't hear a sound," murmured Eddie from a

corner, shaking his head. "Who can sneak up on *us*? No one. These guys were like ghosts."

There were other kids inside the truck, too—a mix of gutter rats and rich kids, some stunned into silence, others all-out shrieking.

"Shush! Stop being a baby!" Pearl hissed at one of the kids, then felt a little bad. "We got to figure this out."

Think, Pearl. Think.

Her fingers fumbled inside her pockets, searching. They closed on something metal, and she exhaled. Her blade.

She was deft with the knife, good at picking locks with her tiny fingers. But there were no screws or seams, and she couldn't find a single weak spot in the metal; it didn't seem like anything an ordinary man had made. And no matter how she worked the blade, the hard bolt wouldn't budge.

Pearl felt real panic rise inside her for the first time. These rough and weathered men were definitely not New Order—so who were they working for?

And where were they taking her?

There couldn't be a new threat so soon. No way. Whit had said they were safe. He had promised.

Pearl squinted through the bars, the capital's distant lights blurring a little in her vision. They were already on the outskirts of the City. Soon they would reach the boundary line, and she had no idea what lay beyond.

Chapter 3

Whit

MY TURN.

I am not an awkward person. But this is one of the most awkward moments of my life. Wisty lives for the spotlight, but me? I'd rather write the script.

I step up to the small platform where Ross, the DJ, was spinning. Wisty hoots "*Woo!*" embarrassingly loudly, and Byron follows her lead with his best off-the-cuff cheer: "Go Whit!!"

The Allgood magic has always felt kind of sacred, something not to be used lightly. I've used mine to escape from prison, heal the sick, and defeat the most evil dictator our world has ever known. But now that he's gone, now that we've won, we all deserve a little joy. So, hey, I've been working on a new use for my M. I start with a poem.

"Brush the ash from your bones."

I concentrate on the power building in me, and make it visual.

"Cast aside your red tears."

The gathered crowd gasps in delight as a three-dimensional scene swirls behind me, morphing and changing with my words. The hologram isn't much—just colors and energy. But it's as beautiful as my sister's fireworks, or the paintings on the wall. It's a bit of performance art that has every soul in the place completely enraptured for a good five minutes. Until—

My head throbs suddenly. I double over in pain as a bright light cuts through my vision.

It feels like it's slicing my brain.

Janine grabs my arm, a worried look on her face. "You okay?" she asks quietly.

I nod, standing up again. The hologram flickers behind me like static. I start reading the poem again, trying to get my bearings. Trying to get the energy back.

"Weep for the fallen, stand against those you fear…"

This time, as I continue, the expressions of the audience members change from concern to confusion and then shock.

Something's wrong. Something's *seriously* wrong.

I turn around, and the three-dimensional images playing out behind me are awful. A sea of black rats scurry over one another, attacking their own tails. Worms crawl out of an eye socket, bathing it in their milky trail. They writhe outward toward the crowd, so real in their holographic existence that a few people jerk backward, shrieking.

It's like the movie has been switched, but it's all in my head.

How are these things coming...out of *me*?

Just keep going, Whit. Get it back on track.

I concentrate hard, my whole body shaking with the effort, but the horrifying images keep projecting behind me.

The image flickers: now a child bangs his head against the wall, over and over, as blood pools in his eyes. A mask is removed from a face, and behind it is the chill of death. An avalanche of snow barrels outward, and members of the crowd turn away in terror.

"Whit!" Wisty yells, a look of horror on her face. "Stop it!"

But I'm utterly helpless as the darkness feeds on itself. I shake my head and jump off the stage, leaving my sister and friends and a roomful of people gawking after me.

I run, and keep running. Out of the room. Out the big double doors, knocking them against the wall on their hinges, and out into the street. I take huge gulps of the night air as I try to keep from vomiting.

Voices are calling in the distance, yelling my name, but I can't face them, not now, not until I shake this diseased feeling. I won't stop running until my lungs are screaming and my legs ache.

I have to escape the thing that's in my head.

Chapter 4

Wisty

"SERIOUSLY, WHAT'S *WRONG*?"

"Let it go, Wisty," Whit warns as I try to keep up.

Okay. Good sister that I am, I'm just going to ignore the fact that my brother had a complete meltdown at a party for our friends that was supposed to be about *celebration* and *happiness*. I'm going to forget that he stormed out of the gallery without any explanation, and then refused to answer a single one of my questions when I chased after him in the street.

Yeah, right.

"If you just tell me what happened, maybe I could help," I prod, turning the key to let us into my sweet new apartment. (The upshot to using your magical powers to save basically the whole world from a psycho villain is that your parents freak out a little bit less when you mention you'd really like to get your own place.)

"There's nothing to tell," my brother insists. He steps

over one of the piles of stuff on the floor, and perches on a counter stool. "Wow, Wisty, you've really done wonders with the space." Whit shakes his head. "Have the rats moved in yet?"

"Organized chaos," I say, cheerfully ignoring the dig. A little mess keeps me sane, and I can do as I please here. "And you're the one living with weaselly Byron Swain. *That's* what I call rodent's paradise."

"Har har," Whit answers dryly.

Then the doorbell rings, and we both glance toward the front door, surprised. Whit raises an eyebrow. "Visitors this late?"

I shrug. "It's probably Janine, wondering why you acted like a total freak and just left her at the gallery."

"Wisteria," Whit warns, looking at me sternly. He never uses my full name.

"Whitford," I reply mockingly, and chuck a couch cushion at his head as I walk to answer the door.

"I said, Let. It. *Go*."

"Yeah, yeah." I smirk and look through the peephole. I glimpse the height, the dark hair...

Oh. Em. Gee.

It's Heath. The guy who asked me to dance at the art festival. Here. At my apartment. I totally spaz out, flattening my body against the door.

"What? Who is it?" Whit asks, standing up.

Ignoring my brooding brother, I finally pull myself together enough to open the door.

"Hi," I say shyly.

"Hey," Heath answers, and it's like a little velvet purr.

Neither of us moves for a moment; we just blink at each other, not sure of our boundaries. Under the porch light, Heath's pale eyes glow a cool shade of blue I've never seen.

"I was thinking maybe you had the right idea," he says softly, finally breaking the silence. "Maybe we should just stand here. Looking at each other. Like this." There's no denying it: this instant connection feels even more intense than before—almost blinding.

I laugh then, shaking my head. "And I was thinking maybe it was time to *move*."

"I'm game if you are," he answers.

"What's going on?" Whit opens the door farther behind me.

"Um." I pull my gaze away from Heath. "My friend just stopped by to . . ."

"I couldn't stop thinking about that magnificent fireworks display your sister put on earlier," Heath answers cordially. Then he looks at me. "I felt like *I* might burst, too, if I didn't see her again."

The line is clearly extra cheesy for my brother's benefit, but it still makes my stomach flutter.

"Okay, lover boy," Whit says, stepping out onto the porch, frowning. "It's late. Let's wrap this up."

"I wasn't planning to take much of anyone's time. I just wanted to show Wisty—"

"My sister isn't interested." Whit's in hostile-big-brother mode now. "Wisty, let's go. Back inside."

"Whit!" I'm sure the humiliation and anger is written on my face, but Heath's eyes sparkle with amusement.

"You're going to keep Wisty locked in her own apartment? Maybe she wants a bit of freedom. Isn't that what you two fought so hard for?"

"Maybe you don't know what she wants."

Heath cocks his head. "Hey, now," he says. "There's no need to feel threatened, big guy."

Yikes. This isn't going to be pretty.

Whit blinks at him. "Threatened?" he asks incredulously, crossing his arms. "By who? You?"

"Okay, okay," I groan. *Boys.* "Relax, both of you." I push Whit back toward the door, then turn back to my visitor, sighing. "I really should go back inside...."

Heath holds up his hands. "Of course. Didn't mean to intrude. Good night, Firecracker." He smiles and places a single flower on the doorstep at my feet, nods to Whit, and walks away, just like that.

I stand on the porch after he leaves, staring into the night. He called me *Firecracker.* He doesn't even know me! I should zap him right to Shadowland, shouldn't I? But there's something about the way he said it—something familiar yet exciting and new. I can't explain it, but I feel incredibly drawn to this boy with the sharp tongue and the strange eyes. The highest part of the sky is in those eyes, cool and vast, and they seem to see right inside me.

Maybe I'm afraid of what they see. *Freedom* . . . to do what?

I pick up the flower he left. It's lovely. Pale silver with a bright flash of orange in the center—like nothing I've seen before.

"I wonder what he wants. . . ." I mutter softly.

"I bet I can guess," Whit says, startling me. I thought he'd gone in.

I roll my eyes and step back inside, brushing past him. "Oh, come on. He seems like a nice guy. And he's right—it *is* my apartment."

"Nice guy? Every guy wants something. Usually the same thing. Trust me, Wisty. You haven't been in a foolball locker room. You learn a lot in there." I roll my eyes at my overprotective brother.

The One Who Is The One wanted me for my power. Since the victory, politicians seem to want me for my fame. Heath said he just wanted to see me again. Not my magic, not my fire.

Me.

I feel a weird sort of vulnerability. Not fear, exactly. I know my power, hot and true, will protect me, and if that fails, my watchdog brother sure will. But with the electricity of my interaction with Heath still making my whole body hum, I'm just not sure I want to be protected.

It can't be that Heath wants to be my *boyfriend* . . . could it?

Chapter 5

Wisty

I'M OUTSIDE. IT'S RAINING. The boy is there.

Heath.

The rain is in my eyes, but I can feel him.

"I just wanted to see you," he says in that velvety voice.

"But I can't see you," I answer. "I can't see anything." I squint, but the water is coming down too hard to see my hand in front of my face.

"I can show you. Everything," he promises. "Just don't look down."

He takes my hand, and I shiver at his cold touch, but I'm warm inside. Full of fire. Like my heart is filling with air, lifting up.

And then we *are* lifting up—actually rising above the City and into the clouds. I hold my breath as we break through into sunlight, eager to see what "everything" might be, but before I can turn, Heath leans toward me, and I sigh, letting him pull me into his arms....

I wake up, disoriented and clutching a pillow. Then I make a mistake: I look down.

And I almost have a heart attack.

I'm floating above my bed. Like, *five feet* above my bed, just hanging out near the ceiling. I blink and fall to the mattress, knocking the wind out of myself, and lie there, gasping.

God, my magic is weird sometimes.

And *embarrassing*, I think, chucking the pillow aside. I can only imagine the faces I must've been making in my sleep.

Fortunately, this is *my* place, my own apartment. For once I don't have to deal with older brothers barging in all the time. I close my eyes again, looking forward to the end of the dream. Right about now, Whit is probably bugging someone else about clean dishes, or hogging someone else's TV to watch foolball. . . .

No. My eyes fly open. *That's not what Whit is doing at all.*

I look at the clock, my stomach sinking. I've already messed up. Whit is where *I'm* supposed to be, right at this moment, on the most important day of our lives.

And I'm late!

I leap out of bed, yelling as I stub my toe on a guitar I left out. Clothes are strewn everywhere. I stumble through them, frantically grabbing at pants and sweaters. Nothing seems quite right for the occasion, and you never know who you'll run into because *he just wanted to see you.* . . .

Settling on a simple black dress, I jump in the shower,

shrieking at the blast of cold water. But it's good. No time to focus on still-lingering dreams when your brain is freezing.

Makeup time. I frown at my reflection. Special day, but same old face, with the added benefit of bags under the eyes and straggly wet hair. And no time!

I pick up a celebrity rag—a guilty pleasure that's back now that actors and other pop idols (who aren't The One) are no longer being exterminated—but I'm not wasting time with gossip right now. Tearing through the magazine, I find what I'm looking for: a picture of an actress who has that professional-yet-pretty look. There's this spell I've been meaning to try....

I touch the face on the page and then brush my fingers across the mirror. As I watch, my eyes seem to transform into smoldering goddess peepers, a hint of rose color blooms on my cheeks, and my lips look—well, like you want to listen to what I'm saying.

I don't have her cheekbones or her pouty lips, of course. It's not a full morph—just a bit of spell-spiked makeup— but it'll do in a pinch. Still Wisty Allgood in there, freckles and all, but with a touch of celebrity chic. Not bad.

I struggle to pull on my high-top sneakers as I yank open the door, and then I spot it there.

The flower.

The dream comes back to me in a rush, "everything" echoing in my head. But what does the offering of a flower say about a boy in real life? Sweet, or stalker? Walking down the steps, I twirl the stem, considering, and then I realize—

I almost forgot the most important thing!

I drop the flower and burst back into the apartment, hastily gathering up the plans Whit and I spent hours brainstorming, and now I'm *really* late. I sprint down the street with the papers clutched to my chest, wet hair streaming.

People are giving me strange looks, but that's normal. It isn't until I get two full blocks away that I realize my right foot is a little chilly. Sure enough, when I look down, I'm only wearing one sneaker.

I *so* don't have time for this right now.

I turn to head back for it, then stop. Instead, I close my eyes, picturing the red high-top sneaker with its scuffs on the side, lying just inside the door.

Then I whistle, and, like a loyal pet, the shoe flies out the window and tumbles toward me down the street. Grinning, I turn and keep running as it gallops behind.

Chapter 6

Whit

WHERE IS SHE?

I watch the giant clock on the wall, the slow click of the seconds echoing in the vast chamber. My pencil mimics the beat—*tap, tap, tap*—on the long table.

Matthias Bloom, self-styled Speaker of these proceedings, clears his throat for the hundredth time. As I glance sheepishly around the wall of faces, I see that he's not alone in his impatience.

She knows how important this day is.

The memory of last night resurfaces then, those horrible headaches and disturbing images, and for a moment I worry something's happened to my sister. Maybe the vision was some sort of omen....

Come on, Wisty. Come on, I plead silently, thinking if my stare drills hard enough into the door, it might creak open.

Miraculously, after an eternity, it bangs open. My sister

bursts through, a ball of flustered energy with red hair hanging in her face. "Sorry!" she shouts as she hops across the room, still struggling to pull on a shoe.

I shake my head, but I'm grinning anyway, because she's *here*. There's no bad omen, and everything's cool, because Wisty's got the papers in her hand—the ideas we spent weeks developing.

With those plans and this Council, the future of our City starts *today*.

"Now that our last esteemed member has arrived..." Bloom sighs heavily, and straightens his tie.

Always the smart aleck, Wisty curtsies in response, then finally plops into the seat at my side.

"May we begin?" Bloom finishes dryly.

"Great!" I stand, eager to address the group. "Since we're reinventing this City now, and not just fixing what was broken, it's important that we do it right this time." I grab the plans off the table and glance at my notes. "We were thinking, start with the City's biggest hope: kids. School should be about creativity and fun, so kids actually want to go."

Looking around at the faces of my fellow Council members—war heroes, rogue journalists, a former film star who survived on roaches for two years underground— my enthusiasm grows. I'm not a natural speaker like Janine, but I'm more pumped about this cause than anything, and these are the people who can make it happen.

"We also need to build a major outdoor community

center, so all citizens can tell us their concerns and ideas,"
I continue. "We can use The One's old compound, and it
would be great for concerts, too." Wisty gives me an
encouraging wink. "Of course, first we'll have to redesign
the streets to make room for more parks...."

Bloom clears his throat again sharply, and it's like a
crack of thunder in the chamber. "Those ideas are all
charming, Mr. Allgood," he booms. "However, this is a
Council, and all members will vote on its proceedings."

I redden. "Right. I know, Mr. Bloom. We just thought—"

"We thought that as *members* of the Council—the
members who freed the Overworld, if we're getting into
specifics—you might want to at least hear our ideas,"
Wisty blurts out.

A couple of voices shout words of encouragement, par-
ticularly the youngest of the seventeen kids on the board,
who totally idolize Wisty.

"*General*," Bloom corrects. He straightens the white
swath of hair atop his glistening forehead. "And who will
fund these projects? Our bankrupt treasury?"

When Wisty and I are silent, he addresses the whole
Council, pitching his voice across the room. "Unfortunately, we cannot just burn away the problems of the New
Order as we did its flags. Along with a money shortage," he
drawls, fixing each member in turn with his gaze, "we're
facing a fuel shortage. A materials shortage. And a water
shortage."

"A sense-of-humor shortage," Wisty quips.

But the rest of the room is silent, and I'm not laughing, either. How did we think it was going to be so easy?

"Okay," I say quietly. "Where should we start, then?"

There's a flicker of compassion on Bloom's face, but his authoritative voice doesn't budge when he replies, "I propose we stick to the agenda."

"Agenda?" I look around. Everyone has a crisp, typed sheet of paper in front of them. Everyone but us. I sit back down with my hand-scrawled notes.

"First item," Bloom reads. "Housing needs for displaced citizens."

"There's been violence in the Gutter lately," says the kid from the streets whose parents were martyrs of the Resistance. "Families trying to build up their bombed houses, but others claiming their supplies."

I think of little Pearl Neederman and her family's basement home in the Gutter. They didn't have much, but they definitely had kinship. "Maybe we could discuss ways to get the communities working together to rebuild neighborhoods, one house at a time," I suggest.

Every eye in the room flicks to the man who seems to know about these things, but he shakes his snowy head dismissively. "The Council must decide how many stones each citizen is eligible to remove from rubble for rebuilding."

"We'll need to know how many stones each rubble pile contains, on average," notes an eager Councilman beside Bloom.

"And what percentage of stones were lost in the bombing," a droopy-eyed man across the chamber adds.

The woman to his right pipes in: "Shouldn't we first vote on whether stones should be determined by size or weight or concentration of minerals...?"

Two hours later, my head is throbbing even harder than it was last night. "Is blood leaking out of my ears yet?" I whisper to my sister.

Wisty looks up at me with glazed eyes, her chin resting on the table. "I didn't think this was actually possible, but governing just might be worse than going to school."

"Before we adjourn, I don't want to cause anyone to panic, but I fear we must address one last pressing issue...." Bloom announces, and the tone in his voice makes both of us sit up straight.

Chapter 7

Whit

BLOOM FIXES US all with a steely look I'm familiar with: like a foolball coach who's about to ask you to do something ridiculous, like provoke the other team's Demon, sacrificing life and limb in the hopes that it's a win for the team.

I clench my jaw and Wisty nervously chews a strand of her hair.

"As the Keeper of *The Book of Truths*," Bloom says with self-reverence, "I have interpreted its messages as faithfully as I could."

All eyes in the room look up at him, hungry for that knowledge. The attention seems to make Bloom grow taller.

"Now I fear we are at a grave point in our history, a new-made City left vulnerable to rising crime and outside forces."

There's a murmur of confusion, all of us alarmed at the same two words.

"What does he mean, 'outside forces'?" Wisty whispers.

I shake my head. There is land beyond the City, of course. To the east lies a wide river whose banks I've been to a thousand times. But the currents are so deadly, no one has ever crossed it, and it's said that all that's beyond is an endless forest. To the north, there's a desert, and to the west, a range of mountains.

But the City has been isolated from those people for almost three generations.

The restless crowd moves closer to Bloom, all of us eager to understand.

"*The Book* warns that there is much to fear from the King of the Mountain People to the west," the Keeper continues. "We are facing a water shortage because every drop running down from the mountain has stopped, and I believe the Mountain King acts with hostile intention, as is prophesized."

The volume grows with this new revelation as real fear starts to take root. "What does this mean?" a Councilman from the outer suburbs shouts.

"It could mean many things," Bloom says ponderously. He seems to be talking slower and more softly now that he has our full attention, savoring our dependence. "First it will mean thirst. It may eventually mean that our truce with the Desert People is broken, since we share our water supply. One day . . ."—he drawls so slowly I want to shake him—"it will mean war."

The shouting reaches a fever pitch then. Bodies are

pushing, voices yelling. The fear is so thick in the air I can smell it now, seeping out through pores and infecting all it touches, but I'm not going to give in, not yet. I wrap my arms around Wisty's shoulders protectively.

We killed The One, I remind myself. *That was the prophecy.*

"I thought he didn't want to make us panic," Wisty says miserably.

There's wild speculation about attacks from the Sand Men who live on tarantula blood and ride lizards to war, or the Ice Eaters who feast on human flesh. "We have no police force!" several voices are despairing.

"Council members!" Bloom steps onto a bench, his doughy body rising above us. "I understand your fear. I have known that fear." He's still talking in that slow, serene voice, so I have to strain to hear. He draws himself up higher, and I swear he's sucking in his gut. "Fortunately, I am a practiced strategist of war."

"He wasn't even in the war," Wisty hisses. "I heard he just hid from the New Order and managed to bury *The Book of Truths*."

But the Council members crowd around Bloom's feet just the same, hungry for his advice.

"Earlier, we agreed to give pardons to those who worked for the New Order but who have renounced their former loyalties," Bloom states, to murmurs of agreement. Surprisingly, that was one of the easier votes of the day, to choose to unite our people after losing so many. "I move

43

that these experienced soldiers be reinstated as a temporary police force," Bloom adds hastily.

"*What?*" Wisty and I gasp together, and I know we're both remembering the sound of the soldiers' boots chasing us through plague-ridden streets.

The room is a wild chorus of dissent. Some of us are survivors of New Order prisons; others were orphaned by their bombs. It's one thing to give a brainwashed kid soldier the chance to start over. It's another to give every old cog in The One's murdering machine a gun and trust him to protect us.

Someone knocks into the bench Bloom stands on, and he clamps a hand on his head as if to hold down his gray toupee. "I understand your concerns," he shouts over the crowd. "Unfortunately, the issues I've mentioned aren't the worst of what our fair City is facing...."

Kidnappings, he tells us. More kidnappings.

There isn't much information. Someone saw a couple of black armored vehicles. A few people heard screams. By late evening, more than twenty-five mothers had registered their children as missing at the Council office.

A stunned silence finally falls over the once-raucous chamber. The news feels unimaginable, yet at the same time it feels incredibly familiar. I vividly remember the day Wisty and I were taken, ripped from our home and thrown into prison. There were lots of other kids there, too. Kids a lot younger than us.

"This feels like the New Order all over again," Wisty

murmurs in a small voice, as if reading my thoughts. "What if—"

"The One is dead," I answer before she can even ask.

My sister is so strong. She's one of the most powerful magic makers in our world, and she defeated The One during the height of his power. Few people can really harm her. Yet I know she hears that mocking voice and sees his Technicolor eyes in her nightmares.

The One is dead. Absolutely and totally. But if there are pockets of still-active New Order in the Overworld...

"No former New Order sympathizer will serve as part of the Over Watch," I say suddenly and certainly, my voice louder than everyone else's in the chamber—even Bloom's.

The Book Keeper raises a cottony eyebrow. "There is no one else strong enough for the police force. I thought I made it clear that these are dire times—"

"We'll handle it," I snap.

"With all due respect..."

"I said, *we'll handle it.*"

Chapter 8

Pearl

"YOU WILL BE CLEANSED," echoed the voice on the loudspeaker, over and over.

Pearl wasn't sure who the voice belonged to, or what the phrase meant, or how long she had been in the dim room crowded with sweltering bodies. At this point, the noise was all she knew. The noise and her hunger. She hadn't slept since she'd been taken.

"YOU WILL BE CLEANSED," the voice boomed, again and again, until Pearl was delirious from her throbbing head, her ringing ears, the heat and the gnaw of her stomach.

"I'm clean," she sobbed. "I swear I'm clean."

When the door opened, Pearl thought she was hallucinating. Or dead.

But the delicious cool breeze on her skin felt real, and so did the ground beneath her feet as Pearl stumbled out into the open air, blinking against the sudden light of the sun. The air was so crisp it burned her nostrils, and she could smell food cooking somewhere.

"YOU HAVE BEEN SAVED," another voice echoed somewhere, and she believed it. She thought she'd gone to heaven.

And then they were herded into a rough pen.

She didn't have a coat or shoes, and as the cold crept into her bones and her teeth began to chatter, she almost wished for the sweaty warmth of the death cell again.

Almost.

"Are you hungry?" a giant man with a matted nest of a beard yelled at them.

Pearl felt her eyes bulging from her head, her tongue swollen. All she could do was nod.

"Then *run!*" he screamed.

Around and around the pen they went. As several of the other kids stopped to catch their breath or winced as sharp rocks cut into their bare feet, Pearl was grateful for her gutter-kid soles, thick with calluses. Because if running meant food, she was prepared to run all day.

So she ran. And ran. And ran. At least it was warming her up.

Finally, just before Pearl thought she would keel over from exhaustion, a horn sounded, and the runners stopped to wait for the next instruction.

"You did well for your first day," an older kid with stick-like legs and arms roped with veins whispered to her. "You didn't even slow down."

"I'm glad someone noticed," Pearl said.

"They call me Eagle. Around here, it pays to keep an eye out."

"Where I come from, it pays to take an eye out," Pearl answered, reaching for the handle of her hidden blade as a warning that she wasn't to be bothered, then realizing it wouldn't be a good idea for Eagle to know she still had it.

Pearl jutted her chin up toward the tower. "Who's the old guy?"

Eagle squinted against the sun to look at the man standing on the castle balcony. "The King. They call him the Snow Leopard."

The old man was wrapped in rough furs and had a yellowing beard that tucked into a ruby-encrusted belt at his waist. Above him flapped a banner with a giant white snarling cat on it. His face looked carved from stone.

"So he's who stole us." Pearl narrowed her eyes and memorized the look of the man she should save her blade for.

"He saved you," Eagle said defensively. "He saved us all. For something greater."

"I don't feel saved," she snapped. "I feel hungry."

Eagle shrugged. "There's plenty of food around here. Just follow my lead."

"How was your run?" the bearded giant interrupted them. "Tell your king everything you saw. Were there any Failures?"

Eagle raised his hand immediately. "That one there.

The scrawny one. He stopped running. I don't think he wants us to win."

The King watched carefully from the tower as a blond boy was dragged to his feet and brought to the center, where everyone could see. His toes were all cut up and bloody. The King gave a clipped nod, and the boy winced, bringing a hand to his head. As Pearl watched, the boy walked to the wall . . . and began banging his head against it, over and over.

"Be cleansed!" the other kids chorused in rhythm with the *thunk, thunk* of skull on rock.

It was awful to watch. A stream of blood flowed from the gash on his forehead, but he kept striking himself, again and again, until the King finally turned away. Then the boy stumbled back, crumpling to the ground.

Two more kids were called out, and the ritual repeated. Finally, when there were no more Failures, the brute dished out a large portion of food to everyone who remained.

"New here, aren't you? You still have the reek of the slums on you." A gangly older girl sat down next to Pearl and the slum boys on the bench they shared with Eagle.

"But we'll be cleansed," Razz echoed mockingly.

"Better you're up here than down there. The other gutter rats will be getting pretty thirsty, now that the King's cut off the City's water supply."

Pearl blinked hard as she thought of her parents, Mama May and Hewitt; of all her aunts and little cousins—all the other Needermans. Living under the New Order had been rough enough, but no *water*?

"No. The witch and wizard won't stand for it," she protested. "They'll demand water, they'll come up the mountain, they'll—"

"The King is counting on it," Eagle said.

A trap.

"They destroyed The One Who Is The One! Whit could take on some stupid King."

"You sure about that, little girl?"

"Of course I'm sure!"

But she had been sure The One was the only threat to the Overworld. She had been sure Whit wouldn't let anything happen to her. She had been sure her family was safe. She looked around her now, at the gaunt kids running the drills, and back at the leopard flag waving proudly overhead.

In truth, Pearl didn't know if she could be sure of anything anymore.

Chapter 9

Whit

"YOU'RE SURE THIS is the place?" I squint doubtfully at the blackened windows of a crumbling old video store near Industry Row—the Resistance's new hideout.

"It says *The Tube*." Wisty looks at something written on the palm of her hand, and back up at the yellow letters painted on the side of the building. "That's what Sasha's friend Ross told me."

I yank on the door. "Then why is it locked?"

"Dunno. I guess Ross forgot to pass along the info about the secret knock or secret entrance or whatever. We'll have to find another way in. How about..."

Her eyes flash, and she drums her fingers absently. I know that look. It's got M written all over it. "Lead on, sister."

Well, being a cockroach wouldn't have been *my* first choice, but I have missed morphing. That first tickle of power moving through your body is such a high, and the

51

sensation of having six legs as I scurry after my witch-bug-sister under the door is definitely a first.

It takes only a second to get in. The paint-coated space looks huge to my little roach eyes, which makes it all the more beautiful. Graffiti of mermaids swimming down the wall toward dinosaurs and marching soldiers crushing giant flowers look so real they seem to be growing right out of the wall. These are remnants of the inspired yet twisted visions of the repressed artists living under the New Order.

Ross looms over us, a can of spray paint in hand, and Sasha almost squashes me as he steps back to admire the incredible mural. The others are crowded around a low table, playing a card game. Emmett looks relaxed, but Byron is sulking, and it looks like Janine is taking them both for everything they've got.

"Hey, gang," I say, morphing back into my human self. Beside me, Wisty does the same, shaking out her limbs, and Ross gapes at us.

"Don't worry, you get used to it," Sasha promises him.

"*You* might," Janine says, laughing. "I don't think *I'll* ever get used to the sight of Whit Allgood materializing out of thin air."

"Out of a cockroach, actually," Wisty points out.

"Charming," Janine answers, but she's looking at me when she says it, and the softness of her voice makes my pulse speed up just a notch.

"The door was locked," Wisty explains. "Next time, give us the secret knock or whatever."

"Nah." Emmett nods toward the broken bricks near the far wall. "See, what you do is, you make another door."

I grin and turn to Ross. "This is an awesome space, by the way."

"Thanks, man. Since the art ban was lifted, my tagging buddies don't really come around, but The Tube's got a history, you know? When you said you needed a space off the grid, it seemed perfect."

"Speaking of which, what's the urgent news? Are you okay, Wisty?" Byron places a hand on her arm, then peels it off when he sees the look she gives him.

"We're fine," I say. "But the City might not be. At least, not for much longer."

Wisty sighs. "It's happening again. Kids are disappearing."

I can almost see my friends' hearts sag with the news. It's exactly what I'm feeling: *We're back here—already?*

Then Sasha jumps to his feet, all anger in action. "Do we know who did it? Do we know where they were last seen? Do we have names? There's still time."

I shake my head. "Bloom didn't tell us much of anything. Just the basics."

"And that we should be terrified of an attack at any time." Wisty frowns.

"Sounds like he knows how to talk like a politician,"

Janine says, her jaw tightening. "Too bad it leaves us at ground zero for those little kids. Just like before."

The guilt I felt earlier washes over me again. *I should've done something.*

"But it's different now, right?" Ross cuts in. "There's no New Order to fear. We have an elected Council now, and they can handle this. They'll find out who did it." He looks around the card table, wanting to believe. "Right?"

I make myself meet his eyes. "The Council isn't exactly... it isn't what we thought it would be. There wasn't a system in place to deal with something like this. It's all talk and no action."

"Sounds familiar," Janine says. "Action always starts at the ground level. That's why we started the Resistance in the first place."

"It's settled, then," Sasha says, eager to move forward. "The Resistance returns, and we'll grow it again. We'll patrol the streets."

"Really?" I gasp. "I know it's a lot to ask...."

"We'll do it," repeats Janine, her gaze meeting mine. "All in favor?"

The hands go up, one after another, and I'm so full of gratitude.

"Kids as cops." Emmett nods. "Could be cool."

"Real justice, without the corruption," Byron adds, and Wisty cocks an eyebrow at him. "What?" he says, incredulous. "What?!"

"She's just teasing you, By." I chuckle. "Don't give her the satisfaction."

"I'm in, too," Ross says. "But if we're the cops, are we still resisting?"

Janine nods. "We're resisting the fearmongering of politicians and the capture of our youth. We're resisting having our freedom revoked."

"Resist or submit!" Sasha crows.

"We'll resist," Janine promises, her clear green eyes as determined as I've ever seen them. "We're not ready to roll over just yet."

Chapter 10

Wisty

"GOOD THING THEY'RE wearing red uniforms," Mrs. Highsmith yells into my ear excitedly the next day as Whit's teammate is carried off the foolball field on a stretcher. "Is that a lot of blood or what?!"

I nod. "Broken nose" doesn't even begin to cover it. The kid is a pulpy mess of broken *face*, courtesy of the other team's Demon. I guess I'll never completely understand the appeal of a sport where boys try to kill each other. I guess that's why they call it *fool*ball. Who else willingly plays a game where a player named for evil incarnate is allowed to do absolutely *anything*—break your neck, tear off your arm, bite a chunk out of your face—as long as he can catch you?

Not *everyone* can be caught, though. No Demon has ever brought my brother down.

When the teams take the field again, Whit sidles up to his place at the center. The whistle shrieks and Whit takes off without snapping the ball. The crowd whips into a frenzy. *"Use the Demon!"* chant the blue team's fans as Whit streaks by, zigzagging around the blue bodies and dodging the Demon's grasp. Whit even shifts the ball like a carrot in front of the Demon's nose, and the crowd eats it up.

Whit pretends to falter, letting the blue Demon in for the kill move at the very last second, and then the snap is so quick that the guy has a useless mouthful of my brother's ear before he realizes Whit lobbed the ball down to the end zone seconds ago.

That's another signature move. Whit has never scored a single point. He told me once that it's not a big deal to him to get that kind of glory, but it seems like a big deal to everyone else, so why not give the other guys the ball? Pretty cool of him. But that's pure Whit for you.

"What your brother's best at is slipping through people's fingers.... Just ask all the heartbroken girls on the sideline!" Dad quips after the play—the same joke he tells every game. Mom shakes her head at his dorkiness, like always.

It's good to have something familiar among all the chaos and bad news. Whit's been pretty shaken up about the kidnappings—we all have—and he almost didn't come tonight. It took Janine to convince him that Sasha had the Over Watch under control, and that it was just as important to lift community spirits and morale by giving them a good show.

So far, it's been a success, with half the City in the

stands cheering. Whit's playing maybe one of his best games yet, despite the usual blood and tufts of hair littering the field. Some people say Whit has a bit of the supernatural in him when he plays, and I can see it coming out tonight. He's slick, he's graceful, and he's fierce.

I guess I shouldn't be so surprised, then, that in the last quarter, the blue team decides to switch in their second-string Demon.

"Whit, *watch behind*!" I yell, jumping to my feet, but it's too late. The Demon is already diving, wrapping my brother in a viselike leg grip and pulling him down. Whit's first fall is hard, and I wince as his helmet strikes with a dull *thud*. The shocked crowd gasps, and then boos the Demon in defense of their idol until Whit finally struggles back up.

This has never happened before.

"He's just got a lot on his mind," I say to reassure my parents as much as myself. "Governing is hard, and then with his weird headaches the other night..."

But when the blue Demon takes Whit down in the next play, and then down a third time, the people start to take notice. It looks like this guy's determined to take my brother out of commission, and he's certainly capable.

He's liquid smooth in his maneuvers, slipping through openings right as they close. He anticipates Whit's exact timing as if he'd choreographed it himself.

But mostly? He's *fast*. Faster than Whit. Again and again, the Demon delivers moves that are quick and clean to take Whit down without injury.

Who is this guy?

At this point, it's like Whit doesn't remember how to play. It's a train wreck, set up for maximum smash effect, and not one of us can turn away as the last few minutes on the clock wind down, the blue team driving the numbers up on the scoreboard.

Afterward, everyone is waiting to see the new second-string-completely-unheard-of blue Demon who took down the legendary Whit Allgood. Waiting and watching as he high-fives his team and does handstands. When he finally removes his helmet, the plastic reflects the light onto his face and a little shiver runs through me.

Heath.

He looks up into the stands and I wave tentatively at him. Heath pumps his helmet in the air a few times, then cups his hands to yell something.

I freeze. He's saying my name. Screaming it like it's some sort of tribute.

His dark hair falls back from his face in disheveled waves, shiny with sweat, and the flush of exercise is still in his cheeks. He's smiling at me in the sly way that makes me feel that scary spark. I look at all the girls drooling at the sight of him and I can't believe it's me he wants.

But I can sense Mrs. Highsmith's tight-lipped smile on me, too, and my parents' confusion, and I feel suddenly embarrassed. Then I see Byron and Whit across the field, looking at us, and I feel . . .

Well, like a traitor.

Chapter 11

Whit

WELL, *THAT* WAS a new experience. I sit on one of the sideline benches in a fog, still kind of in awe. Where did that guy even *come* from?

Byron sits down next to me. "Hey, Whit. Rough game today, huh?"

I shake my head. "Not sure what happened out there."

"You'll like this better—I promise." He plops a manila file into my lap.

"Yeah, sure, Byron." I toss the folder aside as I pull off the heavy padding. I've just lost the biggest game of my life, and this is his idea of empathizing?

"You'll find it interesting, no doubt." Byron glances toward the bleachers. "It's an investigative file on that guy Wisty's—" He sits up suddenly. "No. Oh, no."

I follow Byron's gaze toward my family, coming down the stands toward me, and when I see them together, my heart breaks a little, too.

Of *course*, it had to be Heath under that helmet.

"He's New Order, Whit," Byron says, looking devastated.

"What? Like, *currently*?"

"It's all in the file," he says, walking toward the bleachers. "I gotta tell her."

But Wisty's making a sudden left turn away from me. "Wist!" I yell after her, but she doesn't stop. Every time this guy shows up, doing his swagger routine, she's weird and upset for hours afterward. And now he's N.O. I open the file. Or *former* N.O.?

I'm putting a stop to this right now.

"Hey, Demon!" I yell across the field toward the guy who's still reveling in victory with his teammates.

Heath turns and grins at my choice of address, and I signal him over.

"Hey, man, good game," he says in this superfriendly tone. I look down at Heath's offer to shake hands and back up at his face.

That's not going to happen.

Instead, I reach for my gear—pads and bands and guards—and start shoveling it into my gym bag.

"You're really not going to shake my hand?" He manages to look wounded, enjoying himself in front of the onlookers around us. "You can't respect a guy for playing well?"

"I respect your game." That's definitely the truth. I actually feel a weird sense of relief now that I don't have to maintain that perfect record. "We both know you played way better than well. You wiped the field with me."

Heath smiles. "Humble, aren't we?"

I shrug. "There's always going to be someone better out there."

"Wanna bet?" Then he *really* smiles, all shark's bite, and a tuft of jet-black hair falls over his forehead.

"Humble, aren't we?" I counter, sitting on the bench to lace up my shoes.

"I could've killed you out there today. What's there to be humble about?"

"I'm glad you didn't." I look up at him, not sure if it's a threat. "This isn't about the game."

He grins, amused, and I fix him with a level look.

"Why are you still talking to Wisty?"

He laughs, so sure of himself. So certain life is all a joke. "O-*ho*. Another big brother chat. Maybe you should ask *her* why she's still talking to *me*."

I clench my teeth together.

"I know who you are." I stare at him, detecting the slightest falter in his gaze, like a shadow crossing as ice blue darkens to steel.

But when he leans toward me, he's all confidence. "I know who you are, too," Heath whispers, and his eyes flicker mockingly. "But I don't really see where you're going with this. . . ."

"I know you're lying. You were a New Order Youth Brigade leader with a different name. Byron Swain showed me your records."

"Byron," Heath groans. "Is that pup still nipping at

Wisty's heels and whining for my scraps? The One would say that dog needs a stun gun to the groin."

I glare at Heath, remembering Byron's heartbroken face.

"Hey, just kidding—no need for the silent treatment," he says, picking up the file and flipping through it with casual indifference. "Tell Mr. Swain that in case he wasn't aware, the Council pardoned all former New Order Youth yesterday." He opens the folder then, shrugging as the pages take flight and scatter in the wind. "But you knew that, didn't you? Since you and Wisty sit on the Council?"

"The Council votes for the good of the City. We're talking about what's good for my sister."

"Well, fair ruler, that seems a bit hypocritical, if you ask me."

I look him in the eye. "I didn't."

"Fair enough." He shrugs. "I don't think Wisty asked you what you thought about me, either." Heath starts to walk away, still smirking, but when he turns around suddenly, I'm surprised by his intense expression and blazing eyes.

"You don't know anything about me, because you don't want to know," he says, and for the first time, Heath seems sincere, almost emotional. "I never lied about the Youth Brigade. The One," he spits, nearly choking on the word, "killed my father. Then, like practically everyone else in this City, I had no choice but to join his service." Heath picks up his shining blue helmet from the bench and rubs at a scuff mark. "Maybe I just wanted a fresh start, for once." He sighs. "I hope that satisfies your little background check."

He gets about five paces before the guilt sets in.

Nice going, Whit.

Here I'm ready to write this guy off as a soulless faker, and he ends up being another kid damaged by the system who's just trying to stay afloat.

"Hey," I call after him.

He turns, his gaze accusatory.

"Listen," I offer, "I'm sorry about your father. I'll think about what you said, okay?"

Heath shrugs, the mask of amusement creeping back into his eyes. "Does this little heart-to-heart mean we get to be buddies now and throw the ball around again sometime? Because I can't wait."

Chapter 12

Whit

THE SKY OVERHEAD is darkening with the threat of rain, but the clouds inside my head feel stormiest of all.

The bleachers cleared out long ago, so the touch of a hand on my shoulder takes me by surprise.

"You okay?" Janine asks, her eyebrows crinkled with concern.

"Yeah. Sure." I force a smile. The field is where I've always been able to let go of my anxiety, but with this loss today, my stress over the Council, the missing kids, Heath, Wisty...it's all just been building. "You didn't have to wait for me."

Janine shrugs as if to say, *Of course I waited.* She's hugging her bare arms to her chest, and her hair is damp. I hadn't even realized it was raining.

"You must be freezing," I say, standing. "Here." I hold out my jacket.

Janine tilts her head to the side. "You don't have to take care of me, you know."

"Oh. Um." I shift uncomfortably. "You were just shivering, so…"

But Janine smiles and pulls my jacket over her bare shoulders anyway. "I just meant that everyone expects you to play the hero all the time, and you don't have to do that with me, okay?" She looks me in the eye. "You can be real."

"Great. Then if you wouldn't mind carrying this…" I lift up my gym bag.

Janine's crack of laughter is sharp and bright, and immediately puts me at ease.

"Would you maybe want to get a bite with me?" I ask as we walk together off the field. "I thought we could go to that fancy new place downtown with the awesome view of the mountains."

"Whit Allgood, are you asking me on a date?" She arches an eyebrow.

I grin sheepishly. As lame as it sounds, I've never actually asked a girl out. Celia was a cheerleader, and I was the foolball captain, so we first got together because that's what everyone expected. With Janine, I have to work for it.

"What if I am?"

"Well, then I'm not sure," she answers.

"Since when is a 'daughter of the Revolution' ever not sure of anything?"

Janine smirks. "I'm not sure I want trendy food that looks like whipped vomit and tastes like air. Let's grab a burger instead!"

"Deal."

We end up at a hole-in-the-wall grill that used to have the best burgers and wings in the City.

"It feels exactly the same," Janine marvels. It's the only building left standing on the block, but inside it's still cozy, with the same worn red furniture and loud decor on the walls.

"Last time I was here, I didn't know I was a wizard," I say, remembering. "I didn't even know the Resistance existed, and you were already *running* it."

We stuff our faces with greasy goodness, reminiscing about those early days—the jailbreaks, the protests, the so-horrible-you-just-have-to-laugh-now-because-we-made-it-out-alive mishaps—if you can call them "mishaps."

"I hate to say it, but this barbecue dip kind of reminds me of that time the Lost Ones basted us in roasting sauces," Janine says.

Yeah, that was rough—we were trapped between dimensions in the maze of Shadowland, and hunted down by tormented souls who survive on the flesh of the living. Not one of our finest moments.

"I still don't get why they wanted to eat you." I pick up her hand. "Not much meat," I joke. But feeling the warmth in her touch, I can't help thinking about how I almost lost her then. "That was one of the worst days of my life," I say quietly.

Janine meets my eyes. "That was the day I knew..."

"Knew what?" I ask, even though I remember. It was

the day she told me she loved me. I couldn't say it back, not yet.

"I knew I never wanted to eat barbecue again," Janine answers solemnly, and takes a huge bite of her sauce-covered burger. I crack up, but Janine shakes her head and takes my hand again.

"What?" I ask. She glances down at our entwined fingers.

"I never thought I'd be holding hands with the star of the foolball team, that's all."

"Yeah, because back in school, girls like you wouldn't give us jocks the time of day."

"Ha!" Janine cackles. "Girls like me?"

"Creative, confident, independent, crazy smart..."

"All true!" she says wryly. "I was smart enough to see there was more to Whit Allgood than muscles, even before you read me poetry."

I smile, remembering that first intense moment between us, and the awkwardness after, when Wisty told her I hadn't even written the poem.

Janine drops her eyes and sighs. "But you were always with Celia. It was like you didn't even see other girls, especially me."

"I see you now," I say, squeezing her hand.

Janine looks up at me, and I'm really happy to just lose myself inside the endlessness of her wide green eyes. "I see you, too."

Chapter 13

Whit

I'M WALKING THROUGH darkness where trees are made of bone, and shadows slither under my feet. When I hear wailing in the distance, a familiar terror grips me. I start to run. But then the sky fills with light, the noises stop, and her face is all around me. Her almond eyes, sweet mouth, and rich curls—she's all I see.

"Celia?" I ask, blinking up at her ethereal image in wonder. After she died, even the thought of Celia brought instant tears and a sharp stab of hurt, but right now, I only feel peace.

"It's good to see you, Whit," she says serenely. "How's Janine? I can feel the two of you getting closer."

The accusation makes me wince. "I'm sorry, Celes," I blurt out. "I still miss you every day. You *know* I wish it could've been different, that I could be with you forever, but…"

"But you were meant to live," she murmurs, and her

gaze gets distant. "You're meant to be with someone who is real and *alive*."

I nod. Celia's part of *beyond* now, a face in the sky I can't even touch. And when I try to remember her musical laugh and sweet perfume, there's a disturbing emptiness, a place my memories can't reach anymore.

"How are you, Whit?" she asks in that removed voice, her features blurring in the wind. "Tell me you're happy. Tell me it was all worth it."

Was her death worth it to destroy The One?

"I think it was worth it...." I say hesitantly. But I was never good at deceiving Celia, even when it would've been best for both of us.

"What is it?" she asks, the clouds shifting as her lips purse with concern.

"It's just so much harder running things than I'd imagined," I sigh. "Dealing with laws and kidnappings and the Mountain King threat. And Wisty seems to be pulling away from me and—"

"*The Mountain King?*" Celia breaks in. The light filling the sky flickers like a candle.

"From the Mountain on the western border..."

"The Mountain King is *alive*?" Her detached tone is replaced with alarm.

"The Council thinks he just wants to negotiate the old laws for water usage," I say, trying to stay calm.

"Listen to me, Whit." Celia's voice rises, and the bone trees around me sway. "There are souls here in the beyond, souls of *children*, who became Lost Ones because they couldn't rest after what had happened to them at the hands of the Mountain King."

"I don't understand," I whisper, feeling a cold dread flood my chest.

"The Mountain King killed them, Whit. He slaughtered whole cities of people!" Celia screams, her voice thundering all around me. The force of the sound knocks me to the ground.

"What are you talking about?" I shout up at the sky, but her face is fuzzy static now.

"Promise me you'll stay away from the Mountain," Celia pleads as she fades into red clouds. The shadows start to creep back in as the light dims, and I feel my panic rising. "Promise me you'll be careful. . . ."

I wake up from the dream soaked in sweat, with her voice still echoing in my head. But it's the middle of the night, and Celia is dead. I don't know who to tell, or who to fear, or where to go. I don't even know if it was real.

I'm alone in darkness again.

Chapter 14

Whit

"SO." I LOOK AROUND a table at the tired faces of the Over Watch, trying to keep the anxiety out of my voice. "What's the latest? Has anyone heard any news about the Mountain People?"

Wisty looks at me strangely, but I continue. "Any contact near the border, or changes with the water negotiations? Anything about the King? Any news at all?"

"Whoa, whoa, whoa, brother," Wisty protests. "You sound like our dear General Bloom, and we're not at the Council meeting quite yet. Coffee first. Then business."

"Coffee coming right up," Emmett offers.

As he sets down the mugs, I raise an eyebrow at my sister. "I thought you hated coffee."

"I do." Wisty drains her mug in one big gulp. "I also hate rules. And meetings. And waking up early. Ruling the City is just a barrel of fun. Hit me with another cup, Emmett," she says, and slaps the card table.

"Hey, easy there," Byron groans, lifting his head off the swaying table and rubbing sleep from his eyes.

I guess I can't blame them. It *is* obscenely early—the sun hasn't even risen—but after that dream, I lay awake, the dread slowly turning into icy fear. By early morning, I sent out the alert to the Resistance to meet at The Tube so we could touch base before the eight o'clock Council meeting.

I'm so on edge, even the graffiti looks malicious this morning; all I see are those painted soldiers marching on the wall. But then I catch Janine midyawn and she grins, looking adorably game for anything, as usual. For a moment, the warmth I felt with her yesterday floods my senses. Maybe the dream was just a stupid dream. Everything is going to be okay.

"There were more kidnappings last night," Sasha reports in his typically blunt way, instantly shattering all notions of things being okay. We all stare at him, and he shakes his head dejectedly. "We couldn't get there in time. That's the news."

"I thought we had eyes and ears all over the City," I say, bewildered.

Byron nods. "I used all my connections."

"And no one saw anything?" I ask desperately, the frustration starting to spill out of me. "We couldn't save them?"

"Hey, we're doing everything we can, pulling crazy hours," Sasha says defensively. "I was up all night patrolling."

"We just need more people, Whit," Janine says. "It's

hard to get new recruits because the kids who survived the New Order are still afraid. Don't forget, it wasn't that long ago that we lost most of the Resistance to the regime."

Celia's voice intrudes on my thoughts. *Souls of children,* she said. *The Mountain King killed them.*

"And you're sure *none* of your street ears have heard anything about the Mountain King?" I repeat, fixing Byron with a hard stare until he squirms.

"Whit, stop it!" Wisty snaps her fingers in front of my face. "This is bad enough without you acting like a total jerk. What's up with this stuff about the Mountain King? Did you have another one of those visions?"

Janine raises her eyebrows, and I hesitate. *Just my dead girlfriend shrieking at me to be careful.*

I sigh, feeling like an idiot as I see the wounded looks around the table. "I'm sorry, guys. I know you're all doing the best you can. Just ignore me."

"Always do," Wisty grumbles.

"No visions. Just some bad dreams."

Chapter 15

Wisty

"I'M SO RELIEVED you brought up the issue of security, Mr. Allgood," Matthias Bloom thunders into the microphone as Whit retakes his seat in the Council. My brother just presented his concerns about the threat of the Mountain King, but I'm not sure I completely understand his recent obsession with the guy.

"What's the *deal*?" I whisper to Whit, but he shakes his head maddeningly and hushes me as Bloom continues.

"Protecting our citizenry is our highest priority, as you'll see from our first agenda item today," Bloom says, and nods to a jowly man in the corner.

The man reads from the agenda: "'Sanctions for magic makers.'"

Whit jerks his head back toward Bloom. *"What?"*

Before I know what I'm doing, I'm on my feet. "What kind of sanctions? The City is free!"

"Exactly." Bloom stares down from the new raised

platform he's had installed in the chamber. The Seat of the Speaker, he's calling it. "And by requiring magic makers to register their powers with the Council, we ensure it will remain free and safe for all."

"So...it's just a registry?" Whit asks guardedly. I gape at him like he's crazy. *Just* a registry? This is the first sign of a police state if I ever saw one.

Bloom shifts in his high seat. "Yes. And in addition, as a courtesy, we will also ask that no acts of magic be performed at this time, at least until our City becomes better able to defend itself. Magical behavior is just too unpredictable. Too dangerous."

I clench my jaw. *Behavior?* It sounded like he was talking about a bunch of un-potty-trained toddlers. No one messes with my M. "And if we refuse?"

"Why would any magic makers refuse to comply with such a code, unless they planned to do harm? Steps would need to be taken to control the situation."

"Control?" I feel a scowl searing my face, and I don't even have to look at Whit to know that he's got on that face that's pleading with me not to do something rash.

"How's this for *control*?" My anger is tingling through my body, and as I work my M up into a spell, I see a uniform look of shock rippling across the room on the Council members' faces.

Here's what they saw: my mouth, and then the rest of me, dissolving into thin air as I disappeared from my seat. It feels kind of like needle pricks all over me.

"How exactly are you going to control us?" My voice echoes around the room. "Forcibly? Like The One did?"

I make myself reappear in the rafters for a brief instant, but by the time Bloom's eyes flit upward, I'm dissipating again. It's a lot of work—but absolutely worth every uncomfortable look shared among the Council.

Unfortunately Bloom's wit is sharp. "The One was truly evil," Bloom agrees. "Naturally, we recognize that not *all* magicians pose a threat to society, but without regulating such power, how do we know we won't end up with another person exerting their unique powers over society like The One did?" A tense hum of whispers builds.

But I'm about to make Bloom's golden words disappear, too.

In an instant Bloom's toupee soars off his head onto the floor, hit by my invisible hand, and the room erupts in snickers.

That was priceless. I can't believe I didn't think of doing it sooner.

Bloom finally loses his cool, and his chins quiver with his booming voice. "*Ms. Allgood!* This is an official Council meeting in the sacred Hall of your City! *Will you kindly return to your seat?*"

I can't resist one last retort. Instead of taking my seat, I materialize right next to him, smirking. This time, he flinches.

With the last of the magic energy I can muster right now, I return to my brother's side. I can tell Whit isn't all that amused by my performance—but he's still fighting the good fight.

"These are our rights, and you don't have the right to change them, Mr. Bloom," he says. "You don't speak for all the people."

"I am the Speaker. I absolutely speak for our citizens," Bloom says irritably as he smoothes the few remaining wispy hairs across his head. "Each of us is an elected Council member, and each of us has an equal voice." He looks like a fat cat about to pounce. "So, let us take a vote, then, shall we? All who oppose that magic makers should disclose their potential to do harm to the general public?"

From the way Bloom worded it, I see uncertainty written on every face in the room. Still, the hands start to rise, one by one. Most of them are kids who were elected to be on the Council because of their extreme bravery, but they still look terrified.

"Come on," Whit says under his breath. "Come on, come on."

The revolutionary from the Gutter raises his hand, and the journalist from the suburbs casts her vote. I hold my breath as I wait for more, hoping, hoping...

But as I look around, the rest of the hands are folded. The voting is done, and it's not enough. Eight out of thirty-four.

"All in favor of the proposed sanctions, to secure the safety of the citizenry of the City?" Bloom asks cheerfully.

The speed at which the rest of the hands shoot up takes my breath away. I clutch Whit's arm as I gaze around the circle of the room, and I feel dizzy and nauseated.

We're surrounded by a wall of hands, every one of them ready to grab for our throats.

Chapter 16

Whit

"WHAT DOES *The Book of Truths* say?" I shout, my voice carrying through the chamber. "I believe *The Book* wouldn't allow for such sanctions."

Bloom looks up from his agenda, surprised. "And what makes you believe such a thing, Mr. Allgood?"

I step into the center of the chamber, my shoes echoing on the marble floor. I look around, trying to catch the Council's eyes, spark their trust, remind them why they are here. *To serve the good of the community. To fight for free will.*

"As free citizens, we all have the right to see what Council member Bloom sees in *The Book of Truths*. I move that we reprint the book and distribute it to all citizens immediately."

There are collective gasps and excited whisperings around the chamber at the suggestion. Bloom's eyes appear stone cold from his high chamber seat. "And I move to table this issue for further review. Next agenda item?"

I hear Wisty's sharp intake of breath. *The Book* was supposed to be the property of the whole Council. "What is there to review?" she shouts, starting to reach her breaking point.

Bloom flicks his wrist absently, as if the answer is obvious. "It would be irresponsible to rush into reprinting. In such perilous times, *The Book of Truths* could be dangerous in the wrong hands."

Exactly. Wisty and I share a look. Bloom's hands are starting to seem a lot less clean.

"If we're facing possible war, the community needs that information now more than ever," I point out.

"I agree," Bloom allows. "The community needs to be protected, and they need someone to interpret the insight that *The Book of Truths* offers."

We parry words back and forth like swordsmen matching blow for blow. The other thirty-one Council members look on, their heads swiveling between us as we each try to gain ground.

But my head starts to throb from the effort, and I know Bloom can out-talk and out-twist and out-sell Wisty and me any day. Everything's riding on this debate, and it's only a matter of time before we fail to block.

There's only one final weapon to pull from our arsenal. Wisty sighs and finally says what everyone has been thinking.

"Look. I killed The One Who Is The One myself. My brother and I saved this City when no one else could, and we deserve a little respect. We demand to see *The Book of Truths*, which foretold of our power!"

She's played our ace.

The faces around the room are nodding in agreement. But they're still looking at Bloom the Speaker, Bloom the interpreter, Bloom the Keeper of *The Book of Truths*, to see what he'll say.

The general clears his throat with a guttural hacking. "I'm afraid that won't be possible." Bloom shakes his gray head sadly. "Regardless of your achievements, as magic makers, you're subject to the recently passed sanctions. No wizard may see the sacred words, lest they twist them into spells for their own power."

"By whose authority do you deny us our most basic right?" I shout.

"By the authority of this Council, elected by the people," Bloom answers mildly. "I'm afraid that unless *The Book* decrees, the Council's ruling must stand."

Bloom strikes a large bell and it echoes around the chamber's high ceilings like a wail of frustration. Then he allows himself a rare, self-congratulatory grin as he says, "This meeting is adjourned."

Chapter 17

Wisty

"WISTY?" WHIT LOOKS at me with concern.

I start to heat up. My color is rising with anger, my ears and cheeks flushing red. After all we've fought for, our rights as free citizens are going to be revoked in ten minutes by one well-spoken man in a room of cowards.

And they're *ignoring* us. Papers are shuffling, the doors are opening. They're all leaving. Feeling steam gathering in my head and lava flowing through my veins, I place one of my muddy sneakers onto my chair and push myself up, rising above the Council floor.

"Wisty," Whit repeats, "I really don't think it's a good idea to—"

"*Wait!*" I yell at the dispersing officials, just as my hair bursts into flames.

All the members stop in their tracks at that moment to stare at the burning girl in the center of City Hall. A few of the suits closest to me start to back away as beads of sweat pool on their foreheads. I even manage to singe Bloom's eyebrows. I smirk with satisfaction...until he points a long, bony finger in my direction.

"Fellow Council members, Ms. Allgood wishes us to consider the plight of magicians," he crows. "But *this* is the face of magic—dangerous and out of control. It is the common citizen who is truly at risk."

"I'm perfectly under control," I scowl, letting my flame fizzle out.

But Whit is shaking his head at me, his jaw tight, and I see it's too late.

Bloom's flinty eyes sweep the chamber, connecting with each person in turn. "Remember The One, friends. Remember how unrestricted magic makers remain in power: through trickery, intimidation, and fear!"

I can't believe he's actually comparing me to The One. "Are you really listening to this lunatic?" I ask everyone. But I see few sympathizers here, and even fewer friends. No one moves, no one speaks, and even the kids on the Council won't meet my eyes.

"Fine," I croak, feeling the tears start to brim. I jump off my chair and hastily grab my belongings, my fingers shaking with hurt and anger. Bloom's mouth stays tight in a smug, thin line.

Whit tries to put a hand on my shoulder, but I fling it away, furious he didn't support me up there.

"Prejudice is prejudice," I shout as I storm out of the chamber. "No matter how you spin it."

I can't believe I trusted Bloom, or any of them.

To Shadowland with them all!

Chapter 18

Wisty

I BANG THROUGH the doors of City Hall in a blind rage, papers slipping from my grasp as I try to shove them into my bag. I take the steps two at a time to get away from this corrupt place, full of liars and word twisters and bigots.

But I don't get out of there fast enough, because guess who I spot waiting for me, leaning against a pillar, looking suave as ever?

Yeah: the Demon himself.

Oh, that's just great. I'm sure I'm looking totally stunning right now, with my face flushed with anger and my eyes puffy from tears. My hair is probably still steaming.

I veer away from Heath, hoping he hasn't spotted me, but luck just doesn't seem to be on my side this week.

"Wisty! Wait!"

"Not now!" I yell, but I can hear the sound of his shoes on the pavement as he runs after me. He's at risk of getting as bad as Byron. But at least I can turn Byron into a rodent to shut him up. Heath . . . well, I just couldn't *do* that to him.

"You dropped this." He holds out one of the papers I dropped—where I'd doodled a cartoon of Bloom getting crushed by a book. "Nice," he smirks.

I snatch it out of his hands.

"Look," I snap. "I'm warning you, I'm seriously not in the mood for any games right now. I've already burned one person today, and I'm *thisclose* to bringing the heat again. So just—give me some space, okay?"

"Did *inflamed* tempers *spark* debate with our cherished Speaker?"

I'm not in the mood for stupid puns, either. I storm off toward the square, but Heath keeps pace with me, totally unfazed by my threat. He actually hasn't stopped smiling, and I'm not sure if I want to kill him for it—or kiss him. Because I know he's trying to make me laugh.

"No need to get *fired up*, Wisty," he says playfully. "Don't have a *meltdown*."

I glare at him. Leaning toward *kill*.

"You're so *hot* when you're mad." He grins. "No, seriously. You're *smoking*. There's no *match* for you."

I shake my head, feeling a laugh building despite my anger. "Your puns are really awful."

"But accurate!" he shoots back. "You can't argue with anything I've just said, can you?" He raises an eyebrow and I roll my eyes, but I can't resist a grin.

"See? You're smiling." He looks pleased with himself.

"This is getting a little old, don't you think? *I* think." I walk even faster, not wanting to give any ground. Not yet.

"I guess we don't think the same way," Heath fires back. "That's a good thing, right?"

I whirl around to face him, holding out my arms. "What do you want from me?" We're in the center of the square now, as good a place as any to finally duke this out. "Seriously, what do you *want*?" I yell.

Heath cocks his head to the side, studying my face. "Why do you assume I want something?" he asks.

I purse my lips, thinking of Bloom and *The Book*, of The One and his power, of the guy in the band I had a crush on who sold me out to the New Order. I almost want to cry, but I've done enough crying today. Instead I smile and give a helpless shrug. "Because everyone wants something from me."

"I just like being around you," Heath says simply, and his eyes have so much sparkle in that moment that I almost believe him. "Is that so bad?"

Is it? I drink him in, this boy who can't seem to get enough of me. All sharp lines and long looks. That flirty twist of his mouth that drives me crazy in the worst way... but in the best way, too. He's not giving up.

Maybe this *is* getting old, but is that because I'm finally aching to move forward? To the next level of this... *thing* we've got going?

"Okay," I sigh. "The Resistance is having a party tonight. I guess it would be cool if you came." I try to say it as nonchalantly as possible, but I can feel my usual flush creeping up my neck. I shift my bag to my other arm awkwardly.

"Perfect." Heath gives me that blinding white grin full of perfect teeth, looking more confident than ever. He leans forward, and I hold my breath. "Are you ready to dance?" he whispers.

I bite my lip, feeling the spark. *Keep it together, Wisty. He's just a boy.*

"I might dance." I can't resist my own coy smirk as I walk past him and call over my shoulder, "Who knows if it'll be with you."

Chapter 19

Wisty

MY BROTHER'S PACING across the living room, gesturing wildly to our parents. I've never seen him so agitated, but he seems to be like this all the time lately.

"You should've seen the deadness in their eyes as they just crucified us up there, willing to do whatever he said."

Mom and Dad nod at Whit from the couch, listening intently as they sip their tea, but they haven't said a word.

"The Council ruled that *magic is forbidden*," I say. "Don't you guys think this is serious? Shouldn't we be doing something?"

Our parents share a long, sad look, but they don't exactly look *alarmed*.

"Did you guys know about this?" Whit asks, and folds his arms. He looks like the sensitive little boy I remember growing up with right then, not the well-built athlete with serious magical power that he's become.

"We *suspected*..." Mom begins.

Dad stands and touches Whit's shoulder. "But we couldn't confirm the rumors, or we would've told you."

"But how?" my brother asks, bewildered. "We've got Resistance spies all over the City, and no one had heard a word about this. How did you know?"

"Well..." Mom looks uneasy. "Since the original development of the New Order, we've been meeting in secret with an underground network of magicians to share information."

"Since *before* The One?" I say, shocked. "This could've been really helpful a lot of the times we *almost died*."

"The group dissolved during The One's rule," she answers. "Mrs. Highsmith was the only magician still able to safely operate."

"Did you not find my services useful, Wisteria?" I hear Mrs. Highsmith sing as she suddenly materializes in the fireplace from a puff of ash.

"Always." I grin at her. Apart from her incredible power and the fact that she's saved our hides a few times, this is why I love this quirky, crazy witch: our shared pyromania. Mrs. Highsmith dusts the ash off her clothes—which are as eccentric as ever, including an elaborate feathered hat and yards of fuchsia felt—and plops down into the chair beside me.

"We've only begun meeting again recently because of suspicions among the magic community about Bloom," Dad continues. "The man has a bit of a history of being reactionary...."

"Pfft!" Mrs. Highsmith waves her sooty handkerchief at my dad. "Sweet words. Call a bean a bean, Benjamin. He is a politician, a money hoarder, and the ultimate straight-and-narrow, with no appreciation whatsoever of the arts. The One took power because of people like Matthias Bloom."

Whit rakes his hands through his hair in frustration. "And he's got *The Book of Truths*, so people are listening to him. What are we supposed to do?"

"The solution is simple," Mrs. Highsmith crows. "Do what The One did."

"What?" I say. "Scare them into submission? That's exactly what Bloom's doing."

"I don't mean scare them, dearie. I mean *charm* them."

I look from Mrs. H. to my parents to Whit, nodding. She's right. The One was a dictator, but it was the people who raised him up.

"But we don't want power," I say. "Ruling is pretty much the worst thing ever."

"Worse than school?" Dad asks, and he laughs when I nod. It wasn't so long ago that I was just a girl doing whatever she could to cut class, and I guess some things never change.

"So don't seek power," Mom says. "But if you want to help the City, find a way to make the people listen. Find a way to win them back."

"You already have the three of us," my dad says, putting his arms around me and Whit.

"And we count for *more*." Mrs. Highsmith winks.

"We love you guys," I say, grateful for the millionth time that we'd been able to bring them back from Shadowland. "But we should go. I have to get ready to go out."

Whit gapes at me. "I can't believe you're going to the party when everything around us is falling apart."

"Like you played in a foolball game the day after the kidnappings?" I counter. "We all need ways to let loose, and we can't fix it all tonight."

"I heartily agree with Wisteria," Mrs. Highsmith chimes in. "Now, what about this Heath chappie, dear?" she asks pointedly, as if she can see exactly how my heart pounds inside my chest at the mention of his name. "You haven't said a single word about him. Why is that?"

"I..." I flush tomato red and chew my lip to shreds, but I still can't give her a straight answer. I don't think I know myself.

Chapter 20

Wisty

THIS *SHOULDN'T* BE that awkward, right? Just a simple party. It's just friends. And friends of friends. Everyone knows everyone here....

But no one knows Heath, so they're all staring.

"Let's, um, go over to the corner so we can talk."

But we don't talk, because now that I've finally admitted to myself that I might *really* like him, I don't know where to start.

"Nice shoes," he says, nodding at my shiny silver pumps.

"Thanks." I smile. But they shredded my heels so much on the way here I have to take them off. Heath watches me slip them off, amused, but holds back any obnoxious commentary. "Nice club, right?" I say, and he nods.

We look at the DJ booth and at the red disco ball. We stare for long minutes at the floor tiles or the gum stuck to the walls...just not at each other.

Awk. Ward.

I'm about to call it quits and just head home, but then Heath looks at me with that familiar spark, that electricity that I've been missing all night.

"Look," he says. "We're making this too hard. Let's just dance."

Earlier today, I thought I was going to play a little more hard to get. But right now, I know that dancing is what I need.

I start swaying back and forth, bouncing to the beat, loosening up with the occasional hip shake. The same rhythmic movements over and over, just like what everyone else is doing.

But Heath's doing a lot more than the rest of us. Like his Demon tearing apart the foolball field, it seems like everything he does has to be a thousand times more... electric. Powerful. Maybe even... perfect.

While other people bob like lapping waves, he's liquid motion. His whole body seems to writhe, but he doesn't look stupid. He looks incredible. He merges styles, swaying to the lulls and shaking to the pickups. It's like he anticipates the musical shifts before they happen, and his body responds instantly.

I'm kind of inspired, watching him. I let my arms rise up and swirl around. Then my head and hips get into the gyration. We're dancing by ourselves, doing our thing, but our eyes find each other again and again, stoking the spark.

My hair starts swinging wildly and it whips Heath's

face. He's laughing. I'm laughing. His arm curls around my waist and pulls me in close.

But just then the song ends and we pull apart abruptly.

Heath's cheeks are flushed with the exercise, and for some reason, even the sight of his sweat makes my heart rate rise.

"You're an incredible dancer," I say breathlessly as someone fumbles with choosing another song.

"You're pretty great yourself."

I shake my head. "Not like that. And on the foolball field. No one has reflexes like my brother. But you move like magic."

"Maybe I'm a wizard, too," Heath whispers, his breath hot on my neck.

I pull back, surprised. I see from his expression that there's no maybe. He's telling the truth. "You're not registered," I answer, confused. I thought I knew all the magicians in the City.

"If you could go back and keep your power a secret, wouldn't you?"

I shake my head instinctively, but then I think of the sanctions Bloom is imposing on magicians. I see what Heath is saying. That kind of information is a dangerous secret these days. And he's sharing it with me.

I'm more intrigued by this mysterious boy than ever.

"Now, do you want to *really* dance?" he asks, eyebrow raised devilishly, and I know what he's asking.

Whit and I have merged our power with other people a

few times when we had to. Whit brought me back from near death with the help of a little girl named Pearl, and even Byron and I had a notable moment....

But Whit and I have never merged with other magicians.

I look down at Heath's outstretched hand, then up at those fearless, clear blue eyes. For being one of the most powerful witches in our world, I'm way too intimidated.

"Don't follow me. Follow the music," he says. "Let it *inside* of you."

No more holding back. Time to feel it. Deep inside.

I take his hand and instantly feel the surge of his power as it builds on mine. I feel my heart beating out a rhythm, faster and faster.

I do as he says and let in the music. I let in the beat, the rhythm, and the pulse. I let it shake up through my bones and into my muscles. But more than that, I let in Heath's *power*.

It makes my feet feel light, my hips free. It makes me feel like I'm capable of anything and everything. It pulses hotter than fire, lifts me higher than morphed wings, is stronger than mind control. It *electrifies* me.

Once again Heath's arms find my waist and we're drawn together by an almost magnetic force. Pretty soon it's like our separate moves just start morphing into one pulsing, swaying animal.

The crowd instinctively backs up around us, giving us space, and all the other people seem to fade away until it's just *him and me*. We're spinning now, shoulders shuddering, hips popping, then stopping magically at the same moment. Right now, it's not about us. It's not about what we want.

It's about the music.

After years living under the New Order, sneaking muffled strums on a guitar and trying to keep my movements measured and meek, this is exactly what I needed. After a while, I don't even know how long we've been dancing, because the hum of our energy makes it feel like forever and mere moments at the same time.

I just know that I never want to stop.

Chapter 21

Wisty

"YOU'RE NOT WELCOME HERE."

It's Byron. I can hardly believe it. I should've left him as a weasel.

Heath just keeps dancing. He doesn't say anything or even acknowledge that he's heard Byron. And why would he? It's a ridiculous statement.

"Byron..." I start, but thankfully, he's walking away.

Or not. He pulls the plug to the amp, and the music dies. Complaints erupt around the room, but Byron ignores them all and stands in front of Heath, arms crossed over his chest.

"You're upset. I understand," Heath says, his voice thick with amusement. "But I'm not the problem here. Wisty knows what she wants"—I see where this is going; I start to open my mouth to object, but he's too fast—"and she didn't choose *you*, friend."

Byron gives Heath a sudden hard shove. "I'm not your friend," he spits.

"Whoa," I gasp. "Byron!"

Heath takes a step back, still smiling, but from the tilt of his head, I'm guessing he's not going to give Byron another shot. From what we all saw during the fool-ball game, Byron would have to have a death wish to attempt it.

Of course, he tries to push forward again anyway.

"I said, enough!" I yell, stepping between them. I throw a spark in warning, and the lights flicker. Everyone in the club is watching us now, eyes round. "Just leave us alone, okay?" I say, lowering my voice.

"How could you be with him, Wisty?" Byron pleads, his voice cracking, and I feel totally awful. "After everything we've been through, making magic together."

That was nothing like this. "Byron," I say gently, touching his arm. The heat is gone from my fingers now. "We were never... I—"

"I mean, how can you even *touch* a New Order Youth like Heath?" He shrugs off my hand with disgust.

I stare back at him, agape. Is he serious? Half the citizens in the City are former N.O.... *including Byron.*

Heath cocks an eyebrow. "Think you better quit while you're behind, *friend.*" His voice is smooth as silk, but there's an undeniable edge to it now.

Byron's hair has fallen across his brow. His face is blotchy with fury and his mouth is pressed tight with suppressed insults, but he knows he's beaten.

Giving me a final, withering look, he slinks off.

"What'd you do to Byron?" Whit says accusingly from behind me.

I wheel around, anger flashing. This just gets better and better. Is *everyone* against me today?

The onlookers start to whisper, which makes me more furious. Yes, let's have the famous witch and wizard air out their dirty laundry at what was *supposed* to be the best dance party of the new era. I drag my brother over to a darkened corner for more privacy.

"I didn't do *anything* to Byron!" I say irritably. "And neither did Heath."

Whit's brow furrows. "Weird. I've never seen him pick a fight before. Why would Byron do something like that, do you think?" He crosses his arms and eyes Heath, who's stayed by my side.

"Because he's acting like some jealous child," I say. "Obviously."

Whit sits down on a bar stool and studies me. "Or maybe because he's really worried about the decisions you're making, and how they're going to affect your future?"

I narrow my eyes. Whit's talking to me like Bloom does, all patronizing rationale, and I don't appreciate it.

"Maybe you should ask Byron yourself." Heath looks at Whit coolly.

Ignoring him, Whit continues on his controlling big-brother tirade. "Wisty, do you really trust this guy?"

This is totally about the foolball rivalry. *Just because Whit lost a stupid game...*

"Because I don't trust him," Whit goes on, not even giving me time to answer. "And maybe if you just came out of your little bubble for a second and listened to the people who care about you—"

"I can take care of myself!" I explode at him.

"I hope so." Whit nods, but manages to look extremely doubtful at the same time, and it's all I can do to control my flame and fury. He walks toward the door. "I really hope so."

Chapter 22

Wisty

WHIT LEAVES THE CLUB, slamming the door behind him, and it's like the magic has been sucked out of this night with a vacuum.

The music starts up again, and the party rages on, but the Resistance kids are looking at me curiously from across the room, and while I know what they're thinking, I can't help what Byron feels. I can't help what *I* feel.

I watch Heath move in brilliant sequences and sigh. I feel *a lot*.

I want to keep dancing with him, feeling that electric jolt of connection again and again, but I can't seem to get my rhythm back, and the music just sounds like deafening static in my ears.

"I think I'm going to head out," I shout over the bass.

"Can I at least walk you home?"

We take the back route to my apartment, through the winding alleyways of what was once the Gutter. It's a thrill to be alone with him, to hear the sound of just our feet on the cobblestones, to feel that pulse of attraction growing even stronger since we used our power together.

But I can't quite give in, can't get that awful scene with Whit and Byron out of my head.

"You look like you could use some cheering up." Heath opens his palm, and a flower grows right up out of it. "A gift from my hometown."

It looks like the one he gave me before, with the bright orange center and papery, silver petals. I swallow, remembering the rush of emotions I felt then.

"It's pretty, right? It might look all delicate and sweet, but if you get too close…" He touches the center of the flower, and quick as a flash, the petals pull closed, and stinging nettles shoot out of the stem and into his skin. Heath flinches and drops the plant.

"You didn't have to actually show me." I laugh. "Does it hurt?"

He shrugs, sucking at his finger. "I kind of like the burn."

"Me, too," I whisper.

Our eyes lock with smoldering intensity under the streetlight, and he pulls me to him, inhaling me in a reckless kiss that takes me by surprise.

It's the hottest thing I've ever experienced. My face and chest suddenly feel like they've exploded with my fire, and I don't even care. When he suddenly pulls back, I'm breathless.

I hadn't flamed out. It was all passion. Pure, simple, true *passion*.

"Sorry," Heath says quickly, stepping back. "I, uh, didn't mean to…" His confidence seems to flicker for the first time since I've known him. I don't get it.

"You didn't mean to kiss me?"

Heath leans against the alley wall and shoves his hands in his pockets. "I promised myself I'd never do that until you asked me to," he sighs.

He waited for me to choose. He waited on doorsteps and next to bleachers and outside City Hall. He waited until I was ready.

Byron and Whit were so wrong about him. In every way.

"Well, don't be sorry. I liked it." *I like everything about you.* I step toward him and stand on my tiptoes to lean close to his face, now hidden in shadow.

"So now I'm asking you." My voice comes out raspy, full of hope and need and everything that's been leading up to this moment. I take the leap. "Please do it again."

Chapter 23

Whit

"I'M GOING TO VOMIT." Byron groans as Wisty closes the door behind her.

I know the feeling. Crouching behind someone's porch and watching my little sister make out with a creep in a dark alley isn't exactly my idea of a good time, either. Heath is whistling as he strides away from the apartment, a swagger in his step, and I grind my teeth.

Why did I let Byron talk me into following them?

I look over at him resentfully and notice that he's prying off a rotting wooden board from the porch steps.

"What are you doing, Swain?"

Byron slaps the board against his palm a few times as if testing its weight. "Let's get him," he says, taking a few purposeful steps down the street after Heath.

I yank Byron backward by his collar.

"Are you *insane*?" I demand in the quietest voice I can manage. "First you push Heath in the club, and now you're

106

going to jump him in the alley? Wisty's right—you've lost it. What happened to Byron Swain, the coward I used to know?"

"I was never a coward," he says irritably, struggling out of my grasp. "I was just sensible."

"And where's your sense now? Heath would crush you. Did you *see* him on the foolball field?"

"And did you see him just *now*?" Byron challenges, but he can't quite keep the whine out of his voice.

"It was just a kiss, Byron. Look, I don't like the guy any more than you do, but it's Wisty's choice."

"He needs to know that if he hurts her..." Byron shakes his head and steps out into the street again, right under the streetlight, determination on his face. If I don't go with him, he's going to get himself killed.

"Put the board down." I sigh, knowing this is a bad idea. "We're just going to *talk* to him, and I'll do the talking."

But by the time we catch up, someone else has found him first.

We spot Heath as we round a corner. He's backed up against a car, a massive figure looming darkly over him. I freeze and yank Byron back behind the building before they see us. We flatten ourselves against the wall, straining to understand their low whispers.

It's Heath's voice I pick out first, though his usual snide bemusement is tinged with a hint of desperation. "Everything is in place. If I can convince the witch—"

"My lord is getting impatient," the figure says gruffly, in an accent I can't place. "It's time. He wants the girl out of the way."

Byron looks up at me, eyes wide. "Do you think they're talking about *Wisty*?" he hisses, and I wave him quiet.

"Tell him to stay out of it." Heath's voice again, agitated. "I've earned this."

"Then take what is ours by rights. Bring them home. Your father failed in his mission. Don't *you* fail, too."

I crane my neck around the corner to try to get a better look at the man. A ragged cloak is draped around him, a hood hiding half of his face.

"My father was weak," Heath snaps angrily, his voice carrying down the dark street. But pressed against the car, he looks far from the arrogant heartthrob; he looks like a nervous, insolent boy trying to prove himself.

I've played sports long enough to know that a kid like that is the most dangerous.

"Who's his father?" Byron wonders, and I flinch, wondering if they heard us—the kid couldn't whisper if his life depended on it. "Bring *who* home? What mission? What do you think they're planning? I *told* you Heath couldn't be trusted."

"Shh!" I snap, sending a jolt of power in his direction to seal his lips together temporarily. It's as simple as closing a wound. I'm not as practiced at turning Byron into a weasel as my sister is, but my healing powers do come in handy.

I've already missed the end of the conversation, though.

I curse under my breath as I watch the cloaked giant walking away, a million thoughts racing through my head, most of them similar to Byron's.

What are they planning?

Heath stands alone against the car, and even from here I can see his chest rising and falling in the dim light. Something the man said scared him, and scared him bad. What could scare someone as cocky as Heath?

"And remember," the hooded messenger calls over his shoulder as a last warning, "don't get too close to that fetching witch, either. A witch and wizard can never be together—you know the danger."

My chest tightens at the mention of my sister, and though Byron's lips are still sealed, I can see from his expression that we're thinking the same thing: *Heath is a wizard!*

My breath quickens as I hear the click of boots on the cobblestones, headed toward us. We hold our breath as Heath nears the corner, but he doesn't even see us.

"The danger is what I love," Heath mutters as he walks past.

Chapter 24

Heath

HE STOOD IN the darkness of his empty apartment, pulling off his boots and trying to stop his heart from racing. The merge had been strong—*dizzying*—and the ghost of Wisty's power still tingled on his fingertips hours later.

She made him want to *create*.

Not another flower, though—something that wouldn't wilt. She had told him she loved dogs. He laughed to himself, shaking his head. He couldn't believe he was sitting here thinking about what she'd like as a gift. It was so... *normal*. Simple. Just boyfriend trying to make his girlfriend smile. It made him almost... giddy.

With his mind reeling, Heath sank into the couch—the only piece of furniture in his apartment. He held open his palm and felt the trace of her spark burning within him, melting away all the coldness he was used to, that had been forced on him since he was a child.

Now, he thought only of warmth, and he smiled as he

watched a puppy grow from a speck in his hand to fill his fist and then playfully spill out over his two hands as he lowered it to the floor. It leaped at him moments later, now a huge Labrador with a lolling tongue and eager eyes.

When it licked his face, the weird thing was, he actually *liked* it. He liked the way it felt to scratch the dog's ears, too, and the way it nipped at his fingers happily. When he chased it around the room and it skidded across the floor on clumsy paws, it was like he could almost feel Wisty in the room with him, and hear her giggling at him.

He made another puppy, and another, addicted to the warmth in her power, the *life*. The dogs bowled into him, tails wagging, and now *he* was the one laughing as they jumped happily around him. He couldn't remember the last time he had laughed for real. *And he'd probably never laugh again after tonight.*

The smile fell from his lips as his thoughts drifted back to the dark messenger who had visited him in the alley. His orders were clear: "Bring them home in chains."

Home. After all he'd been through, all he'd worked for, it was *finally* happening.

Of course, if he went through with the plan, he'd never see Wisty again. He cradled his head in his hands, the conflict eating him up inside.

He could still remember the first time he saw her, when she'd infiltrated The One's New Order camp where he'd been working. Even though she was dressed like everyone else in the Youth Brigade, the red shimmered in her hair and the fire danced in her eyes. It was right before she'd openly challenged The One. He'd felt her pull even then.

She did what she wanted, and that's what he loved about her.

As he rubbed the dogs' big heads, Heath suddenly felt disgusted by their blind loyalty. Just like him. Always listening to orders—his mother, his grandfather, The One. All telling him to control himself.

To stay away from witches.

Never again.

The prophecy said a witch and wizard's power was limitless. He just hadn't expected to actually fall for her.

Such a love would destroy the world, his mother claimed.

Touching his own cheek, he was surprised to feel the wetness. He hadn't cried in years—since he had lived with his grandfather. In the moonlight, his fingers glistened with the tears, and he wasn't surprised to see they were as red as before. Some things would never change.

He laughed harshly as the dogs licked at his face, their slobbery tongues washing over his tears of blood.

"Of course you have a taste for blood," he told them. "You're part of me."

Chapter 25

Wisty

I'M HOLDING MY toothbrush like a microphone, rocking out to some superhappy, loud music and feeling like I'm walking on air. I look up in the mirror and see that, actually, I *am* levitating a little—that's how fluttery I'm still feeling.

Then the door to my apartment bangs open on its hinges, and my feet slam to the floor. Could it be *him*? My hair's frizzed out and my ratty pajamas aren't exactly flattering, but I still can't help feeling a little pang of hope as I peek over my shoulder with wide eyes....

But it's only my brother.

"You really know how to make an entrance," I say through a mouthful of toothpaste. I spit in the sink and resume hip shaking in my pajamas, trying to remember exactly how it felt with Heath on the dance floor.

Whit's still all worked up from earlier. "Wisty, listen, I really don't trust this guy," he starts in immediately.

"Byron and I did some digging, and I need you to listen to me this time."

I roll my eyes. "You guys just don't know him," I say, walking past him to close the front door, since he didn't bother to. "Heath's actually a total gentleman. Tonight was the best night of my life, despite you and Byron trying to ruin it. There was magic in everything—the dancing, the flower, the walk home...."

I sigh, flopping backward onto the couch, remembering the suddenness of the kiss, the *wanting* burning through every part of me.

"Wisty, forget about the stupid kiss. I'm trying to warn you—"

Wait, did I say that out loud? No, I didn't even mention the kiss. *Did Whit's power turn telepathic or*...I sit up, understanding finally breaking through my blissed-out state.

"Wait." I narrow my eyes at my brother. "You were *spying* on me?"

"I was protecting you!" Whit's eyes fly open defensively. He walks over and clicks off the loud, happy music, and the sudden silence seems to press in on me from everywhere. "When Byron and I saw Heath leaving your apartment, we trailed him. And it's a good thing we did, because—"

"*Byron* was with you?" I gape.

"He was worried about you, too!" Whit says angrily, but he's looking a little guilty now. "Actually, Byron wanted to come back here with me. You should be grateful I sent him home." His eyes soften, but I'm still feeling full of sharp edges.

"Gr-*grateful*?" I stutter, my eyes bugging with disbelief. "You *followed me* out of the club with my date, *watched us* kissing, and then *barged into* my apartment, shouting accusations...." I can feel my color rising with my voice. "And I should be *grateful*?!"

"He's a wizard, Wist. The messenger said—*oof!*" Whit glares after the pillow I throw clocks him in the head.

"I know he's a wizard!" I cut in, exasperated. "He *told* me, because that's the kind of relationship we have: an honest one."

"We have no idea who Heath could be involved with— Bloom, the Mountain King...even Pearce."

At the mention of The One's creepy protégé, I totally lose it.

"Pearce is *dead*!" I explode. "Just like The One Who Is The One. Can't you just let me be happy for once? I told you—I can take care of myself!"

Whit looks at me coolly. "So you said. Is that why you pulled that stunt in the chamber earlier, without even running it by me?"

"Oh, like you've been explaining your little Mountain King paranoia to me?" I fire back. "And since when do I need your permission to use my magic?"

"When you're speaking to the Council on behalf of all magicians and playing stupid pranks! Do you ever think about how your short temper affects anyone else? No—you only think of *you*. Yeah, you really seem to be doing a great job of taking care of yourself, Wisty."

I blink at him, fighting back tears. That might be the meanest thing my brother has ever said to me.

"Well, maybe if you had my back instead of shaking your head at me like Bloom and the rest of those cowards, I'd actually *trust you* enough to talk to you about Heath."

Whit gapes at me, the hurt plain on his face. The one thing we've always had between us was ultimate trust, but it's not my fault he broke it.

"You know what? I don't care about your personal issues anyway. Date who you want. Just don't cry to me when it blows up in your face."

"Fine!" I shout, throwing another pillow. "Get out of my apartment!"

But Whit's already slamming the door.

Chapter 26

Whit

I AWOKE THIS MORNING wanting to fix things with Wisty. Apparently she didn't feel the same way, though. By the time I spot her strolling across the square, very obviously ignoring me trying to catch up to her, I'm so angry I wish I had another door to slam in her face.

"We're late again," I snap in greeting when I finally reach her side. "Thank you, as usual."

"It's not my fault you're late," she says coldly, clicking along in her heels. *Since when does my sister wear heels?*

"I waited for you for half an hour!"

Since that first day, we've met with the Resistance at The Tube every morning before the Council meeting and walked over to the chamber together. This morning, Sasha and I went over updates from the City Watch, but Wisty was a no-show.

Wisty shrugs. "I was meeting Heath for breakfast," she says sweetly.

She just had to throw that in my face, didn't she? *That explains the heels.*

"Do me a favor, Wist. Don't say that name to me."

"Real mature, big brother." Wisty rolls her eyes, starting up the marble steps to the chamber. "No problem. We don't have to talk at all."

"And *that's* mature?"

I stop at the foot of the steps and watch my sister walk away from me—an image that's starting to feel familiar. I can't believe this morning I thought we could just move on. The rift between us isn't a crack; it's a canyon.

But something else is going on at the Capitol.

I was so caught up in bickering with my sister, I somehow missed the huge crowd gathered at the top, near the doorway. There are cameras and microphones set up overhead. Reporters vie for spots near the front. And in the center of all of them is Bloom, the flash of a snapshot illuminating his stern, pudgy face.

He's holding some kind of press conference.

It makes sense. The water supply is dangerously low, and with no fresh rations coming from the Mountain, Sasha said the Watch is overwhelmed with crime in the streets. The Council needs to issue a statement to calm the people before panic and fear build to a fever pitch.

I just wish Bloom wasn't the one doing the talking.

Chapter 27

Whit

I'VE LOST MY SISTER in the crowd, and I can barely see the podium, let alone claw my way up there to make a statement.

I look for an opening in the mob of people, trying to figure out what's being said, but Bloom's gesturing someone else to the mic. "We will continue to field questions in one moment, but first, Dr. Wells, if you please."

The man looks like a worm—he's bald, with a narrow pink face and lips that seem to blend into it. He looks nervous behind his glasses as he addresses the press.

"Magic is an unstable condition, as it manipulates our perception of reality," Dr. Wells the Worm begins, his pink lips pressed too close to the mic. "All the magic has seeped into our world through wormholes in the universe. Some of you may remember them being referred to as portals. Whatever they may be called, they are akin to an open wound that allows damaging foreign organisms to enter the healthily functioning ecosystem of a human body, and wreak havoc upon it."

He pulls out a series of charts and diagrams, awkwardly holding them up and trying to explain the physics of supernatural forces to an impatient crowd. Even *I* can't follow the terms he's using, and I *am* a supernatural force.

"Put simply," he says, clearly noticing the bewildered looks on the faces of onlookers, "magic is what happens when the laws of nature in our world are disrupted by the laws of nature from another world. The two must not intermingle. Chaos results...as we have clearly seen illustrated in recent dark days."

Finally, when Bloom signals to wrap up, the Worm adjusts his glasses and looks nervously at the cameras with huge, watery eyes and says, "In summation, these holes that the magicians call *portals* must be permanently closed."

"*What?!*" I gasp. I think of all the times we needed those portals in the past: to cover ground, or escape The One's grasp. To see Celia in Shadowland, and to get our parents safely out. They've been crucial to our survival.

I try to push forward to make my voice heard, but a hundred other people are shouting questions at the podium.

"How does this relate to the water shortage?" a reporter asks.

"Or the missing children?" another shouts.

Bloom is reclaiming the podium. "We all know the dangers of magic running rampant in the City," he booms over the crowd's roar. "Have you forgotten The One Who Is The One?"

The mention of that name still strikes fear in the hearts of every citizen, and even the most eager journalists fall silent.

I spot movement near the stage, though, and for once I'm grateful for my sister's love of the spotlight as she squeezes herself under the Worm's arm, pressing into the microphone.

"The One also tried to close the portals!" her voice echoes.

The Council may have turned on her, but these citizens haven't forgotten that Wisty once saved them. All eyes and a hundred cameras look from their old hero to the man who claims to be their protector.

"His mistake was not closing them all, according to our new discovery," Bloom says as *The Book of Truths* is wheeled onto the platform. The cheap parlor trick is getting old, but the cameras love it, and everyone zooms in on *The Book*, now wrapped in chains and displayed behind glass.

"*Oh, come on!*" I shout. "Don't you see what he's doing?" But my voice doesn't carry in the open air, and Bloom clears his throat into the microphone.

"*The Book of Truths* refers to the hostile Mountain King as the *Wizard* King," he reveals. "He rules with *black magic.*"

Like The One.

My mouth goes dry, and the words die on my lips. I

knew it, I realize. Though Celia never said it in the dream, though my vision was a jumble of images, though we couldn't trace the kidnappings, I *knew*. That's why my panic was so irrational, and why I couldn't tell Wisty—I didn't want to admit it to myself.

We're dealing with a darker power, and we don't know anything about it.

"Closing the portals will protect us from his magic as we prepare for the trying days ahead," Bloom continues, looking authoritatively into the cameras and into the fearful hearts of the people watching from home. "This Wizard King has taken our water from us, so the Council has declared war!"

I stare up at Bloom in shock and swallow hard. It's time to find my voice.

Chapter 28

Wisty

"DOES ANYONE IN this City remember how hard we worked for peace?" my brother asks, his voice cracking with emotion. Whit hates speaking in public, much less on television, but he does have a gift for it, and right now he's hovering above the crowd, desperate to be heard.

"Remember how the Council members *earned* their spots, standing up for your rights? And making our streets safe?" Whit reaches down for my hand.

"Together," I shout, levitating up to join him. "With *magic*." A hundred flash bulbs go off to capture us floating together. We're just a few feet up—we don't want to scare them—but now we've got their attention. And Bloom's.

"I know we desperately need water, and I know many of you are afraid," Whit says. "But war is not the answer. War is more starvation, more innocent lives lost, and more ash-covered skies."

"But our streets aren't safe, even with the Watch," a

reporter in a bright pink pantsuit protests, and others mutter in agreement. "How do you plan to protect us?" She points her microphone up at us.

"We have to at least *try* to negotiate for peace, and if I have to, I'll…" Whit swallows, looking out across the crowd. "I'll lead a mission up the Mountain to meet with this so-called King myself."

Our eyes burn into Bloom now. Witch and wizard, a united front.

Bloom clears his throat with a deafening rattle into the microphone. "Magicians will always look out for their fellow magic makers." Bloom leans forward, and his gray toupee shifts. "Perhaps the Allgoods have formed an alliance with the Wizard King. This Council has seen them defy law and use magic with force."

I want to destroy him in that moment, just like I destroyed The One, but I have to remind myself that the cameras are rolling.

Bloom is well aware. He doesn't look at us, but right at the camera when he says gravely, "We suspect magicians may actually be responsible for kidnapping the City's children and smuggling them up the Mountain."

"That's not true!" I protest, but my voice is drowned out by the aggressive crowd. They need a cause to unite around, a common enemy to rally against.

And this time, *we're* the enemy.

I feel arms tugging at my ankles. *We should've gone*

higher, I think, but it's too late. People are pressing in from all sides, grabbing at us, and I start to freak.

The strong emotion makes my M go haywire, and I can't help heating up defensively. *No*, I think. *Not now.* But the people grabbing my legs are already shrieking as their hands blister.

I stop my magic abruptly and crash to the ground. *I have to fix this*, I think. *I have to explain.*

But the roiling panic of the crowd has boiled over, and the conference is collapsing into a hate rally of antimagic slurs.

"Dark demon!" a woman spits at me. "Child killer!"

No one seems to care that this is all based on the claims of one man. They're afraid. And fear makes people very dangerous.

I look around for the most dangerous coward of them all, but he's slipped out of sight.

"General Bloom," I yell. This isn't over yet. "Speaker Bloom!"

One of Bloom's lackeys leans into the microphone. "No further questions," he says, and all I can do is gape at the chaos Bloom left in his wake.

He just crucified us on TV—with lies!

Chapter 29

Wisty

AS WE PUSH through the sea of reporters shouting angry questions, I wish I could stay and answer them—grab each microphone and erase the poison of Bloom's lies with truth.

But right now, we just have to get out of here.

In my rush to escape the frenzied crowd, I trip in my stupid heels and fly forward down the last few steps of the Capitol building, my face nearly smashing into the stones of the square.

"I came as soon as I heard." Heath pulls me up and hugs me against him. I bury my face in his neck, trying not to sob. I've never been happier to see anyone in my life. I'm thankful that Janine's here, too. "This is madness," she says with wide eyes as she corrals us down a side street, away from the cameras. I see other Resistance kids farther up the block—Sasha and Emmett, and . . .

"Mama May?" I ask, barely recognizing the disheveled woman calling my name.

It's Mrs. Neederman, all right—the woman who once sheltered me and Whit when we were wanted criminals. Even in the darkest days of the New Order, her bright voice kept everyone's spirits up. I remember her whole body shaking with laughter as she hugged me, her huge arms swallowing me up.

Now, her face is thinner and drawn, and her eyes have given up.

"We saw you on the news," she tells us as we walk. "What the Speaker said, about you being involved with the kidnappers—"

"He's lying!" I grasp her hands desperately, needing her to believe me even if no one else does. "Everything Bloom said was a lie!"

"We would never do something like that," Whit reassures her.

"I know you wouldn't, honey," Mama May says. She looks from me to Whit, her big chin quivering. "I know because my baby Pearl Marie is one of those kids."

It's like another punch in the gut.

"Pearl?" My brother gapes, anguish written all over his face. "We didn't even know she was missing...."

"The Watch investigated every kid," Sasha says, distraught. He pulls a notebook from his pocket and starts thumbing through it. "I swear, she wasn't on the list!"

Mama May worries her apron in her hands, looking ashamed. "We were afraid to report her. The One used lists...." She shrugs helplessly. "And Pearl was so smart. She knew the streets so well. We thought she would come back, but she..."

Her eyes overflow with tears, and this time I'm the one comforting Mama May, cradling her against me like a child.

I can picture Pearl's small, pointed features and her honest, gray eyes, holding everyone accountable. She acted so jaded, waving her pocketknife, but she smiled at the Holiday lights like any other seven-year-old would.

For all the terrible things that have happened today, this feels worst of all.

"I'm going to find Pearl," Whit promises. He puts a hand on Mama May's shoulder and squeezes it. "I'm going up the Mountain."

My heart stops. *What did he just say?*

Chapter 30

Wisty

"HOW COULD YOU promise her something like that?" I demand, my voice scaring up a flock of pigeons from the street.

Whit says I'm impulsive, but I at least had the sense to wait until Mama May left before I confronted him.

"How do you know the Mountain King is even the kidnapper? You're going to trust *Bloom*?"

"No," Whit says tightly. "I'm going to trust my instincts." Then he looks at me, his face softening, and for a second our old closeness returns. "Remember that night with the visions, Wist?"

I remember the horrible images, and the way he winced in pain. He was acting so weird afterward, too, so not like my brother—so agitated and *scared*.

"I was feeling what Pearl was feeling, even if I didn't understand it then."

I nod. I know Whit and Pearl had a special connection,

and I don't blame him for wanting to risk everything to go after her. I should go, too. I should *trust him*, but...

"You can't leave the City now!" Heath says, seemingly reading my thoughts. Whit wheels around and shoves him against the stone wall.

"Does it interfere with your *plans*?" Whit asks, his glare full of daggers.

"I just didn't think you'd enjoy seeing your parents behind bars again," Heath answers icily, and straightens the collar of his leather jacket.

"Stop it!" I look from Heath to Whit angrily, but I know Heath is right. That press conference was a horror show. If we leave, every citizen who watched the news will believe Bloom's claim that magicians are working with the Mountain King. Who will stand up for our rights? Even if we make peace with the Mountain King, we'll return to another prison state.

"What about what Mom and Dad said, about winning back the people?" I remind my brother, trying another angle. I know that as strong-willed as he is, he trusts our parents. "If we can just deal with Bloom first..."

Whit's jaw tightens. For one long moment, I think he's swayed, but then he shakes his head, and I know there's no changing his mind.

"Bloom's not the biggest threat. Celia said the Mountain King is a psychopath. And if he has Pearl..."

Celia? Where does Celia fit in here? She's dead! *Gone!*

"What are you talking about? When were you going to tell me this?"

"I don't know—when you were babbling about your date? When you were throwing me out of your apartment?" Whit sighs heavily and rubs his forehead in frustration. "I'm telling you *now*. Someone has to try to negotiate with the Mountain King, no matter what the Council says. I'm going."

"I'm going with you, then," Janine says, standing next to my brother.

"I'm going, too," Sasha says. He looks at me apologetically. "We haven't caught any of the kidnappers. It's time to go to the source."

Emmett puts up his hands, unwilling to choose, but Whit isn't looking at him anyway.

"Wisty?" His eyes are pleading.

"I . . ." There's a knot in my chest, and my eyes flit between Whit and Heath. *Do I really have to choose?* "I . . ." But I can't get the words out—my throat is so dry.

Heath slides a hand around my waist. I'm not sure if it's because we merged our magic, but I can almost feel the power in it, the support. *You're needed here*, that touch seems to remind me. *Stay. Stay.*

"Think of your parents, Wisty," Heath says gently. "You told me you lost them once. You can't lose them again."

Heath is right. Whit is trusting his instincts, and I have to trust mine.

I drop my eyes. "I'm not going, Whit," I say finally, sighing.

"So that's how it is? You're choosing him over your own family?" My brother's words burn like acid in a wound.

"That's not fair," I start to protest. "I need to be here for Mom and Dad. For the people who are our family now, too."

But Whit's face darkens. "You know that's not the real truth. You'll be here babysitting an old politician and cozying up with your boyfriend."

I'm furious with him, but my heart is aching, and I'm already doubting my decision. Whit's not even looking at me now, though.

He's walking away, with Janine and Sasha on his heels.

"Don't do this," I plead, stepping out from under Heath's arm toward my brother. "Whit—"

"We're going to try to stop a war," he says. He looks back at me one more time, his expression unyielding. "With or without you."

BOOK TWO

THE SECOND TRUTH: TRUST IS A FLICKERING FLAME

Chapter 31

Whit

IT'S SO MUCH WORSE than we expected.

I expected these towering trees, creaking and swaying around us like drunken giants. And I expected this cold wind that rips through to our bones. But we didn't expect this:

A man behind bars.

A woman shot through with arrows.

A head with a dripping axe next to it.

The silhouetted face of a wolfish creature with a gaping mouth full of spearlike teeth.

There are signs posted on trees every ten or twenty paces, crudely drawn on barklike parchment, painted in what might have been blood.

"What do they say?" Ross asked, peering at letterforms on the signs that we don't recognize.

"Rest stop ahead," Sasha answers, deadpan, but panting

in between words. "Fuel, food, beds, and clean bathroom facilities, one mile."

Ross jabs Sasha playfully. "That's what I thought. For a second, I thought they might be warning us of our imminent deaths."

"Silly you," Janine quips, just before the rocks break away under her feet and she scrambles to gain footing as they tumble down the hillside. With an instant protective reflex, I steady her.

"Don't say the words 'imminent death,'" I tell Ross. "You just jinxed us, man."

"So does that mean if I say 'clean bathroom,' one will suddenly appear?" he asks, and it's good for a chuckle.

I'm thankful that I have friends here to help keep spirits up as we struggle endlessly through the harshest environment we've ever been in. Janine and I are up in front, followed by Sasha and Ross behind. I picked up Feffer, our trusty dog, from my parents' house, and she wanders through the woods next to us, her ears pricking at the tiniest sound.

When the conversation lulls for a minute, the sound of our teeth chattering hard feels almost deafening, so I keep talking to distract us. "So, Sasha, did you say Emmett's heading up the City Watch?"

Sasha nods. "He wanted to come, but someone had to stay behind and keep things running." He frowns at the sheet of rock rising up in front of us. "I noticed Byron didn't jump at the chance to come on this little adventure, either."

"I asked him not to. I need him to keep an eye on

Wisty." I shake my head, thinking of heartbroken Byron Swain. To be honest, I don't think I could've dragged him away from her if I'd tried.

"That sounds like something Wisty will really appreciate," Janine says, giving me a wry look from under her ice-encrusted scarf.

I sigh in frustration and slash at the branches blocking our path, my arm getting sore from the constant work. "Wisty's going to do what she's going to do. But she shouldn't be left alone with that creep."

Why wouldn't you just come with us, Wisty? I think for the millionth time. After Bloom's little TV show, the City will be a dangerous place for magicians—perhaps even more dangerous than here.

"Another one," Sasha says as he plucks the weathered sign from an ancient tree. *Okay, maybe* not *more dangerous than here…*

The sign shows a figure that's headless, armless, and leaking dark fluid. The knot in my stomach tightens.

"Maybe you guys should head back," I say uneasily. "I can go on alone."

"And miss all the excitement when the welcome party shows up?" Janine smiles through cracked lips and gives my hand a squeeze. "Shut up, macho man. I'm staying with you."

"I'll turn back when all of us do," Sasha agrees.

"Besides, old Feff here will tell us when we have to worry," Ross adds, patting the dog's side.

I nod doubtfully, noting that Feffer's looking a little wary already, though whether it's from a current threat or a lingering skittishness, I couldn't say—the pup's been through a lot in the past year.

We've all been through a lot.

I look at my friends' flushed faces, resigned to the task, and wish it didn't have to be this way. A normal person wouldn't ask this of people he loved. A smart person would turn back. A sane person would be terrified.

And I am.

I shiver, looking at the horrific image on the sign and at the white cliff of rock before us. I try not to think of the million dark corners of the forest at our back, a million hiding places where eyes might be peeking out, watching us, readying their attack. *Oh, yes, I'm terrified.*

But the Mountain King has threatened the City.

He's taken our water supply.

And he has Pearl.

I snap the bloody warning sign into pieces and fling them aside, and push on toward the next boulder.

What choice do I have?

Chapter 32

Wisty

I LIFT MY HAND to the knocker, holding my breath.

The wooden door swings open on its hinges, and a familiar, weathered face peers out. His long gray braid hangs over his shoulder.

"Hi, Hewitt," I say tentatively, hoping I'm still welcome at the Neederman home.

"Wisty!" His eyes light up. "Mama May told us she saw you. Have you heard from Whit...?"

The guilt twists in my stomach again. I shake my head, hating to kill the hope on his face. "No news. I just wanted to come by to say I'm sorry. I was just going to leave these...." I hold out a tin of cookies—store-bought, since I'm likely to blow up an oven if I try to cook anything.

"We're all sorry, Wisty girl," Hewitt says, linking his arm in mine. "But don't think you're getting out of a full family visit."

I smile, my eyes welling up as I follow him down the basement stairs.

After Whit left, I paced my apartment for days. *Was my brother okay? Did I make the wrong choice?* Seeing Heath made me hurt—it made me remember how I'd chosen someone over Whit for the first time in my life. I was paralyzed with doubt and guilt.

Somehow my feet found their way down these winding streets before my heart knew what I was doing. This was the only place I needed to be.

"We own the rest of the house now, all the way up to the top," Hewitt says proudly. "I even repaired that burned-up staircase."

"That's great," I say, seeing dozens of Pearl's relatives milling in the small space as a throng of grubby-faced kids tear around the furniture. And there's Mama May, laughing as she chases after a couple of them.

Hewitt shakes his gray head and laughs. "We just can't seem to make ourselves use all those other rooms, though, all that empty space."

"It feels better together," Mama May agrees as she arrives at our side. "Some things never change."

I nod. The Needermans' basement is different than I remember, for sure. The leaks have been patched, and the walls have been painted. New couches replace piles of ragged clothing. But the *feeling* is the same.

"Pearl Marie wanted to help redecorate," Mama May

explains when she catches me admiring their new light fixture above.

Looking closer, I can see Pearl's mark. The chandelier is haphazardly put together, with pieces of shattered glass mounted on coat hangers and other things dug from the garbage.

"She always had fancy ideas when it came to that stuff." Mama May smiles sadly. "I'll get a plate for those cookies you brought," she says, hiding her face as she hurries away.

I see the candles on the wall then, right where I remember them. None of them are lit this time, though. . . .

At least I can do this *for them*, I think. *I can do this for Pearl.*

I snap my fingers and there's a *whoosh* of air as a hundred pale candles spark to life.

I pluck one off the wall and hold it close to me, watching the flame dance. The other Needermans follow suit, smiling at me with shining eyes as they pass the flickering fires between them, each one burning for little Pearl Marie.

"No!" Mama May shouts when she sees us. She slams the plate of cookies down as she hurries across the room, and all of us flinch with her angry footfalls. I'm so shocked by the outburst that I almost drop my candle, but I cup my palm around the fire to save it from winking out.

No matter, though, since Mama May licks her fingers and snuffs it out anyway.

"*No.* No candles," she says firmly. Her face is blotchy with anger as she pinches the flames out one by one.

"I—I'm sorry," I stutter, but I don't understand what I've done wrong.

But Mama May turns me to face her and looks at me with kind understanding. "Candles are for the dead and gone. Pearl Marie is coming back to us," Mama May says, her voice full of unshed tears, "but we can still pray."

She combs her fingers through my always-knotted hair, and then takes my hand and Hewitt's in each of hers. "Lewis," she calls across the room, "sing the old songs to bring our Pearl Marie back to us."

A little boy begins to sing, his voice a high, clear bell, and one by one, the other voices are lifted up, and the Needermans join hands.

As I look around the circle of faces, the hazy memory of the last time I was in this house resurfaces. I was on the floor wrapped in rags. I heard the singing in a fever dream, heady and distorted, and saw the flicker of light between plague hallucinations. As I hovered between life and death, it was *me* they prayed for that time.

I won't give up on them now.

I don't know their religion, and I don't know the old songs, but I might be an expert in hope at this point. I've rationed it out, stocked it up, and lived on it for years, and

I believe sometimes, if you hope enough, then someone will listen.

My solemn prayer of hope, sent out into the universe through the clear, pure voices ringing together:

Please let Whit find her and bring every soul home safe from that Mountain.

Chapter 33

Whit

"DON'T MOVE, JANINE. Not an inch. Don't even blink."

The wolf has her backed into a corner of rock. Its eyes are red and terrible, and blood drips from its bared teeth. Patches of gray fur are missing from its hide, exposing bone and gristle and rot. It looks like an animal that has already died, and maybe that's exactly what it is.

"Are you nuts? Of course I'm not going to move!" Janine says, her voice rising toward hysterics.

I've seen a wolf like this before—it's some kind of zombie dog pulled straight out of Shadowland, surviving on death and remains. The New Order used to use them to hunt *people*, but even those killers were kept on chains. This thing is just roaming free. It's horrifying, but I might be able to take it with magic if I can get it away from Janine.

Another snarl makes me whirl around, and there's a second wolf, with foam bubbling up at its terrible mouth. Every nerve on my body is prickling with terror.

There's no way I can take two at once.

Seeing the second wolf moving in, I take a protective step toward Janine, and both wolves look at me, panting.

I freeze, my body flooding with adrenaline.

The wolf that has Janine cornered bares its teeth, a growl of warning building in its throat. The two wolves lunge at each other threateningly, jaws snapping.

Janine cries out, terrified.

They're fighting over us, I realize with sickening clarity. We're fresh meat, and they're yipping over who gets to rip us apart.

That's it—I have to morph while they're distracted by their greed.

What can beat a wolf? I think, my head a fuzzy mess of panic.

"Guys..." Sasha's voice quavers.

I take my eyes from the two wolves for a flick of a second...and almost lose it when I see three more behind us. But beyond that, there are *men*.

They're massive figures—giants, really—with long hair and dreaded beards and leather vests wrapped around their thick chests. There are at least eight of them, but somehow we didn't even hear them coming.

We're completely surrounded.

The Mountain soldiers are heavily armed, all of them wielding strange metal tools, like axes and maces and knives that extend from the arm and curve into deadly points.

The Resistance kids are war veterans, but none of them are trained in hand-to-hand combat. I don't think my skills battling fooball demons count, either. Never mind the wolves; in a battle with these men, we're dead in our tracks.

"Whit—" Janine says nervously as the shadow wolves press in on her, the reddish saliva dripping from their jaws.

I need to morph, I think again. *It's the only way.*

What can beat five wolves and eight men? I reconsider, just as one of the men yells some kind of war cry.

Now.

I feel my shoulders shift up, my skull expand, and my hands explode into giant paws. I scream at the men and the wolves, and what comes out makes the bark on the trees shudder. Even some pinecones are shaken from branches as the deep growl penetrates the icy air.

Grizzly.

I run at the wolves first, lunging at the two that have Janine trapped. The wolves snarl and spit, gnashing their bloodied teeth. I clamp my jaws on one's leg, and the other backs down, whining as it slinks away.

The men come at me two at a time, yelling gruff words I can't decipher. I rake my claws against a heavy club a soldier is trying to wield, splitting it apart like kindling. When two hairy men lunge at me with knives, I take a chunk out of one's thigh, and the other screams as one of the wolves attacks him in the confusion.

"Break away!" I hear Janine yell. I keep fighting as I see the team scatter.

Three wolves leap on me at once, sinking in their razor teeth. I roar in anguish but manage to rip two off with my giant paws, and sink my teeth into the third's throat.

I glance around, roaring another challenge and tasting the metal tang of blood in my mouth. But the wolves have limped away and the men are backing off to regroup.

I tear through the trees after my friends. The wind rustles my fur and I'm running faster than I imagined, but the morph is fading, and I can feel my features returning.

Sasha, Janine, and Ross are waiting for me at a river.

"Guys...I think the Mountain men are coming for another attack," I say nervously, picking up their scent before the last of my bear senses leave me. But there doesn't seem to be any way across the rapids, and none of us want to return the way we came. "We have to jump in and swim it."

"It's freezing!" Ross states the obvious.

I nod, trying to figure out how to explain my idea. "I think I can monitor your vitals and use my healing power to repair your organs as they start to fail...." All three of them are gaping at me in disbelief.

"Don't ever say 'organs start to fail' to me again." Sasha shakes his head.

"Those rapids are really fast, Whit," Janine says uneasily. "We can't just morph into fish like you can if it doesn't work."

I look into Janine's eyes. "How much do you trust me?"

She sighs. "More than I probably should." Janine grips my hand at the edge of the river, but the guys are still looking doubtfully at the terrifying rapids.

Unfortunately, their uncertainty lasts for just a split second too long.

Our enemies are back.

We didn't hear them near the boulders, but this time, the giants are crashing through the forest, and it sounds like a stampede.

"There's no time, guys!" I scream as the Mountain men round the corner screaming for blood. "This is the only way out!"

One of the biggest soldiers flings an axe and it thuds into a tree about a foot from Ross's head. His eyes bulge, staring at the giant gash in the old tree. "So what do we do?" he asks quickly.

"Grip hands, kick your feet, and don't let go, no matter what."

With just one step into the ice water, the current sucks us into its freezing torrent.

I hope I know what I'm doing.

Chapter 34

Wisty

"WHIT, *LOOK OUT*!" My shriek rips me from sleep, and I take a gasping breath as the dream dies.

I can barely remember it now. Chains and cages? The One or the Wizard King? But the terror of the dream seems to echo around me even after the images have faded, making my own apartment feel hostile.

It's over, I think. *You're awake, and safe.* I sink back into the pillow, closing my eyes.

Then I hear it: the click of a window as the lock shifts out of its place in the next room.

I bolt up in bed, every nerve alive, my heart thudding in my ears. I stand, gripping the bedpost as I strain to listen for sounds.

Again—a creak in the floorboards.

Someone is in my home.

For a moment, terror takes hold. But as I stand here

149

waiting to be ambushed, anger replaces the fear. *Someone is in my home!*

I feel the M heating up inside me. My confidence returns as the itch starts in my fingertips. *I'm nobody's prey. I'm a witch.*

Someone is about to get fried.

I tiptoe to the doorway, and peer around the corner. Dim light from the street stripes the floor with shadow. And as I creep across the room to inspect the open window, I see one of those shadows shift.

"Hey—!" a man starts to say, but only gets half a syllable out before I wheel around and lunge, throwing sparks.

The intruder anticipates it, though, and deftly leaps out of the way and pivots. I stumble after him, but he seems to whir past my focus. I concentrate on my power instead, the buzz of heat, but before I can go full torch mode, he tackles me in the darkness.

We bowl into the coffee table, shattering its glass top, and a raw, piercing pain shoots through my hip. I see spots.

Then he's on me!

With his back to the light, he's just a terrifying silhouette looming over me. We roll as I try to throw him off, but he's got lightning reflexes and flexible joints, and every blow seems designed to inflict the most pain possible.

"Gahh," I groan as he pins my arms.

Focus on the M, Wisty. Focus.

But all I can do is thrash wildly in his grip.

I claw across the carpet with my free arm, searching for a lifeline....

My fingers find the broken glass from the table, and I grip a shard tighter than anything as I slash. The jagged edge of the glass is an inch from his throat, maybe less, when the man catches my wrist.

"You trying to kill me?" the intruder asks—in Heath's bemused voice.

I drop my makeshift dagger, speechless. We're breathing heavily for a few seconds as I try to make sense of what just happened. I'm wild with rage that he nailed me to the ground like an assassin—and is now acting like it's some *joke*—and yet strangely thrilled to have been rolling around on the floor with him.

It's that crazy raw power that just takes over when we're together.

Heath starts laughing, but I don't see what's so funny. He lets go of my arms and sits back on his heels, a patch of streetlight finally exposing his crooked smile and chiseled face.

"You could've said something earlier!" I say testily as I scoot out from under him. "What exactly were you trying to do?"

"Surprise you, I guess." He shrugs. "You attacked me before I had a chance to do it right."

"Oh, like *you're* the victim here," I protest, rubbing my hip where it smashed into the coffee table.

"I'll admit, I kind of enjoyed seeing the fighter in you

come out. It's so..." If I'm not mistaken, I think Heath might *almost* be blushing.

"*Hot*, right?" I roll my eyes. "Okay, seriously. Why did you come here in the middle of the night?"

"I thought you might be ready to get out and do something," he says as he takes my wounded palm and examines the cut. He starts to wrap the hand in a stray sock, and his eyes flick up to meet mine, like they can see right into me.

All my anger evaporates as he says, "I thought maybe I could help you find that little girl."

Chapter 35

Whit

WE EMERGE FROM the rushing river, bodies shivering and lungs heaving, choking up water. The vital signs monitoring trick worked a *bit* less seamlessly than I'd hoped, with Ross dipping into critical territory a couple of times. We're all shell-shocked and colder than we've ever been. But we're alive.

Ross lies on the riverbank, still gasping, and I sit next to Janine on a wet log as she coughs uncontrollably. Sasha's the only one not feeling too bad.

"Up here," he gestures, and we stumble up the steep bank after him.

He's found a promising path—flat and smooth—and it's even kind of pretty, with snow falling down all around us. For a few moments it seems like the worst is over, if we can just get dry.

Then the arrows start to rain down on us.

We're in the perfect target strip for the archers, and the

153

attacks seem to come from everywhere. Arrows fly from cracks in the rock face above, and whistle from the trees on the other side of the river. Sometimes it feels like they're falling from the sky.

"Back to the bank!" Sasha yells, and we scramble down, running as fast as we can in our wet clothes. But the bank is too gravelly, and we can't get our footing. We slip and stumble, ducking arrows with every movement. I hear myself yelping involuntarily as an arrow clips the side of me, ripping through my heavy coat. If we keep this up, we'll look just like that NO TRESPASSING sign: human pincushions.

I have to do something.

I try to remember that feeling on the foolball field—the dance of bodies in motion and the anticipation of another's intention—and channel it as I summon every ounce of power I have left.

I feel the M in my heightened senses, turned to turbo speed in my reflexes. I feel eerily aware of everything happening at once—every movement, every sound—and see each bow poised. I can see the shift in the rock when the Mountain men move a hair, and hear their breath rustling the leaves of the trees.

I can smell their fear.

They *should* be afraid, too. Because at the instant each arrow is released, I focus everything into the spin and turn it back around—right at the archers.

We never see the soldiers, hidden in their cracks and

caves. But screams seem to come from all around as the Mountain men turn from us, fleeing their own arrows. The weapons fly by in a blur, my hands conducting their movement like a maestro with his orchestra.

And then it's over abruptly, and the forest seems to swallow up every man and every motion. I stare at the trees, breathing heavily, and feeling *incredible*.

"Whit!" Janine's shout cuts through the quiet. The terror in her voice makes my blood run cold.

It's Sasha. Janine kneels on the ground next to him. I blink, not comprehending at first what's happened. Or how.

I must not have seen it. I must've missed one, somehow. I don't understand it, but a single arrow made it through.

It's sticking out of Sasha's chest.

Chapter 36

Whit

SASHA IS DEAD. It's not possible.

The thought takes my breath away, and I stand there stupidly, staring at the arrow, the crumpled body, the blood. So much blood, leaking right out of him.

How did I let this happen?

Then I see his head lolling against Janine, and the faint fog of his breath in the frigid air. He's still alive, but barely. He's fumbling at his clothes, trying to get them off as the heat of the pain rages inside him.

Janine and Ross are staring at me, because right about now I should be helping Sasha, healing him with my magic.

But here's the horrible truth: *I don't have any juice left.* It's killing me. And it's killing him.

The bear, the river, the soldiers... they took every ounce of M I had, and it'll be at least a day until I can heal a paper cut, let alone something like this.

Janine must see the truth on my face, because she goes into crisis mode.

"Help me hold Sasha up," she commands as I kneel next to them. "We have to get it out of him."

As I prop him up, she snaps the point off, and Sasha screams. The anguished, whimpering cry tears through me as sure as that arrow.

Ross is freaking out, pacing behind us nonstop, and he shrieks out something that sounds like half prayer, half curse as we pull out the rest of the arrow, its shaft glistening darkly.

Janine works with quick, deft fingers, pressing Sasha's signature bandanna against the wound and tying her scarf tight around it, but it's not enough—in moments, the cloth is soaked through.

"Help him," Ross pleads. He looks at me, the tears freezing on his cheeks. "Whit, help him, please."

He's right. I have to help him. I have to *try*.

I sit cross-legged on the frozen ground and hold Sasha's head in my lap. The sweat is beading on his forehead now, and his breath is coming in short gasps. I put my hands on his chest and take a long, slow breath. I think of every healing poem I've ever invoked, every spell, trying to feel the magic and bring back the power.

Please, I beg silently. *Please work.*

My fingers twitch, and I concentrate on that buzz of life that makes them itch at first. I wait for the jump, for the surge of energy as it builds and transfers between us.

But it just...doesn't...happen.

There's nothing left.

"I'm sorry, Sasha." I choke back a sob. "I'm so sorry."

"It's okay, Whit," Sasha whispers. His eyes are starting to lose their focus.

This isn't possible.

"I know it's time." He coughs, and blood spatters bright against the fresh snow. "I'm ready."

But I'm not.

I keep desperately trying to work up any last bit of M I can find in myself. For a moment, I think I feel a spark. A spark is all it takes to light a fire....

"It was for the Resistance." He grips the bandanna, soaked through with his blood, and manages a weak smile. "You'll tell them that, right?"

I shake my head, the tears blurring my vision. *I don't want to tell anyone that we lost you*, I'm thinking. *We can't lose you.*

"You're a true hero, Sasha," Janine says, giving him a strained smile of good-bye, a look of peace for Sasha to take with him.

"No!" I wail. She's giving up. *He's* giving up. *I can't... let...this...happen!*

Then the last breath leaves him, its smoky trail barely visible through the falling snow.

Ross collapses to the ground and hugs Sasha's body, rocking as he cries.

Janine brushes the snow from her knees and turns

away silently, staring into the forest. Then she wraps her arms around me, and I'm suddenly aware of how I'm trembling. I can feel her shaking, too, inside her layers of coats. Ross's wails bounce off rocks and trees, and seem to echo all around us, so it feels like everything in the world is grieving for our fallen friend.

"You'd think it would get easier, losing our friends," Janine says finally, the tears thick in her voice. "But death is worse every time."

I nod. We lost so many during the time of the New Order, but this feels different—more raw, somehow. It just feels so, so wrong.

I couldn't save him.

Stifling a scream, I slam my fist into one of the ancient trees and feel the skin of my knuckles split.

It wasn't supposed to happen like this.

This was supposed to be a peace mission.

Chapter 37

Pearl

PEARL CLUTCHED THE PAPER in her hand as her bare feet lit over rocks and tree needles. She ran up and up the boulders, her lungs straining in the thin air as she climbed higher above the treetops. It was quite a long way from the new training camp, but they'd picked her to be messenger because she was the best runner by far now.

She thought of her mother then, suddenly remembering how Mama May would send her on errands around the Gutter—"Because you're my best runner, sweet pea."

The memory made her sad in a vague way, but she didn't know why. She was starting to forget what Mama looked like. Already she couldn't remember her brothers and sisters.

There was only the camp, its days defined by the ringing of bells and the rules of the games. *Don't stop running* was the biggest one during the drills, but Pearl had a list of her own rules, too, to make sure she could keep winning—like *Don't do what the Failures do.*

Some couldn't stop shaking, and some started to look all cross-eyed. Eddie had turned out to be a Failure, and he had hunched over like a gargoyle in the City, not moving all afternoon as his lips turned blue.

Don't let your lips turn blue, Pearl had added to her list of rules.

Some of her toes had started to turn black, though. If she delivered this message quick enough, she might win a pair of rough leather shoes, like Eagle wore. *Faster*, Pearl thought. *Winners go faster.*

Finally, she padded through the dreary castle, breathless, and handed over the crude paper to its recipient. The man's glass eye caught her in its frozen orb. She felt rooted to the spot, but then he turned from her, starting to read the letter, and she was able to breathe again.

Pearl knew she should go. But the room was so warm with its crackling fire, and if she just stayed for a few minutes, just slipped into the corner, she might be able to move her toes a little. . . .

"It's the wizard," she heard the man with the glass eye say. "He's already killed a few archers."

"I told you they'd come, Larsht," answered the King. "Kill them both."

Seated at a large square table, the old man looked anything but regal as he hacked into a hunk of meat, the grease dripping down his beard. Pearl's stomach complained, and she backed farther into the corner.

"The witch isn't with him," Larsht said carefully.

"Excuse me?" the King asked, setting down his knife and turning his gaze calmly on Larsht, who visibly flinched.

"We—we were told they'd both come," Larsht sputtered nervously. "We can hold the wizard, maybe use him to lure the witch up. Or merge his magic with ours. He could be useful...." Larsht was so much bigger than the old man at the table, but somehow, even seated, the King seemed to dwarf him.

"Like the Allgoods were useful to that bald fool they took the City from?" the King said icily. "Power is dangerous, Larsht. It's so easy to abuse."

Pearl jumped at Larsht's sudden bark of laughter—she hadn't realized the King had made a joke.

The old man went back to his meal. "We'll get the girl later. Better to kill Whitford Allgood now, before he even reaches the kingdom. Send him something better than archers this time," he said thoughtfully. "Something magical."

Kill Whit?

Pearl felt a sharp jolt through her fingers then, like the twitch of a phantom limb. She forgot about the rules, and getting back to camp. She even forgot to keep being afraid of Larsht.

She only felt the weight of her blade, still hidden in the folds of her ragged clothing. Underneath the fur and the leather, the King's old neck was a papery stalk, thin and vulnerable. *He'll bleed the same as any other man*, she thought as she crept closer.

She lunged, sinking in the knife.

Only he didn't bleed like other men, and a force flung her backward onto the floor with a hard *smack*.

The old man looked at her strangely as she scrambled up.

Larsht stalked toward her, a towering shadow that blotted out everything else, and she remembered to be afraid again. "First I'll kill this curious little City rat," he growled, and Pearl shook so violently with panic that she couldn't help it—she peed her pants.

"You've got it backward, Larsht," the King said, picking at his rotting teeth with a bone. "This one's only a child. We know how fickle children's ideas can be. How *moldable*. She probably believes the witch and wizard's parlor tricks are *special*. She doesn't understand what true power is, in its purest form."

The King looked at her then and smiled. He didn't move an inch, but Pearl couldn't look away from his intense stare, so forceful it seemed to physically push her toward the fireplace.

Suddenly, Pearl understood what she needed to do. Why hadn't she done it before? She turned to smile at her true King, regal and wise, and he nodded his encouragement.

Then she thrust her hands into the flames.

Pearl felt the fear melt off her, cleansing her. *Wisty's not so special after all*, she thought absently as the skin on her hands started to bubble and twist.

It doesn't even hurt.

See, Witch and Wizard? I'm a magician, too.

Chapter 38

Wisty

I REALIZE I'VE missed Heath so much these past few days when I was holed up in my apartment, sulking and fretting about Whit.

But I think I might've missed this even more: fighting injustice, working for change...*doing* something about all the ugliness.

We head toward the inner neighborhoods, figuring the City Watch might be a good place to start. Sadly, the two kids we find don't even seem to see us until we're standing right in front of them.

"You Sasha's guys?" I ask, nudging the bigger one's toe.

He jolts awake. "Yeah. Um. Yes." He blinks rapidly, trying to fight sleep. "We're the Watch."

"What are you watching?" Heath asks dryly, but the joke's lost on this one.

I nudge the younger kid, whose shoulders are slumping

against a streetlight. "Any new information about the missing children? Any leads?"

"What?" He squints up at me, blind as a mole under the light.

I roll my eyes. No wonder the citizens think the Watch is such a joke.

I sigh and take Heath's hand, and we comb the streets for hours looking for a single clue that might help us figure out what happened that first night when Pearl was taken.

But there's not a scrap of clothing, not a trace of a fingerprint, and with every dead end, my spirits plunge a little further.

"This is a waste of time!" I finally shout. "Whit was right. I should've gone up the Mountain with him. While he's off actually *doing* something, I'm here just hanging out—"

"Don't. Don't regret staying here with me," Heath pleads. "Listen. I think I have an idea."

"What?" I step closer to him, studying his face, but he's staring into a storefront window strangely, peering at our reflections: a boy with a face of sharp lines and a girl with a mess of red hair.

"What if we could *see* what happened?" Heath asks. "What if we could *re-create* the scene of the kidnapping that night?" I stare at him, puzzled, trying to figure out if he's serious. "Then we wouldn't be in this situation, would we?"

"No, but..." I furrow my brow. "I've never been able to do that. Have you?"

Heath turns to me earnestly. "No. But—what happened the other night...with us...that was like nothing I've ever experienced."

"Me, neither..." I say honestly.

He holds up his palm. "So what if there's *more* that we can do together? Don't you want to find out?" His grin is all mischief, and like always, I can't resist him.

"I do want." I lay my hand against his, aligning our fingers. "I want to do everything with you." My hand is shaking a little with anticipation. "And first, I want to find Pearl."

"So..." he says, still gazing at me, "let's think about her." Then his lids fall shut, and I close mine, too. At first, I'm distracted by how our palms go sweaty; there's such heat generated at the touch of our skin. But when I'm *finally* able to forget about Heath and think only of Pearl... *bang*.

There's a surge between us so fierce that the energy almost knocks me down.

I cry out and almost let go, but Heath squeezes my hands, and as I grit my teeth against the intensity and the heat of the current, the colors around us blur, and the storefront window pulls out into a long tunnel that we seem to be careening down.

I squint down the tunnel and see fuzzy shapes of hulking men in dark clothes and hoods. Trucks in front of

Dumpsters. Then kids, and more kids. It's almost like I'm seeing the scene play out underwater. And then—

A giant of a man has Pearl Neederman by the throat.

I lunge forward in alarm, but a vortex of swirling, waterlike air seems to push me back. I can't move. I can't stop it.

Then Pearl's head turns and she seems to look through the tunnel and see me.

There are tears in her eyes.

Chapter 39

Wisty

"HEATH! I THINK I know that place!"

It's hazy, but I can just remember the smell of sickness in the Gutter that day, Whit running with me on his back as crowds pushed in on us. And the taste of blood...

I tear off toward that wretched place.

"Wisty, wait—" Heath yells, but I don't stop.

"It's not far!" I promise. We race across the City. Though I was barely conscious when I was last here, somehow my feet know the way beyond the boarded-up food carts, and I hang a right into the alley. Rats look up at us defiantly as we slow to a stop past the rows of giant garbage containers.

"I told you," I say breathlessly. The setting looks just like in the vision.

Right down to the hooded men loading kids into trucks.

"Oh my god!" I gasp. "Heath!"

They may be different from the group that took Pearl,

but they're here—the vans, the men, the kids.... *It's really happening. Right now.*

Heath protectively tries to pull me to a crouch next to the containers, but one of the men jerks his head toward us at the sound of our voices, and I know we've been spotted.

The villains make a break for it then. "They're getting away!"

It happens too fast for us to join forces, but as Heath and I move to attack, our separate strengths are undeniable.

I see the electric lines above and clench my hands into fists, pulling the power into my body as the severed lines go haywire. Then, when I'm absolutely brimming with M, I fling it out through my fingers. A shower of sparks rains down over the hulking men.

Just like the fireworks on the night they took her.

The kidnappers yell and cover their heads, and as they scatter, Heath goes into Demon mode. He whips forward, a ferocious force of speed and pain zeroing in on each hulking, hooded target in turn.

While I'm trying to get to the kids in the back of one van, I hear a screech of tires and whip around as the second van starts to peel away.

"Wisty, stop them!" Heath yells as the van whips down the alley, its back doors swinging on their hinges. Before I have a split second to come up with a plan, the van swerves to avoid the live wire I left still sparking in the street.

"*No!*" I scream as the van smashes head-on into the

side of a building, and the sound...well, that explosion will echo in my dreams forever.

I start sprinting toward the flames, wailing. *If there were any children in there...*

"Wisty! Come back!" Heath yells above the roar. "Get away! That van didn't have any kids in it!"

I sink down to the pavement, collapsing with relief.

"Move back!" Heath cries. I look up and leap away just before another explosion pounds my ears. Trembling, I stagger back toward the first van.

Now only one man remains, and without laying a finger on him, Heath brings the man to his knees on the filthy ground in front of us.

"Where are you taking the captives?" I demand breathlessly, tearing off the captor's hood.

Underneath, the man is balding, with wind-whipped cheeks and hatred in his eyes. He doesn't say a word.

"What do you want with these children? *Who is your leader?!*" I try again, but the man scowls at us and spits at my feet.

At that, Heath narrows his eyes. A sheet of ice slowly starts to grow from the ground beneath the man's knees. The ice eats its way upward, over knees and fingers, slowly covering his body. When the frost starts to choke at his neck, the man groans.

"Heath—" I cut in. I'm getting uncomfortable with where this is going. "That's enough."

"If we let him go, he'll tell his leader," Heath says

confidently. When I don't say anything, he looks up at me. "Wisty, do you want to be able to save more kids or not?"

I bite my lip and nod. *That's the only thing that matters.*

"You're not—" the man whispers through chattering teeth.

"What's that you say?" Heath leans in, and I want to look away; I just want this to be over.

"You're not...supposed to...use...magic," the kidnapper chokes out.

Heath shrugs, and with a flick of his wrist, the man's whole head becomes encased in ice, his eyes frozen open in their judgmental stare.

"So I've heard," Heath mutters.

Chapter 40

Whit

SASHA IS REALLY GONE.

It doesn't feel real. Even after hours of chipping away at the hard ground to dig his grave. Even after I watched the soil slowly cover his face as Janine talked about his life, and listened to Ross cry until his throat was raw, I can't process it.

He was my age. He was my friend.

And he's dead.

We sit next to the fresh mound, the snow soaking into our clothes.

"What are we doing here?" I whisper, my heart breaking with hopelessness. "We should go home."

"No." Ross wipes his eyes and straps on his pack. "We can't give up. We have to keep going. It's what Sasha would do, and I'm not going to let him down."

So with our friend dead and our spirits shattered, we trudge on for hours through the sleet and the snow. We

173

don't speak, and the quiet of the forest somehow feels both mournful and peaceful at the same time.

By the time the first stars spot the twilight sky, my legs can barely carry me forward. I start looking for a place to make camp, grateful for an end to this awful day.

Janine stops, but she has a strange expression on her face. "Do you hear that?" she asks.

"It sounds like laughter," Ross says.

I tilt my head, listening hard. What I hear makes me tremble. *It can't be.* I look at my companions. "It sounds like—kids."

We race through the trees toward the noises of children playing, and hope starts to creep back into my heart.

But when we peer over the ridge at the valley below, my excitement withers.

It's worse than I'd imagined.

"What are they *doing* to that kid?" Ross gasps.

I shake my head, unable to look away. The scene below is grotesque. The boy is slashing at his own legs again and again with a stick, and its thorns leave screaming red stripes where they hit. His thighs are a mess of blood and welts.

And what's worse: there's a mob of children of all ages leaning in toward the spectacle. They're *cheering him on.* Every slash provokes another roar of applause.

The camp is small, but there are hundreds of kids milling around the space, waiting for direction. When the torturous performance is over, one of the burly sentries sounds a deafening bell.

The kids immediately take off at a trot, like they're racing, only there're no markers and no finish. They just circle the small yard over and over, hiking their knobby knees up with dogged concentration. They jump over the kids who are lying on the ground—the ones who aren't moving—or sometimes they step on them instead.

As they run, I can see most of the other kids aren't in much better shape than the whipped boy. They're thin and poorly clothed, and their cheeks are hollowed, their eyes sunken with exhaustion. Some are missing fingers, others toes. I spot one little girl with a dirty rag wrapped around the stump where her hand should be, and I feel bile rise up in my throat.

"Pearl," I croak, lurching up from behind the ridge.

"No," Janine hisses, tugging at my arm. "They'll see us! It's not her, Whit—it's not Pearl."

I know she's right. This girl's hair is too light, and her legs are too long. Her face is too old to be Pearl Marie Neederman.

But it *could've* been. These monsters could've done the same to Pearl. Tortured her. Maimed her. *If she's here . . .* Who knows what they've done.

"We have to break into the camp," I say, trying to keep my voice steady.

"Now?" Ross's eyes are as wide as saucers. I know he's

thinking of how Sasha died, but the kid is brave, and he nods.

Janine, on the other hand, isn't having it. "No. We scout it out tomorrow," she says. "It's almost dark."

"It would be so easy to bust them out of there right now," I point out. "There's no fence, and they only have a few guards—"

"We don't know what they have. *Something* made the kids do those things. Something made that boy…" She shakes her head. "Tomorrow," she says firmly. "We're not going in there at night without knowing what we're walking into. It's suicide."

Chapter 41

Whit

I CLENCH MY JAW as we set up camp on the rocky platform. Wolves howl in the distance, and the wind whistles against the rock. I'm trying to keep my teeth from chattering with cold, or grinding in anger and frustration.

Tomorrow. I settle back into my crude bed, sighing, and promising once again: *If Pearl's inside that house of horrors, tomorrow we'll bust her out.*

"You're shivering," Janine says, putting a hand on my cheek.

I hold her smooth, gentle fingers to my face. "My clothes are still damp from the river," I answer, not mentioning the thoughts that are really chilling me to the bone. "It'd be kind of unreasonable for me to expect to be warm at this point."

Janine shakes her head. "Not unreasonable, really." I notice she's got her sleeping bag balled up in her arms. "I was thinking Ross and Feffer have the right idea." She points over at our sleeping friend, his arms wrapped around the dog. "Shared body heat," Janine explains, and her wry smile is the first thing that has truly made me feel warm since we started up this Mountain.

"That's better," I say, once she's curled up beside me. I breathe her in, a sweet smell of pine and dirt all her own, and the night feels a little less dark. For a long time we lie quietly, listening to the screech of bats and the rustle of leaves.

"It wasn't just for the warmth," Janine finally says, her voice muffled by my chest. "I just...I didn't want to be alone tonight, you know? I see his face every time I shut my eyes."

"I know. Me, too." *All their faces. Their eyes, most of all.* I see Sasha's eyes as the life went out of him, Wisty's eyes brimming as I turned away from her, and the dead eyes of the girl with the missing hand.

"How do we ever sleep again?" Janine asks hopelessly. "I mean, how do we get past this?"

The moonlight catches in her eyes, making them glisten with life, and suddenly I can't help it—I'm not thinking about the sadness, or the tragedy, or the cold anymore. I'm thinking about the heat in the spot where our legs press against one another. I'm thinking about the outline of her body under the blanket, about how smooth her skin must feel....

I'm thinking about a night spent under the stars with a girl who drives me crazy. *Janine.*

"Maybe we remember the people we still have," I whisper, and hear the desire in my voice. "Maybe we act like each day is all we have left, and go from there."

Janine tilts her head up to me. "So, what would you do if we just had right now?"

I kiss her fiercely then, and she kisses me back, her hands pulling me closer. Even if the world is crumbling around us, tonight Janine and I will feel as completely alive as we ever have, and hold each other tight until the last star is gone from the sky.

Chapter 42

Wisty

AFTER OUR TAKEDOWN of the kidnappers' vans, Heath makes a point I've been trying not to think too much about.

"Makes you wonder what else we could accomplish together, doesn't it?" He smiles mischievously.

Something comes over me when I see that devilish grin, and I can't *not* kiss him. I savor the taste of his sweet lips and drape my arms around his neck, inhaling him.

"Ahem," I hear a young voice say nearby.

A dozen children are still huddled together by the abandoned truck, staring as we smooch near the still-smoking wreck.

I cough awkwardly, dropping my arms from Heath's neck. "What are you guys doing out this late, anyway?" I scold the kids, but they just gape at me, still too shell-shocked to move.

The group is a mix of older and younger kids, ragged

and well dressed, dark and fair. Whoever's taking them seems to just want numbers. *But for what?*

"Haven't your parents told you that monsters come out after curfew?" I ask, going for a lighthearted tone. Still no one speaks.

Unless... *it's* me *they're afraid of*, I realize with a pang. I'm *the monster that comes out after dark*, thanks to Bloom's antimagic rhetoric. And now they've just witnessed us starting an electrical fire, blowing up a car, and freezing a man. Not exactly the stuff sweet dreams are made of.

I sigh. "Go on, get out of here!" I clap my hands, and that seems to shake a few of them out of their stupor. They start to scamper in all directions. "Go home to your mamas, and tell them you saw the fire witch and her horrible spells!"

And maybe tell them how we saved your lives, too.

"Thank you, Missus Fire Witch," a tiny girl in a pink jumper says. She kicks the frozen man as she passes. "He's better that way." She reminds me a bit of Pearl Neederman with her wise, old eyes.

"Hey, what's your name?" I ask.

"Bettina Alexandra Gannon." She leans forward conspiratorially. "My mom says you have to say your whole name if you want people to remember you. You won't forget, will you?"

I put my hand over my heart and look at her solemnly. "I won't forget."

I'll remember these kids, remember what it took to save

them. Maybe we did do something good here tonight. And maybe we could do it again.

After the last kid has run home, I look at Heath, grinning. "Thanks for getting me out of the house. Even if you had to break in first."

He's smiling, too, but it's a different sort of smile. He gazes at me from under those lashes, that unflinching look he first hooked me with at the celebration. He takes a few slow, deliberate steps across the cobblestones toward me, his steady, suggestive gaze making the distance feel like miles.

"Speaking of home..." Heath brings my bandaged hand to his lips, kissing the knuckles tenderly one by one, and I hold my breath. "May I show you mine? Would that be all right?"

I feel the flush on my neck as I nod. I chatter constantly as we walk. Not doing a great job of hiding my butterflies.

"So," Heath says as we reach the steps of the building's front porch. "Do I still frighten you, Wisty Allgood?"

"I had a shard of glass at your throat a few hours ago," I say wryly, and Heath smirks. I stand up straighter, meeting his bold gaze. "You've never frightened me," I answer.

Heath leans closer. "I wish I could say the same," he murmurs.

Then his lips are on mine, gentle at first, then pressing hard. As Heath moves slowly backward up the porch stairs, I lean into his kisses, letting him pull me upward.

Another step. Another.

The fever spreads over me, up my legs and chest, up my neck....

Oh, no, I think, just as I feel my hair catch fire. *Please, not now.*

I start to jerk away from Heath, afraid I'll burn him, but he only grips my body tighter, his hold firm, his lips insistent.

The fire streaks across my skin as any sense of caution I had a second ago falls away. The pale yellow flame climbs higher and hotter, roaring between us.

I don't even care. There's no pain. Only pleasure.

It feels like all I've ever wanted.

Chapter 43

Wisty

THE AIR VIBRATES with our white-hot heat, like nothing I've ever known. It's like my blood itself is boiling. The sensation spreads through my body like a match to gasoline, snaking in seconds from my toes up into my feverish brain.

We stop to draw in a breath, and our eyes connect. It's just a fleeting moment but it feels like time stops. His eyes wrap me up with a look of complete devotion.

No one has ever looked at me this way.

And there's something else in Heath's look, too: power.

The power of love and lust and heat, controlling my body and my brain and my magic. A power fed by every touch. It's there between the frenzied kisses, crackling and hissing in the flames.

It's so intense between us, like every thought, every emotion is shared and translated into the very real, very physical fire raging around us.

Getting hotter. And hotter. And hotter.

There's a sudden *whoosh* as the roof above the porch goes up in flames.

Heath doesn't even seem to notice. He's still pulling me toward the doorway to his building.

But suddenly I don't know if that's what I want. Suddenly it feels like I can barely see through the smoke, or breathe through his kisses. And the fire is spreading, the heat choking....

My magic has never felt so totally out of control.

"Wait." I step back abruptly, breaking the embrace.

"What's wrong?" Heath asks, breathless.

Nothing. I shake my head. *Everything.* My hair is still sending off sparks, betraying my desire, and I can't explain why I don't want to step through that doorway.

I just don't know if I'm ready.

There's a final swell of heat before my fire starts to sizzle out. But the front of the building is still burning. *What have I done?*

Heath reaches for my hand. "It's okay, Wisty." There's concern in his voice, but his touch is still too hot, and I involuntarily pull away. Even as I do it, it's breaking my heart.

"I just can't," I whisper, and before he can say another word, I turn from him and—hearing that sirens are already on their way—I flee.

Tears streak down my cheeks as I run. *It's not supposed to be like this.* Until this moment, I'd taken pride in the strength of my magic. But right now, running from a burn-ing building because I'm afraid of what power a kiss could have, I just feel humiliated.

And angry.

Shrieking, I light up the alley with a handful of light-ning bolts, and a dozen windows shatter as a frustrated sob tears out of my throat.

I throw fireballs at garbage cans, and they erupt into blazing bonfires.

With a frustrated yell, I kick one over, and the fire shoots outward as the air hits it. It blazes up a nearby building and seems to chase me down the block.

I'm aware of people watching me now—of frowning faces and wide, fearful eyes peering out of the cracks of doorways and from behind window shades.

The fire is reflected in mirrored windows on both sides of the street. It feels like it's just getting bigger and bigger, surrounding me. My hair is still sparking, and the smoke trails after me all the way down the street.

No wonder they're afraid of me.

Chapter 44

Whit

"YOU PROMISED ME, WHIT!" Celia moans, distraught. "You *promised* me you wouldn't come up the Mountain."

"I actually promised I wouldn't go to the King," I say, guiltily. "And I haven't."

Her withering look makes me feel like an even bigger jerk. I don't think Celia's ever been *really* angry with me—not like this. "I'm sorry, Celes. I didn't have a choice. You wouldn't believe how bad it's gotten in the City. Someone needed to negotiate—"

"I'm telling you, the Wizard King does not negotiate!"

Celia's not a floating head in the sky this time. Not a far-off voice. Not even a shimmering Half-light in Shadowland, capable of emotion but not of being held.

This time, she's pacing the rocky terrain of the Mountain, right in front of our camp, and Celia looks like she did in high school that day her grandmother died, with red-rimmed eyes and a sniffling nose. Her tears drip down skin that doesn't even glow. This time, she's flawed and blotchy and angry.

And she seems so, so *real*.

"Is this still a dream?" I wonder aloud.

I keep reaching out to see if her arms are solid, and if I can pinch her thick, curly hair between my fingers. The forest is weird, though. I think she's in front of one tree, but every time I reach my hand out, I realize she's somewhere else.

"Are you even listening to me?" she demands, turning. Even her agitation seems so... human again.

"Are you alive?" I blurt out, before I can stop myself.

The question itself seems to rattle her even more. "No, baby. I'm dead and buried." Celia looks at me hard. "Remember?"

"I remember..." I say, uncertain, but it's so hard to deny what's in front of me now.

Celia shakes her head. "You're confused. I came to warn you, but it's too late. You can't even see me, not really."

The accusation makes my heart ache. "I can see you," I protest. "You're more beautiful than ever." But Celia shakes her head, and my step toward her seems to take me backward again, to the other side of the boulders.

"Get back to Wisty, *now*, Whit!" she commands urgently. "She needs you."

Her mention of Wisty makes me nervous. Hopefully Byron is looking out for her.

"I'm going back to the City soon. I just have to get Pearl first."

"Pearl's already lost!" Celia insists. "They're all lost. The Mountain King takes them."

"The kids? We can take them back, though. I saw the camp—"

"No, he *takes* them," she repeats, eyes wild. "*Cleans* them. The children aren't there anymore. They're all washed away."

I shake my head sadly, thinking maybe she means the river that the dead cross to Beyond. "I'm sorry, Celes. I don't understand."

"Listen to me!" she screams angrily. "I tried to warn you before. I tried to warn you because I love you!" Her shoulders heave as she starts to cry.

"You know I'll always love you, too, Celia, right?" I tell her. But she sobs harder, burying her face in her hands. "It's okay. Don't cry. Look at me. Please."

But when she looks up at me, there's only blankness. Her face is *wiped clean.*

I recoil and jerk awake, and I'm in the same place in the forest, but still in my sleeping bag, and colder than I ever remember being.

Janine hovers over me, her head filling up my view in place of Celia's, and I'm relieved to see her face is still there, with all its freckles and her emerald eyes, spilling over with tears.

What's wrong?

189

"You were talking in your sleep." She shakes her head. "About Celia."

Oh, no.

"Wait," I say, sitting up and touching her hand. "Janine, that wasn't—"

"Even now, even after everything, you just can't let her go," she says, pulling her hand from my grasp and marching off through the thicket of the trees.

I'm struggling to free myself from the blankets when I hear her scream.

Chapter 45

Whit

JANINE BURSTS BACK into the clearing, stumbling into me as she looks over her shoulder.

"What happened?" I ask urgently, looking around for the threat. "Are you okay?"

"It's Margo," Janine says in a thin, whimpering voice, her eyes wide.

Margo? I frown, looking for a head wound or a sign that Janine is injured. *That makes no sense.*

Feffer starts barking, and Ross blinks up at us sleepily from his rocky bed. "Who's Margo?"

"The original Resistance badass," the girl answers as she steps from behind the pines.

She *does* look like Wisty's best friend, purple camo pants and all. Only there's no ash in her blond hair, and her eyes positively sparkle with life. Which explains the shock on Janine's face: Margo was murdered by The One.

She's been dead for over a year.

"Hey, guys," says the walking, talking, *breathing* Margo.

I gape at her in disbelief. *I saw the execution. I watched you go up in smoke.*

Didn't I? The One killed a girl that day, a girl who wore Margo's punky, star-covered sneakers. A girl whose face we never saw under the hood. It *had* to be her, though. Right?

"Hey, Margo," I answer uneasily, not knowing where to start. *Where have you been all this time? How did you find us on this Mountain? What does dying feel like?* "What's . . . up?"

"We thought it'd be fun to get the old crew back together." She cocks her head.

We?

Sasha is walking through the trees in our direction.

"Ohhh," Ross manages to squeak before he passes out in a dead faint.

I'm not feeling so well myself. We buried Sasha yesterday, spent hours chipping at the cold ground to dig his grave, and here he is, lumbering toward us.

Feffer whines—a high, nervous plea.

The blood is gone from the bandanna Sasha wears tied around his head, and there's no trace of the hole the arrow blazed through his chest.

"Hi, pup." He holds out a hand, but the dog backs away from his touch with her tail between her legs.

"Whaddaya say we find us some Mountain boys to kill?" Margo suggests. She picks up a hefty rock with a sharp edge and tosses it up a few times.

Janine's eyes flick to mine. It's Margo's voice, but tough or not, she was too scrawny to lift a rock like that, and she *never* would've been excited about killing someone.

I start to back away, and feel arms lock around my waist in an embrace.

I turn, and it's just like in the dream.

Celia's here, in these woods, not a floating head in the sky.

"I've missed you, Whit," Celia says.

I guess it's not like the dream, though, because this time, her cheeks are pink from the cold, and I can feel her arms solid around me.

Real.

For a moment I'm dizzy, and feel the tears freezing on my cheeks.

"Whit—" Janine says sharply, her tone more terrified than hurt.

When I look toward her voice, I see Margo's smiling face transform as her eyes overflow with tiny white worms.

Dead and buried.

I jerk back in revulsion, but Celia's grip on me tightens as she opens her sweet lips that I used to know so well… and a cloud of black insects erupts out of her mouth.

Bees.

I swat at the air, trying to dodge them like I've dodged so many Demons, but there are too many swarming around me. I drop to the ground, trying to cover my head from the stings as my ears pound with their furious hum.

Feffer is barking frantically now, Janine is screaming, and I'm gagging on the buzzing bodies, invisible fingers tightening around my throat.

"Enough!" a woman's sharp voice warns.

The air clears, the buzz stops, and I squint up from my fetal position on the ground, wondering what to make of our savior. In the bright morning light, she seems to blend in with the Mountain. She wears a cloak of speckled white feathers, with a few in her silvery-blond hair. Piercing eyes look out with distaste at the figures around me.

But...they've changed. Sasha and Margo have been replaced by large men with dreadlocks and beards. Where Celia stood, a boulder of a man with a glass eye fixes the woman with his unsettling stare.

This seems to be magic unlike anything I've ever seen.

"We were sent to kill them," the big man says gruffly. "By the King himself."

"*I'll* answer to the King," the feathered woman replies. "As for Whit Allgood..." She turns to me. "I hear you're a healer. Can you prove it?"

Chapter 46

Whit

WE RIDE FOR HOURS, higher into the frigid air, until it seems that the Kingdom must be built on clouds.

"We were supposed to kill them, Izbella," the man with a glass eye says to the feathered woman. He still looks gigantic and vicious as he glowers down from his fierce-looking warhorse.

"I said I would handle it, Larsht," the woman says icily. Larsht scowls, but doesn't say another word.

We creep along a narrow, treacherous ridge, bowing dangerously outward over the emptiness. When we round the corner along the cliff, a great Mountain Kingdom unfolds out of nowhere, its lands sprawling across the valley below.

The buildings are short and squat, nestled like teeth in the snow of the sloping hillside, and vast mountain lakes are as flat and peaceful as the cloudless sky. Something stirs in me—something like poetry—and Janine seems to feel it, too.

"It's breathtaking," she gasps, shading her eyes from the sun.

"Isn't it, though?" asks Izbella, urging her horse onward.

Above the Kingdom's gates, a banner with a white leopard streams, and inside, it's not at all what I expected. There are no towering buildings here, or signs of busy commerce. But the squat structures of rock and wood are anything but crude, and the uneven rocky path of the journey has been replaced with smooth, paved streets.

"Much cleaner than your City, isn't it?" Larsht says as we approach the modest castle that looms ahead. "No rats, no disease, no filth. The people here are cleansed by the King himself."

"It's a superior way to live," Izbella agrees.

I study this strange woman—so full of contradictions I don't know what to make of her. She's brought me here to save someone, but isn't concerned with tortured children. She has obvious authority in this Kingdom, but defies her King to save people she disdains.

"If you have all this already…" I ask, "why do you want *us*?"

Izbella shifts uncomfortably in her saddle. "That's something you'll have to ask the King." She clicks her tongue, and the white horse gallops ahead of us down the street.

Larsht leans toward us. "Because your kind of idiot can't be trusted," he sneers, his eyes menacing and his breath sour. "You've never been able to take care of your-selves. Don't you know that children are made to work, not rule?"

I let out a shaky breath as we pass under the last row of banners before the castle, images of white cats flapping violently in the wind above us.

Let's see what you're made of, Whit Allgood.

Chapter 47

Whit

FROM THE MOMENT I set foot inside the castle walls, I know it, deep in my bones: *Something is terribly wrong here.*

The chamber is dimly lit, bitter cold, and stinks of death.

Guards stand posted, holding us at the doorway until the signal is given for us to enter, and so I can't really tell what's going on.

The windows are blacked out, and though there's a fireplace, no coals warm the hearth. Shadowy shapes move across the room wearing masks, and they seem to be performing some dark ritual.

I crane my neck to peer in and suddenly understand why I'm there.

A kid lies on a table near the back of the room, naked to the waist. By his face, I'd guess he was about thirteen or fourteen. But the bones protrude from his frail body, and his twisted, underdeveloped legs make him appear smaller and younger. He writhes in pain.

The hooded figures hold scythes over him, I realize with dismay. The long, curved blades are gruesome, made for messy work, and I'm reminded of the mutilated children.

The gloved hands are lowering the blades. *Oh, god, oh, god.*

"Don't," I bark, lunging forward into the room.

Right before Larsht's giant hands yank me roughly back, I see my mistake: it isn't limbs the scythes are for— it's ice. Huge blocks of ice are mounted on a stand, and the hooded fingers are shaving it into long, frosty strips over the boy. Even his table is made of ice.

I don't understand, though. Don't they see? They're just making it worse.

The kid coughs hard, the sound rattling in his chest, and he shudders as the ice water runs over him, melting as it touches his feverish skin.

The masks are to prevent the spreading of the infection. It's so virulent, you can almost smell it on him.

"You won't fix him that way," I tell the icemen. "He needs the fever to help him heal. He needs the warmth to burn the sickness from the inside out."

"He wants to make my boy filthy with fire!" Larsht says, shoving me into the wall.

"Can I just see him?" I ask. "I might be able to help."

"We don't want your poison." Other soldiers join in the taunts. "Make the stranger clean!"

Two sentries step from the shadows with dirk and axe in hand, edging me backward, and I start to press against the wall like a cornered animal, my nerves raw.

This could get ugly, and after the bizarre episode with our dead friends, I have no idea what any of these Mountain magicians is capable of. I watch for sudden movements, for just one hand reaching for an axe....

"Let him come inside," Izbella says in a low, even voice. It seems like she's materialized out of thin air. As the soldiers clear a path, Izbella's feathered cloak rustles as she leads me across the floor. Janine and Ross stay behind.

"Can you heal him?" asks a woman who can only be the boy's mother, clasping my hands in her own. Her face is masked, but the desperation in her eyes reminds me of Mama May Neederman.

Can I heal him?

"I…" I think of Sasha, and how I couldn't save him, how the magic wouldn't come. I'm strong again, though. I can do this—I've done it before. "I think so." I nod, looking up into the kid's mother's shining eyes.

"Don't touch him!" Larsht is elbowing his way into the chamber again. "The King said the ice would mend him— that the cold would cleanse him!" the grizzled man protests stubbornly.

"And *have* his lungs cleared?" his wife cries. "I can feel

him slipping away from us, Larsht." She touches his arm, pleading. "Can't you see the life going out of him?"

Larsht flings her hand away. "There's only one person here who's going to die today," he barks. "And that's Whitford Allgood."

My temper flares at this death warrant, but right now there's a child suffering, and it doesn't matter which side of the enemy line he's on.

"Step aside." Izbella's voice is sharp and unyielding this time. "Leave us," the feathered woman commands Larsht.

He glowers over her, but some of the fight seems to go out of him as he watches his crippled son wheeze and tremble on the table.

"If you would see your son live, let this boy do his work."

Chapter 48

Whit

IZBELLA'S WORDS IGNITE the buzz of power within me. Somehow I know now: I was meant to be here, at this moment, on this forsaken Mountain. I was meant to save this boy.

On Izbella's command, the guards retreat from the claustrophobic chamber, and the dark cloaks shuffle out of my way, melting into the shadows.

I move closer to the table, where a dim glow from the single flickering bulb makes the ice shimmer. The block glows with a cold light as if lit from within, but the boy's life light is almost extinguished.

"What's his name?" I ask gently.

"Njar," Larsht answers, his harsh voice finally softening. "His name is Njar."

I stare at the crippled, emaciated form before me. "Njar," I repeat, the syllable feeling awkward on my tongue.

Healer's hands, I remind myself as I place my palms on his chest. *Don't fail me now.*

Some of the soldiers shift forward again, grunting their displeasure, but Izbella holds them back, and I keep my attention focused in one place only.

There's a pulse beneath my fingers, faint and quick as a bird's, but it's there. This guy wants to fight.

Like Wisty during the Blood Plague, when she almost didn't make it....

"This isn't your time, Njar," I whisper softly, like I did to my sister that day.

His skin is damp with sweat and chilled to the bone, but as the M starts to move through my fingertips, the warm surge of it leaves red spots on his chest, and I know my own brand of medicine is working through him.

I close my eyes, keeping my hands steady on his chest, and concentrate on reaching in and seeking out. I feel myself, my power rushing through the veins, toward his lungs, like a healing serum doing its work.

I seek out the blackness and the death, and root out the pain. I consume it all.

"Come back to us, Njar," I whisper, feeling my hands lift strangely as his body warms and strengthens. "Come back to all these people who love you."

I shudder as I feel the fever leaving him, snaking away in retreat.

When I open my eyes, Njar is floating above the table, as high as my shoulder blades. He starts to tremble from his ankles all the way up to his neck, and as the movement spreads, he's ... *changing*.

His muscles start to fill out. His breathing starts to steady. And color floods his cheeks.

There's something else, too. It's this light that seems to be emanating from his pores, making the whole room glow with healing energy.

I finally let out a breath. He's saved.

Family members blink up at the boy suspended before them, and when they remove their hospital masks, I see that tears are flowing freely down their cheeks.

A few of Njar's relatives lay their cloaks over the block of ice, and I grip his shoulders and slowly lower him back to the table.

Njar opens his eyes and smiles like he's just awoken from a sweet dream.

"You came back," his mother says, weeping.

Njar looks at her, his lucid eyes shining. "I came back for the people I love," he says with gratitude, and turns to me. "Like you said."

Color is returning to his face and he's shed the smell of death like an old robe. Everyone is hugging—Njar, and his relatives, and even Larsht.

"You've saved my nephew and the King's grandson," the feathered woman announces. "You've rid us of this terrible illness and scoured death from this Kingdom. We are greatly in your debt."

I don't even have a moment to relish the triumph before the chamber's huge wooden doors fly open on their hinges, and soldiers flood the room.

Chapter 49

Wisty

"HEY," I CALL UP from the sidewalk.

Heath grins as he opens his front door. "Hey," he shouts down to me. "I'd invite you up to the porch, but..." He looks around at the piles of ash and burnt cinders where the porch used to be, and we both laugh.

"I guess we ran a little hotheaded on that one, huh?" I ask, blushing, and Heath nods.

"I just wanted to say—" We blurt it out at the same time, in the same awkward, rushed tone. This triggers another fit of laughter, of course. But laughing's okay. Laughing is good.

Better than crying, for example. Or fleeing.

Heath motions in my direction. "After you."

I clear my throat. "I just came to say that I'm sorry about running off the other night."

He starts to wave it off, but I've been rolling this over in my head ever since, and I need to get it out.

"Ever since The One—well, was destroyed," I begin, stumbling over that whole concept of Whit and me *killing him*, "I haven't had to use my powers like I did during the New Order. And I'm realizing it's…kind of *scary* that I don't really understand them anymore, don't really know what I'm capable of. And you…" I swallow. "You're pushing me to places I didn't know I could go."

Heath looks sympathetic, but I'm not done yet. My throat has gone dry. "The One did that to me, too, you know." This time I gulp. "Not that I'm comparing you to him or anything…"

Heath's face clouds over. "I would *never* treat you the way he did, Wisty!" he says passionately. He hops down from the doorway.

"I know, I know.…" He comes over to me and lets me bury my face in his chest.

"The truth is, Wisty…" His dark hair falls forward. "You're pushing me to places I didn't know I could go, either. Ever since we first merged our power…do you ever still sense that connection when we're apart? Like you can feel…"

A ghost of the other's power. A whisper of a thought. An emotion. A surge.

I nod. "All the time."

"So it's my fault for pushing you too fast, really. I just… started to want that feeling all the time. I *crave* it. Like I crave you."

His gaze is burning into me, as intense as ever, and I

207

remember all those dizzy moments after I left him. *Yeah, I guess I crave him, too.*

"But I can slow down," he adds. "We can cool off."

"We don't have to cool off," I say quickly. Heath flashes that wicked grin. "I mean, we still have so much work to do in the City. Why don't we keep exploring our magic in ways we've already tried so far, so we can get it more under control? Like..."

"There still are lots of kids to save," Heath suggests.

"And plenty of ways to use that crazy tunnel vision to dig up information," I point out.

"And ways to stay fired up about the cause in the meantime." Heath cocks a mischievous eyebrow, and I grin, shaking my head again at the blackened porch kindling.

"Definitely."

The network of magicians was right. The City is falling apart too fast and I *can't* do this on my own. I'm just not quite ready to go running for my big brother yet, either.

The City needs a witch and a wizard, they said, and that's true. So here we are. I think again of our window reflection as we merged—the girl with the nest of red hair; the boy in black.

A witch. A wizard.

I'm not trying to replace Whit forever, but he's gone now. He left.

So for the moment, I need to make do. And this feels right.

Heath lifts up my chin, and the sky is reflected in those clear blue eyes, vast and true. When we kiss this time, it's more like a cloud kiss—soft and light and dreamy, a promise of things to come.

Chapter 50

Whit

IT'S LIKE A POLICE RAID.

Armed men storm into the chamber where I healed the boy. Everyone is screaming, and terror and chaos seem to blot out everything else.

The moment the old man enters the room, however, it falls eerily silent, and I swear, the temperature drops another twenty degrees.

"Having a celebration?" he purrs, stalking around the chamber.

This man wears no crown, and is draped in rough, dirty animal furs, but the instant he speaks, I know that this is the infamous Wizard King. The Mountain Man. The Snow Leopard.

This, without a doubt, is the man who does not negotiate, who I have to try to reason with.

The King's fury is palpable—it almost hums off him,

to practice magic in this village, *in my house*?" His voice thunders louder, and the heat of his sour breath hits me full in the face. "You may be a healer, boy, but you'd best remember that *I* am the king of destruction."

I'm trembling, but I don't dare open my mouth.

"Now tell me," he asks in a falsely pleasant tone. "What did you want to negotiate?"

Remember what you came here to do. I step forward, trying to find my voice again.

"We want to restore the water agreement," I finally answer. "And we request immediate release of the City's kidnapped children, or the penalty is war."

"Yes, it is," the King says ominously. "It always is. Now, what do *I* want?" The King drags a long, thick fingernail slowly down my face, from forehead to chin. I try not to flinch.

"Well, I want you dead, to start with," he says simply. "You and your sister both. I have you already...so tell me, boy, where is the little witch?"

The Wizard King doesn't negotiate, Celia had insisted. She knew everything, all along. Why didn't I listen?

I set my jaw. *I won't go out like that. Not where Wisty is concerned.*

"*Where. Is. Your. Sister?*" he repeats in a low, threatening voice.

I look this sick old man square in his creepy eyes and clench my jaw.

"We just got word the kid's on his way up the Mountain

with his sweetheart," Larsht interrupts. "He'll deliver the firebrand to us."

Wisty, I think desperately. And then: *Heath*.

"Wonderful," the King says. When he looks at me again, his expression is rife with nastiness. "Put them in the Vault with the leopards, then. My kitties haven't eaten in two days—they deserve a little treat for their morning feed."

Chapter 51

Whit

WHEN THEY SHOVE me inside the Vault, my whole body feels paralyzed in alarm. I flatten myself against the iron door, my eyes bugging out at the scene across the room.

The Wizard King wasn't bluffing: *Our cell really is inside the leopards' den.*

The enormous cats run pink tongues lazily over their jowls and squint sleepily at one another. I see those fangs peeking out, though, and their tails swishing back and forth.

They could attack at any moment.

"Aren't they gorgeous?"

It's Janine's voice. I hadn't even noticed her in the room, along with Ross, sitting cross-legged on the floor. For a second I'm overjoyed to see them, and then I'm crushed again.

They shouldn't be in the death chamber here with me.

Janine pulls on my leg and I slide down beside her. "Don't worry—there's glass between them and us."

215

Not for long, I think with queasy dread as I remember the King's final words: *a treat for their morning feed.*

A slot on the door clicks open, and a pair of eyes scans the room.

I leap to my feet and crowd the opening. *I know those eyes.*

"Pearl?" I ask, and the irises jump inside the metal slot.

Those are Pearl Neederman's eyes, all right—silvery gray and old beyond her years.

"Pearl!" I exclaim.

"Shut up, Wizard," she says, narrowing her eyes. They're harder somehow, I realize. *Cold*, like they weren't before. "I don't talk to the Failures."

"You . . . you don't know me?"

"Of course I know you," she spits. Relief floods through me, but it's only for a moment. "You're the one playing at magic from the City of Scum."

"It's me, Pearl Marie. It's Whit." *We had a connection from my magic. I felt your pain when you were taken. Please, remember me.*

"My name is Rat," she says. "Because a rat can always be cleaner." She says it like she's said it a hundred times before, and my world begins to crumble.

Her deft fingers move over the bolts and pulleys. "Pearl," I say, with a glimmer of hope, "do you know how to open the door?"

She scrunches up her face like I'm the stupidest person she's ever met—it's a very familiar face from the old Pearl,

216

and it gives me hope. "Of course I know how to open the door!" She rolls her eyes. "Since I'm the fastest runner in the whole camp, I catch the rabbits for the kitties."

"Pearl, if you could just open the door, or give us the keys..." I say gently. "We could get you out of here."

"My name's Rat," she says firmly. "And why would I want to leave?" Her bottom lip starts to quiver. "You're not gonna take me away, are you?"

"Stop it, Whit, it's no use—she's been brainwashed." Ross sighs.

The King takes them, Celia said when she was so upset and trying to make me understand. *He wipes them clean.*

"No." I shake my head in disbelief. "No, Pearl, not you."

Maybe she's just pretending, though. Maybe someone is listening....

She slides her hand through the slot in the door to set in the meal tray, and I spot the burns. I grab her wrist and pull it back through.

I gasp at the bubbled, burned flesh snaking across her tiny palm. "Pearl!" I exclaim in horror. "Oh, no. What have they done to you?"

She's trembling all over. "Please let go," she whispers pitifully, all the bravado gone from her voice. She just sounds like a little kid—a little kid who's been tortured. "Wizard, please let go."

"Whit, she's terrified. Let go of her!" Janine yells. I release Pearl's burned hand, and she yanks it back through the window.

"But the burns—" I start.

"Can't you see she hates being touched?" Janine hisses at me.

My heart lurches at the thought of the torture she must have suffered.

The slot is opening again, and this time, an aimed crossbow slides in through the crack.

"Whoa! What are you doing?" I shout, leaping away from the front of the door. The tip of the arrow follows me around the small Vault.

"Strip!" she yells in her tiny drill sergeant's voice, leveling the crossbow at my head.

"What?!"

"The kitties need to be able to smell you," she says matter-of-factly. "For the morning feed, when we pull up the glass door."

"Why are you doing this?" Ross asks, his voice shaking as we reluctantly strip down to our shorts, socks, and undershirts.

Pearl/Rat shakes her head, her dark fringe falling into her eyes. "I didn't do it to you; you did it to yourselves. The King likes winners, and you lost." She cocks her head. "How does it feel to be a Failure, Wizard?"

218

Chapter 52

Wisty

I'M HAPPY. No, *more* than happy. I'm in a fog of romantic bliss.

Heath and I have spent every second together all week, merging our power and saving more kids and—well, yeah, kissing whenever we have a spare moment. And talking. And kissing. And laughing. And kissing.

Everything finally feels like it's coming together....

"Everything's falling apart!"

I swear, if there's a bubble you ever need bursting, Byron Swain will be there in record time, guaranteed. He'd been pounding obnoxiously on the front door buzzer of Heath's building, so I came down to see what he had to say. And that was it: "Everything's falling apart!"

"I admit, it could use a coat of paint," I say, sticking my head out to examine the charred remains of Heath's porch. "And here I thought you were just being melodramatic."

"I have to show you something, Wisty. You have to come with me," Byron urges. "It's just across town—"

"Byron, we've been through this…." I sigh from the doorway, crossing my arms. Since the night he spied on me with Whit, Byron's not exactly on my most-trustworthy list.

"You're on private property." Heath steps behind me and slides a protective arm around my waist. "She doesn't want to talk to you," he adds.

Byron shoots Heath a scowl, but at least he's no longer swinging fists. He shifts uncomfortably.

"Please, Wisty," he begs. "This isn't…." He lowers his voice. "This isn't about you and me. This is more important than all that. It's confidential info I've been trying to crack for weeks." His eyes shine with self-congratulatory purpose. "This is something big."

"So what is it?" I ask doubtfully.

"You have to come see it. I'll take you there right now," Byron says. "I guess the Demon can come, too," he adds begrudgingly.

It turns out "just across town" is actually the westernmost part of the City. After following Byron Swain's speedy shuffle for over two hours and enduring hateful glares from almost every corner of the City, my patience is wearing thin.

"Byron, where are we going?" I huff. "We're almost to the desert—"

"Exactly," Byron says without slowing down. The heat

seems to close in on us suddenly and we're upon it—the border with the Desert that has no name, where the Lizard People supposedly live under the sand, and where legend has it that no City dweller has ever set foot.

But right on the edge of the City line, instead of the usual endlessness stretching out before us, there are buildings. Rows of crude, half-finished structures, crammed almost on top of one another. A towering, mean-looking fence surrounds the development, with barbs and wires sticking out all over.

A memory resurfaces—a memory of drills, degradation, and death—and I realize what this reminds me of, what this looks exactly like: the New Order barracks. My stomach clenches into a knot.

"What is this?" I whisper.

"We already knew Bloom was planning for war," Heath says flatly. "So he's building a place to train an army."

But Byron is shaking his head. "This isn't for training an army," he insists. He grips the fence and looks out across the construction.

"Well, what's it for, then, Swain?" Heath asks, irritated that Byron is drawing this out.

It's me who Byron looks at, though, and his expression is troubled. "It's a ghetto," he says. "Bloom plans to move all the magicians here when the City seizes their homes. And who knows what comes after that? Gas chambers?"

Our rights, gone. Our people, persecuted. A return to the police state.

Byron shakes his head. "I'm sorry, Wisty."

I feel dizzy, and for a second it feels like the ground is coming up to meet me. I lean into the fence for support.

A jolt of searing pain slams through me then, and I see a flash of blinding white. Somehow I'm sailing backward through the air, my whole body ringing like a bell. I smash into the sandy ground fifty feet away, and gag as the impact knocks the breath out of me.

Yes, there's always room for things to get worse.

Chapter 53

Wisty

"WHAT EXACTLY WAS THAT?" I mutter groggily. "A star exploding in my face?"

"A high-voltage shock, if I had to guess," Heath answers as he leans over me with concern. "Thank god you're alive, Wisty."

"But Byron didn't get shocked," I wonder aloud.

"There must be some sort of barrier for magicians." Byron steps back, frowning, with his hands on his hips as he assesses the fence. "Some sort of new technology to incapacitate, to control..."

A prison.

"We have to mobilize," Byron says excitedly. "We have to infiltrate the Council, and rally the people, and set up a petition—"

"I have to bring Whit back!" I exclaim, sitting up abruptly. My head spins.

"What do you mean?" Heath says in alarm.

I struggle to get up after the massive shock, and Heath assists. But once I'm up, I'm steady. And determined. "He needs to be here. This is too big. I can't do this alone, and I need—"

"Whit *left* you, remember?" Heath interrupts. "And you have me."

"And I'm so grateful," I say, and kiss him softly. "But..." *But he doesn't understand how it is with Whit and me. I love Heath, but I need my brother.* "I still have to bring Whit back," I finish. "If Bloom's planning for war, Whit could be caught in the crossfire. I'm going up that Mountain."

"No!" Heath yells suddenly. His eyes flash with panic. "Wisty, you can't!"

Byron and I both stare at him in surprise.

"*Excuse me?*" I ask. If it's not clear by now, I don't exactly love being told what I can and can't do. Even by people I love.

"You don't understand." Heath is pacing now, raking his hands through his hair. "The Wizard King doesn't just want to attack the City." He stops in front of me. "He wants your power, Wisty. And if he can't control it, he'll kill you."

"But Whit—"

"Are you listening to what I'm saying?" He squeezes my shoulders a little too hard. "Your brother's probably already dead! They wanted him dead before he even started his stupid mission!"

Whit...probably dead? I feel like Heath just socked me

in the stomach. *And...how would Heath know they wanted Whit dead?*

"What are you talking about?" I almost spit out at him. When he doesn't answer, a mix of rage and desperation starts to take hold of me. I hardly even realize I'm shaking him. "Heath, tell me what you know!"

"I grew up on the Mountain," he says quietly, his cheeks reddening with shame.

I gape at him. *The Mountain.* As in, where we believe all the kids are disappearing to. As in, the place no one else seems to know anything about. As in, the Kingdom that is about to invade us.

"You *what*?" I demand.

"I knew it!" Byron shouts victoriously. "I knew he was hiding something! I knew he was a traitor—"

"Byron!" I snap. He shrugs and shuts up. "Just because Heath's from the Mountain...doesn't mean he's a traitor," I reason aloud, talking to myself as much as to Byron. "Right?" We both look at Heath questioningly.

"Of course I'm not. I wanted to leave that place behind. I hated it and everyone there." His frown is getting deeper and deeper. "I wanted to start over. I'm no traitor, Wisty."

"But how would you know that the Mountain King wanted Whit dead before he left to go there?"

"Because I know the way the Mountain People think. They think they're superior. They'll kill anyone who they see as a threat to their superiority. *And that includes you.*" He grasps my arms. "Don't go, Wisty."

I fling his hands off me and stumble backward in the packed sand. "How could you not warn me before I let my brother go up there?!"

"I had to keep you safe here," Heath says quickly, moving toward me. Byron steps in front of him. "I couldn't let Whit get in the way of that—"

"I have to go," I snap. "I have to find a portal to get up that Mountain."

"The portals are all closed," Byron says helpfully. "I saw it on the news."

"Then I guess I should start running!" I say, turning. I know I can do this. Even alone.

"Wisty, wait!" Heath pleads. He brushes past Byron.

"I've waited too long already," I say, and start to jog away from him. "Thanks to you."

"I know a better way up the Mountain!" Heath shouts in desperation.

I stop abruptly. "Which way?"

"The way is with me. It's *through* me." His eyes are penetrating me. Commanding me. "Take my hand, Wisty."

Chapter 54

Whit

WE'RE ALL GOING TO DIE. Those are the only words I can think, over and over again. *We're going to die. Painfully. Gruesomely. And very soon.*

"We have to get out of here!" Ross is shrieking. He's flattened against the Vault's door, I'm pacing the small space, and Janine is sitting silently in the corner with her knees pulled up to her chest.

We have to get out of here. If only it was that easy. We spent the entire night trying to break open the iron door through magic, then lock picking and body slamming. It didn't budge.

The glass across the room did, though.

At dawn, the viewing screen that separates us from the group of powerful, hungry snow leopards started lifting. It's continued to move an inch every fifteen minutes or so, and each time it rises, so does our panic.

"We have to stop it!" Ross cries desperately as the glass jerks up again.

Three inches now.

The big cats stalk back and forth in front of the glass, their predators' eyes watching us hungrily.

"If I have to die, I'd rather go like this," Janine says. "Better than some coward with a gun. This is a noble death, at least." Her voice is strong with conviction, but her body is shaking from head to toe.

"Noble?" Ross's fear is reaching a fever pitch. "They'll tear us apart, limb from limb. There's no dignity in that." He starts to suck in agitated breaths.

Janine doesn't answer, but I can see the terror on her face.

I hope they kill me first, I think miserably, watching the powerful muscles ripple beneath the spotted coats. It's a coward's thought, but I don't know if I can bear to watch Janine die first—to see what they'd do to her.

Another inch.

Already? The leopards start to claw at the opening now, their big paws swiping under. I grind my teeth as I pace, back and forth, faster and faster.

Think. I have to think of something!

I could try to freeze the leopards in place, but when the spell wore off, we'd still be locked in.

I could turn into a cockroach and scuttle into a crack in the wall, or morph into a grizzly again and lead the attack. But with nowhere to run, where does that leave my friends?

Think! But the minutes are flying by as my thoughts careen in hopeless circles.

The glass edges up another inch.

And that's it.

"Get back!" I scream at Janine, scrambling frantically away from the glass.

We flatten ourselves against the far wall with Ross, waiting for the first one to squeeze through and tear into flesh.

But the leopards can't get in. Not yet. They flatten their ears, hissing and baring those awful teeth, anxious to get at us. It won't be long now. An inch more, maybe two...

I hold my friends, counting the seconds in my head as I stare at the hungry beasts. Their golden eyes stare right back, the pinlike pupils zeroing in on me.

So this is what it's like—to look death in the face.

"I don't want to die," Ross says hysterically, over and over.

And Janine, though I never thought she was religious, starts to pray.

Then there's a sudden click, and we all nearly jump out of our skin.

Chapter 55

Whit

THE LOCK! THE IRON DOOR is sliding open.

Njar stands at the entrance to our prison cell, leaning on a cane, and for a moment, all I can do is stare, dumbfounded at his courage.

"You saved my life," the crippled boy reminds me. And that's all he has time to say before we fly into motion. Just when we fling ourselves through the door, we hear a terrifying yowl as the cats rush to pounce.

Another inch, another second, and we would've been a feline feast.

I lift Janine into the air, deliriously thankful as the door slams behind us, and Ross hugs us both.

"Thank you!" I gasp, embracing Njar into our little group. He smiles, but I can see in his fearful eyes what a serious risk he's taking.

"There is one more thing we require of you," Izbella

says, stepping out of the shadows. She steeples her gloved fingers, and her eyes pierce right through me.

I nod, waiting for her request. Izbella beckons us to follow her, and Njar waves, staying behind to keep watch.

"You love your sister, don't you, Whit Allgood?"

"More than anything," I answer without hesitation.

"Well, I love my son." Izbella's feathers rustle as she walks ahead of us through the dark catacombs. "Unfortunately, they seem to love each other."

Heath is her son, I realize, stunned.

"We share a common interest," Izbella agrees. "If either of them is to live, you must keep them apart."

Protect my sister from a guy I already hate? I nod, tightening my jaw. *My pleasure.*

"Then go. Quick as you can," Izbella says as we approach a hidden exit. "Stay on the east road. The cats know your scent, and when he frees them, you won't have much time. And take these." She throws us a couple of rough pelts. "They won't be enough, but they'll help."

"Thank you." I squeeze her hand as we step into the blinding light toward our escape. "Thank you for your kindness."

"Remember, don't stray from the east road!" the feathered woman warns.

231

Chapter 56

Whit

THE ROCKS LOOSEN under our feet and we stumble forward down the steep incline, racing as fast as our bodies will carry us. Our legs are pumping and our knees are close to buckling, but it's still not fast enough.

With only the pelts from Izbella to keep us warm, we're losing more body heat with every step. We're at grave risk for exposure, and we don't have much time before the hypothermia sets in. Not to mention the soldiers and snow leopards…

Only…I *have* to stop.

Ross plows into me from behind as I try to get traction on the pebbles and skid to a halt. "What are you *doing*?" he asks between gulps of air.

I put my head between my knees, trying to think of how exactly to say this to the friends I've already put through so much.

"I'm turning back here," I say, looking him in the eye.

"What do you mean? You can't. . . ." Ross frowns in confusion. "Izbella said to stay on the east road."

Janine knows me too well, though. "He's going back to the camp," she explains to Ross. She looks at me for a long moment, her green-eyed gaze never faltering, and I think I see the hint of a smile. "Whit still wants to save those kids."

But there's something else, too: Larsht said Wisty was on her way up the Mountain. If that's really true, I have to warn my sister. Whatever happens to me.

"Guys, we don't have a chance if we go back into the forest!" Ross exclaims, and darts a worried look behind us. "You *know* they're tracking us by now!"

I nod. "Probably. It's a slim chance and a huge risk, and I don't want you to take it this time."

"Whit—" Ross starts, his eyes troubled.

I shake my head. "Really. You've both done more for the Resistance, for the City, and more for me than I ever could've asked for. I know it's insane," I say, blowing on my fingers. "And I can't guarantee that I'll make it back . . . but I have to try."

"I'm sorry," Ross says. His eyes overflow with tears. "I want to, but I just . . . I just can't."

"Don't be sorry." I put my hand on his shoulder and squeeze. "You're a true friend, Ross. Now go. Escape. *Survive.*"

Ross nods and starts to turn, but then realizes Janine isn't following.

"You, too?" he asks sadly.

She shrugs. "I guess in the end I'm just as crazy as he is." Janine gives him her most good-natured tough-girl smile, and a hug.

"Be careful," Ross warns, and then he leaves us, looking over his shoulder with one last look of regret.

"We have to be quick," Janine says. Her lips are blue, and I know that we don't have more than an hour or two before we get stuck out here. We cut inland on the pine-shadowed path and then dart between trees and over rocks, across the snow at a speed we wouldn't have thought was possible a day ago.

But the camp is nowhere in sight.

"We're going in circles," Janine says as we pass a familiar scarred rock.

"It was in a valley," I remember. "Maybe we just need to get to lower ground."

We trek down a steep ridge into the heart of the Mountain. But when we get down there, it's just another bowl-shaped dip, with no camp, and nowhere to go but back up.

I grit my teeth. *You had to be the hero, didn't you, Whit? You couldn't just let it go.*

"We've lost too much time," Janine says between chattering teeth. Her lips are a deep blue, and I can see she's getting groggy. I hug her close to me, rubbing her shoulders under the fur and trying to get her circulation going.

"We can still turn back," I say desperately. "We can still make it down—"

But at the top of our shallow ridge, I can already see them.

The snow leopards are prowling over the steep rocks, and right behind them, the soldiers are spilling down the narrow trail on horseback, their crossbows poised to fly.

We're trapped.

Chapter 57

Wisty

"TAKE ME UP your precious Mountain, Heath!" I scowl. As much as I don't want to be around him right now, I know he's right: Magic is the only shortcut to the Mountain. I narrow my eyes. "Now."

Heath nods and holds up his palms.

Let's do this thing.

I line up my fingers and immediately feel the current between us. I won't meet his eyes, though. There's our power and then there's *us*, and it's hard to keep them separate when it feels so intense every time we touch.

The energy builds, but I don't have to push against it this time—*we're getting stronger.*

I don't know what I expected, but I'm surprised to see the tunnel pulling out of the fence, foggy and swirling. We peer into it and I see my brother. He's running, and there's fear in his eyes.

What's he running from?

I step forward, but it's distant and unreal like before; I can't get to him.

I drop my hands. "You said you could get us there!" I accuse as the tunnel evaporates. "We're not even moving. What good is it to see what already happened?"

"Look, I'm just as new at this as you are, Firecracker," Heath says. "Do you want to try again, or would you rather walk?"

"Don't call me that," I say irritably. But he's right. I shake out my shoulders and take a deep breath. Once again, I place my hands against his.

"Think of trees. Think of snow and cold," Heath whispers. "Think of the flower I made you." The heat starts to build between us.

Think of Whit, I tell myself, closing my eyes.

Sparks crackle between our fingers.

We have to get to the Mountain. Have to. Get there.

Then there's a surge of power so strong that my body starts to convulse with the insane pressure and my eyes fly open, but my vision is a blur.

I think we're spinning. Or is it everything else that's moving? My hair whips against my face and I slide my grip up to Heath's forearms, holding on for dear life.

The streets warp and change. It's almost like going through a portal, except instead of feeling my cells dissolve and reform, the whole world seems to rearrange itself around us, and when it finally settles, we're someplace else.

Someplace with dark trees and white snow and cold, cold air.

"We actually did it!" I say breathlessly. I focus on the rocks at my feet, still fighting the dizziness and nausea.

"What'd I tell you?" Heath asks, but his voice sounds uneasy. "Oh, no..." he murmurs.

I look up, and the wind whips my face so hard it blurs my eyes and steals my breath. Heath's looking out across the ridge of the Mountain, and my eyes follow.

We're looking at the scene of distress that we saw in the tunnel.

Whit and Janine are a hundred yards to our right, running up and away from us out of the valley. They're wearing fur vests, and they're both obviously weakened; Whit is almost dragging Janine as he stumbles forward. I still can't see what might be chasing them.

"Hey!" I yell, trying to reassure my brother. "I'm here!"

He stops in his tracks and turns his head to look at me, confusion written on his face.

"Wisty?" He squints, wrinkling his brow.

The smile of relief starts to spread across his face, and that's when I see it: the enormous spotted cat on the boulder above him, pouncing for the kill.

There's no way I can get there in time.

"Whit!" I scream, and point desperately. But he doesn't see the threat, doesn't understand. *"Whit, look out!"*

Chapter 58

Whit

WE'RE RUNNING FOR OUR LIVES, but suddenly, my vision is a series of images that don't make any sense:

Wisty, somehow here, on the Mountain.

Janine, darting in front of me, shoving me out of the way.

The leopard, falling from the sky.

And then the blood.

Everything comes back into sharp focus with the blood. That, and the sound of Janine's screams.

The snow leopard's paws are wrapped around Janine's body, its teeth sunk deep in her side. It shakes her violently back and forth, and blood sprays from another gash in her neck, soaking the snow.

It's killing her.

I'm on my feet now, charging at the animal. But with Janine limp in its jaws, it turns and bolts toward a tree. *Once it drags her up there, there's no hope.*

With supernatural speed and instinct taking over, I

239

leap forward before it can start to climb. As I slam into the leopard from behind, it *yowls* its protest, losing its grip on Janine. In that brief millisecond of opportunity, I fling the creature away from her, and she collapses to the ground like she's boneless.

I don't know what her wounds are, or if she's conscious. I don't even know if she's alive. And it's killing me that I can't tend to her. Not yet.

The other leopards are crouching just overhead, and the first is already moving in again.

Now I've come between the predator and its prey. I stand over Janine defiantly, and the cat flattens its ears and puffs out its nostrils, snarling.

It leaps, but I'm ready.

We clash midair, and then tumble to the ground. I wrestle with the writhing beast, gouging at its eyes and pulling its tail, and somehow I manage to work my arms around its neck. It swipes at me furiously, but my arms stay locked in a viselike grip, and it's not long before I've beaten it.

I'm breathing heavily already, but the other leopards are on me now, too. Faced with such horrible odds, something takes hold of me and I just...*snap*.

Forgetting the cold, forgetting the exhaustion, and forgetting that I'm not immortal, I go at them with everything I have. I don't even morph. I attack with my bare hands, fighting for my life and Janine's, hitting and punching with furious abandon.

Before long, my arms are shredded with deep scratches, but incredibly, I find strength I didn't know I had, and I know I can take them. I slam one cat against the rocks, throw another out over the cliff. It sickens me to do it, but I don't have a choice.

When the last leopard hisses and slinks away, I sink to my knees next to Janine. I stare at her gouged flesh, her open wounds, and it doesn't seem real. A cold numbness is spreading over me, and my brain clouds with static.

The soldiers are coming, I realize vaguely, as arrows start to bury themselves in the trees around us with low *thunks*. I'm pretty sure someone is screaming, too, but the white noise in my head is so deafening, I barely register anything else.

Nothing matters without her.

I swallow hard and move closer. I touch Janine's broken body with shaking hands, feeling for a pulse, but I'm too late.

She's not breathing.

BOOK THREE

THE THIRD TRUTH:
KNOW LIGHT FROM DARK

Chapter 59

Wisty

IT'S A WAR ZONE.

Giants gallop toward us on huge horses. Arrows whiz past my ears. Somewhere, wolves are howling.

And my brother's there, in the middle of it all, kneeling over Janine.

I look around wildly. It's complete and utter chaos, and the attackers are almost upon us. The ground shakes under my feet and small rocks start to fall down on us from the rock walls above as they thunder down the path. It already feels like we're surrounded, with no escape.

I can see their faces now, their mouths contorting with hatred as they scream for our blood. And their weapons, held out from their arms, with the sharp ends aimed toward us.

Whit has his back to them all, though. He's concentrating hard, trying to heal Janine after that horror show with the leopards. His hands are on her shoulders, and they're covered in blood. Tears stream down his face, but I've never seen him look so determined.

I'm thankful—the thought of losing Janine is devastating.

But Whit's so vulnerable himself now, so exposed, and *that* makes me panicky. I couldn't scramble across the rocky ridge fast enough earlier, and I thought I was going to have to watch him get eaten by those monsters. Now that he's in danger again...

I have to defend him this time.

The strong, defensive feeling makes my M boil over. With an angry yell, I thrust my arms toward the charging warriors, lighting sparks around their horses' feet and sending jolts through arms holding weapons. A few axes clatter onto the rocks, and some of the horses rear up.

But more come, and more.

The black dots keep pouring down the pass into the valley. I can protect myself and lash out before they get to me, but some of the men are shooting arrows now, and they're coming closer and closer to Whit. There are just too many to attack one by one.

I need something bigger.

"Give me your hand!" Heath shouts, as if he heard my thoughts.

I frown uncertainly. Can I trust him now? Here, on his home turf?

"Wisty, *now!*"

I nod finally, and grasp his fingers with all my strength. It's the only way.

We turn to face the onslaught, and the power explodes out of us full force. Streams of fire cut across the forest like shooting stars. The brush begins to smoke and catch, and soon the trees in front of us are blazing, creating a terrifying barrier for our attackers.

This power—*our* power—is stronger than anything, I realize. It has me in its grip, and it is a terrible force to behold. It destroys a century-old forest in minutes. It flattens a whole line of men when a tree falls with a deafening crack. It eats up plants, and animals, and air, and all it spits out is falling ash. There's no dulling it or taming it as it burns a path of total destruction.

But I don't want to tame it, anyway. My brother is in serious danger, Janine is probably dead, and my fury has no bounds. I'm done hesitating or negotiating.

I want to make everyone pay.

Chapter 60

Whit

WISTY HAS SET the whole world on fire, and I don't even care.

My eyes stream from the smoke, I'm coughing uncontrollably, and the heat is so intense I feel like I'm roasting from the inside out.

But somehow, Janine's still getting colder.

Her lips are blue and her hands are icy. Life is draining right out of her.

"Come on, Janine," I say through gritted teeth. "Come on, come on."

I might be able to heal, but I haven't conquered death. My power can fail, and I keep forgetting that. And right now, it's not working, and Janine's not waking up.

It's just like with Sasha.

"No!" The scream rips through me with the thought. I can't go through that again. Not with her.

Men are screaming all around me, running for their

248

lives. We're still in range of a few archers, though, and for a moment, I *want* their arrows to hit me. I want to feel the pain, to curl up next to Janine and go to sleep with her forever so I don't have to deal with this loss. It already hurts so much I want to tear out my own heart.

Because I don't know how to fix this.

Janine is the clearheaded one. What would she do? She always seems to have the answers, but I can't ask her now.

Stop the blood, I can almost hear her saying. *Keep her warm, get her conscious, and stop the bleeding.*

I tear off my rough vest and press the mangy fur against her, but the bleeding is too widespread and the cuts are too deep. I need to stitch them up, or cauterize the wounds— something I've only read about and have no idea how to do. For a healer, I'm totally useless when it comes to these basic skills. I don't have any supplies anyway.

All I have is my magic.

And it's failing me. Again.

No. I bite down hard on my tongue, controlling a sob. The flames climb around us and I can feel the heat pressing in dangerously, but I can't turn away from her. Not yet.

It doesn't have to be like with Sasha. I healed Wisty from worse. And Njar, who seemed so lost when I first saw him. He came back, didn't he?

He came back for love, I remember.

I *do* love Janine, I realize with crushing agony. I love her so much I can't imagine leaving this Mountain without her.

I kiss her cheek and taste her blood, and think of the first time I felt the beginnings of that love. Even though I couldn't admit it to myself at the time, it started with that first poem. I recited it just for her, and her bold smile made me blush.

Poems used to turn into spells for me, before I could call the magic on my own. They used to have so much power....

I prop Janine up in my lap one more time.

You can control this. You can stop it, I tell myself. *This is what you were made to do.*

I concentrate intensely as I touch her shoulders, and even though I thought I barely had anything left, the M feels alive on my fingers again.

"*Methought that joy and health alone could be / Where I was not...*" I start, surprised I remember it after so long.

The poem becomes a spell as I say the words, and I think of Janine's intelligent eyes, her sharp laughter. I hover my hands over her torn neck and her exposed ribs.

The air around us moves with the force of my magic, and the heat from my sister's fire seems to help fuel it. I clench my hands into fists next to Janine's head, urging the power out, shaking with the incredible effort.

At first I can barely see it, but it's there. It's happening. The wounds are mending. Before my eyes, the fibers of the muscle are weaving together; the cells are regenerating; the skin is covering the bone.

She's healing.

I pull her body toward me, rocking her. *Please, please.*

Janine's eyes flutter, and I inhale sharply, so afraid to hope—so afraid I imagined it.

Then I feel her hand twitch. Her fingers squeeze mine weakly, and I totally lose it. Before she can speak, I'm laughing and sobbing and kissing her all over her face—her eyelids and her cheeks and her teeth and her hair.

I don't stop until she starts to cough, and then I help her sit up, still holding her as she spits out blood.

I'm weeping openly now. "I thought I lost you," I sputter. "I thought you . . ." Even now, the word feels too terrible. *"Died."*

"I did for a minute, I think," Janine murmurs. "I saw Celia, wherever I was. She told me to come back here. She told me I would never find a better person than Whit Allgood. She—" Her eyes fill with grateful tears. "She told me to love you with all my heart. And I do."

I cradle her against me. "I love you, too, Janine," I choke out. "I love you so much."

"I get it now, Whit," she says. "It's *our* time to be together."

Chapter 61

Wisty

THE SMELL OF burning wood is intoxicating. Our fire rages on, a wall of orange spreading from tree to tree, and with each second it blazes, I feel stronger.

It's the horses that run first. With white eyes bulging, they throw their riders as they flee.

There are screams and warnings in a rough, guttural language as Mountain People stumble through the smoke. The arrows keep coming for a long time, but eventually, even the bravest turn in terror.

All but a strange woman dressed in white, walking right through the flames.

"Stay back!" I yell.

I raise my fist to throw a lightning bolt, but Heath stops my arm, breaking our connection abruptly. Something's wrong here: Heath, a powerful wizard at his most fearsome and unforgiving seconds ago, seems to shrink as the wispy figure glides toward us across the snow, closer and closer.

Who is this mysterious woman?

Close up, she's tall and elegant, with milky, ageless skin and a severity to her gaze. My eyes flick to Heath uncertainly. I stay on my guard, ready to attack, but I won't make a move until he does.

She studies me with glittering eyes. "So *this* is who all the fuss is about."

I feel awkward under her gaze, but Heath looks even more uncomfortable. He looks guilty. And almost, almost... *apologetic.*

"Mother, this is Wisty," he mumbles.

I stare at him, shocked. This is his *mom*?

"Who could forget Wisty Allgood, the volatile, hot-headed girl who's destroying the world?" she says.

"Excuse me?" I bristle. Not exactly the warm welcome you envision when you meet your boyfriend's mom.

Heath's mother gestures at the blackened trees. "You come to our home and burn down the forest?"

"We were attacked," I protest, my cheeks reddening.

"Tell me, would you burn your people, too?"

"That's enough, Mother," Heath warns.

"Have I taught you nothing?" she snaps at him. "A witch and a wizard must never be together."

"Those were your rules. Old rules, from a different time."

"And I play by my own rules," I say defiantly, and snatch up his hand again. I don't know exactly how I feel about Heath right now, but I know I don't appreciate being told I *can't* date someone.

The woman in white purses her lips. "The magic is sweet, isn't it?" she asks, and her voice is softer, nostalgic. "It gets in your blood. It makes your heart race and rage with its power." She nods knowingly. "And then it drives you mad."

"I know what I'm doing," Heath says tersely. "I'm in control."

"Your father thought he was in control, too."

Heath grinds his teeth. "I'm not my father."

"The power warped his mind," she continues. "He wanted more and more. He needed another witch whose magic he could harness and exploit. I can see why he was obsessed with this one." She looks me up and down, and frowns. "He always had a thing for the color red. I thought you knew better, son."

"What are you talking about?" I interrupt. "I didn't even know his dad."

She stares at Heath. "You didn't tell her?"

When he doesn't answer, the woman looks at me with pity.

"Tell me what?" I ask Heath with growing unease.

He scowls at his mother but won't meet my eyes.

"Tell me what?" I'm almost shouting now. "Heath, *who was your father?*"

Chapter 62

Wisty

"THE ONE," HEATH says quietly, and my skin crawls like a thousand spiders are swarming over me.

I'm not sure if I heard him right, though, because I feel like my head is in a vise all of a sudden. The pines are closing in on me, and the ground is rising upward.

"I'm sorry—*what*?" I manage to choke out, steadying myself against a tree trunk. It's the only thing my brain seems to be able to come up with right now: *WHATWHAT-WHATWHATWHAT*, filling up my skull and pushing out my ears.

"My father was The One Who Is The One," Heath says again. He has the decency to look me in the face while he stabs me in the back, at least.

I may vomit. Repeatedly.

"She doesn't seem to be taking it well," his mother observes. "Maybe you should sit down, child."

"Shut *up*, Mother!" Heath explodes at her, and she goes silent as his voice echoes through the still-smoking forest, scaring up birds.

He steps forward, reaching for my arm. His tone softening, he says, "Wisty, listen to me—"

"No!" I shake my head furiously, backing away from him. I'm not sure what to do—whether I should run or rain fire—but right now, the thought of Heath's touch is unbearable. "Don't come near me," I warn, narrowing my eyes and waving a threatening finger.

"Okay." He holds his hands out in surrender, palms up. "I know it's hard to see it this way right now, Wisty, but this little . . . piece of information . . . it doesn't matter."

I gape at him, finally starting to form clear thoughts.

"Of *course* it matters!" I retort.

The One was the most evil beast to walk the earth. I thought I destroyed everything he stood for, but somehow, Heath is his flesh and blood. How can it not matter when my whole world has been flipped upside down?

"Look, nothing's changed. I'm still me. Everything we had—it was real."

I stare at him—at the thick, dark hair, the broad shoulders, the lips that I still want to touch. Still Heath. But, even though I don't see it, still *The One's son*, somehow. I let him get close, and closer. I let him kiss me. I *asked* him to.

I shake my head defiantly, trying to put that out of my

head. "I could never love someone who came from something so . . . so evil."

"I know you did, though," he insists. "I know you felt
this—"

"Everything I felt was a lie!" I shriek. "Because you lied
to me the entire time! How could you not tell me that?
HOW?"

"I wanted to tell you, Wisty! There were so many times
I almost did. But I knew you'd hate me for it. Just like this.
Hate me for something I didn't do." His face crumples into
a grimace, and he sinks to his knees and grabs my hand,
begging. "Please don't hate me. Please."

"Don't," I sneer, yanking them back. "Don't come
near me."

Whit walks toward us through the smoking trees with
Janine in his arms.

I look up at him miserably, humiliation written on my
face. He's the last person I want to see me like this, but also
the only one who could possibly understand. It's all I can
do not to run to him.

"What's going on?" Whit asks, narrowing his eyes protectively when he sees the state I'm in.

"I'm fine." I step away from the boy I thought I loved,
fighting back the tears. "Let's go."

"You're safer here, Wisty," Heath insists, and reaches
for my hand as I pass him. "I can protect you."

"Don't touch me!" I snap, wrenching my fingers away.

"Izbella—" Whit starts. *How does he know her?*

"Go," she urges. "The old Snow Leopard is sharpening his claws, and soon blood will flow into your City instead of water."

Then the woman in white places a hand on Heath's sagging shoulder, and they both vanish into thin air.

Chapter 63

Whit

THE SOUND OF our feet crunching in the snow is the only noise I hear for hours as Wisty and I carry Janine in the rough pelts.

This journey has definitely taken its toll, and my emotions are raw, a tangle of defeat and relief. I can only imagine what my sister is feeling.

Is she hurting? Is she heartbroken?

I want to ask her. To listen hard and tell her it's going to be okay. To get angry if she needs me to. To hug her close.

It's what I'd normally do without hesitation, what I've always done.

But her face is a stony mask behind me, and the awkwardness left over from our last fight still lingers, so we haven't said a single word. I listen to my feet snapping the branches instead.

It's going to be okay, I keep thinking as we pass the

259

warning signs from the way up and count down the miles. We're on our way home, and Janine is going to recover.

What about Wisty and me, though? Will we ever be okay again?

The silence weighs on me more as the day drags on, making the stretcher seem heavier, the Mountain steeper, and the air colder on my bare skin.

Finally, when we're almost on level ground and can see the jagged outlines of City buildings poking up on the horizon, we stop to adjust our grip on the pelts, and I can't hold it in any longer.

"Wist—" I start.

"You don't have to say it, Whit."

Her composed face crumples before I can say anything, and the words tumble out with the tears.

"I never should've trusted Heath and I shouldn't have let you go up this awful Mountain without me and if something had happened to you I'd probably have thrown myself off a cliff." She shoves me angrily. "So you don't have to say it, okay? I know I messed up and you were right about everything and I was wrong!" Her lip quivers, and she looks up at me with anguished eyes. "Okay?!"

I blink at her for a second, and then I wrap my sister in a fierce hug. Like I should've done from the beginning.

"No," I say when it finally seems okay to pull back. "Not okay. I was wrong. I should never have left you behind, and everything blew up in my face. If you hadn't shown up when you did to bail me out..." I look at Janine's sleeping face and have to fight back the tears. "We both would've been done for."

"I was kind of a mess after you left, too," Wisty admits. "Without you to boss me around I basically just broke windows and set fires." She smiles sheepishly.

Janine squints up at us. "You'd think you'd have figured out by now that you really sort of need each other," she points out sagely.

I nod. "I'll remind Wisty that next time she's being bullheaded and annoyingly independent."

Wisty rolls her eyes. "And I'll remind Whit when he thinks his way is the only way to do everything."

Both of us laugh and hug again.

"Is that...Byron?" Wisty asks, looking over my shoulder. I turn and sure enough, it's him—a one-man welcoming party.

"I came to warn you," Byron shouts as he stumbles up the path. He collapses at our feet, heaving. Byron is *not* a runner.

After a dramatic coughing fit, he manages to tell us that the Council passed some sort of decree that all magic makers would be deported.

But that doesn't make any sense.

"Already?!" Wisty gasps. She looks at me apologetically. "Bloom built a ghetto. It's why I came to get you. I thought we had time...."

"It actually happened as soon as you left," Byron says. "They rounded everyone up."

"We have to tell our parents." My mind is buzzing with alarm and confusion.

Byron looks at me like I'm an idiot. "They were the first to be loaded onto the bus. You're not listening to me. You have to go into hiding, right now, before the Sweepers find out you're here."

I stare at him, the things he's saying finally sinking in: magicians, persecuted; our parents, captured.

I meet Wisty's eyes, and they're just as scared as mine, but they're determined, too. I nod.

Together. That's how we work from here on out.

Byron promises to get Janine safely to the Resistance hideout as Wisty and I investigate the situation in the ghetto.

"Come on, big brother. I know the way." Wisty squeezes my hand.

We're going to need each other more than ever.

Chapter 64

Whit

I SMELL THE GHETTO before I see it.

The people huddle around the unfinished cells, cooking in the hot sun, packed so tight they can hardly move. They remind me of those kids in the Mountain camp: afraid and vulnerable. Like trapped animals.

Something in me dies when I spot my parents crammed inside that awful place, and I run toward them.

"Don't touch it!" my mom and Wisty scream together, just before I hurl myself against the fence.

I skid to a stop in the sand, my hands held up.

"It's electrified," my sister explains. "Or something."

Though it's just at the edge of the desert, the sun is intense, and I'm already sweating. Even Mrs. Highsmith looks wilted in the heat, and I notice my dad's shoulders are bright red.

"They just left you out here in the sun all day?" I ask angrily.

Dad brushes the sand off his sticky legs and shrugs. "We can go inside the barracks, but it doesn't really matter. They came equipped with skylights!" He tries to smile, and his lip cracks open.

"I can't believe they didn't even finish building them," Wisty says, marveling at the roofless structures. "I never thought they would move this fast."

"It was on the news," my mom says. "Some sort of Council decree, a mandatory relocation, but we never expected them to come that same night."

An older woman I don't know bobs her snowy white head. "The siren went off just before dawn. They confiscated everything we own and herded us onto the buses, snapping sticks at our legs."

"The buses were the worst," adds Mrs. Highsmith, who typically travels by teleporting. "All the swaying and the sobbing. I'll never get the smell of vomit out of my clothes."

My mom looks away. I know she'd never tell us these details—she wouldn't want us to know the pain she suffered. But from the way her mouth twitches as the women talk, I know what they say is true.

Seeing she's upset, Dad weaves his hand in hers. "They said it was for our protection, that it was just temporary." He sighs. "But when we got off the bus...we couldn't leave."

We were elected to the Council. We swore to protect

the community. *We can't even protect our own parents.* I'm shaking with fury and despair.

"I'm so sorry I failed you," I say, trying to keep the anguish out of my voice. But I can't help it, and I break down, hanging my head.

"Don't say that, son," Dad pleads through the fence. "Don't ever say that. This isn't your fault. Bloom did this, and he alone is responsible."

"Alone?" Mrs. Highsmith cuts in. "Perhaps. Yet there are the rumors. . . ." She arches her eyebrows suggestively.

"What do you mean?" I ask, and my parents exchange a look.

"What is it?" Wisty echoes.

"Well, there's a barrier on the whole place—not just the fence," Dad says, gesturing behind him. "None of our magic works in here."

I scan the ghetto again, taking in all the huddled bodies, all of them magicians. That's a *lot* of power, all stopped up.

"Do you think it's because they closed the portals?" I ask, shocked that Bloom's stupid theory might actually be valid. Wisty scoffs.

But Mom shakes her head. "It's more than that. The network of magicians has been suggesting Bloom couldn't have done this alone, that he must have someone working with him."

"Someone powerful!" Mrs. Highsmith adds, her eyes flashing.

This has gone too far.

"We have to go to Bloom," I say, and Wisty agrees.

"We'll squeeze him like the worm he is," she promises our parents. "And we'll get you out of here, no matter what it takes."

Chapter 65

Whit

WE STORM INTO the chamber, and the doors bang against the wall on their hinges.

"Let them go!" I roar.

"If it isn't the Allgoods." Bloom's voice echoes around us. "We were actually just talking about you. Though I admit, we'd stopped expecting you at our little get-togethers."

Feeling like an ant in the middle of the chamber floor, I stare up at this ridiculous man, perched atop a chair that is now so high it almost brushes the domed ceiling. I don't have time for his taunts, not when my parents' lives hang in the balance.

"Release the magicians," I repeat in a threatening voice.

"I assure you," Bloom matches my tone, "the magic makers are only being held for their own protection."

"Their protection?" I scoff.

Bloom nods, readjusting his toupee and leaning forward.

"Relations between the magicians and the, eh, normal members of our society have gotten a little, well, strained."

"Yeah, because of you!" Wisty yells. "Because of the propaganda *you're* spewing." She points her finger up at him, and though there's no spark, Bloom still flinches, and I smirk.

Gotta appreciate the small things in life.

"Look, we've just come from the Mountain," I say, trying another approach, since Bloom was so hot on war at the last meeting I attended. "You were right—the Wizard King is getting ready to attack. Don't you think the City needs to band together, not segregate and imprison half of the community?"

Bloom and the other old men share a meaningful look.

"Yes, the magicians will be an integral part of the war effort," Bloom says cryptically.

Wisty rolls her eyes and I sigh. It's obvious we're not going to get anything from Bloom. *Have we ever?* We'll have to dig deeper to flush out whoever's helping him, or figure out a way to break through the barrier.

As I storm across the chamber toward the door, I notice for the first time that the feel in the room is seriously different. I look around, and see that only half the Council seats are filled....

And they're only filled with adults.

"What's going on?" I demand. "Where are all the kids?" The goose bumps rise on my neck as I imagine what Bloom might've done to them. "They were elected by the people! You can't just rearrange the Council however you want!"

Never mind that that's exactly what he did when he kicked us out of it.

"Oh, this isn't the Council," Bloom says smoothly. "This is merely a smaller part of it that deals with specific operations. We're the Inner Circle, if you will."

"And what 'specific operations' would those be?" I ask coolly.

"We find that children are ill-suited to some of the more hardened aspects of government. It takes a more mature character to address certain situations."

"Like when you rounded up the community of magicians like dogs and carted them off to be tortured?" Wisty spits.

"Traitors in our midst do call for a strong stomach," Bloom says, and for a second I think my sister is actually going to fry him. I don't think I'd have the willpower to stop her, either.

Fortunately for the General, the massive screen rolling out from the ceiling has caught both of our attentions.

"While we're on the subject of traitors..." Bloom says as a projector clicks on. "The Council was reviewing a short film." He looks down at us with a worrying smile and steeples his fingers under his wobbly chin.

"Would you like to see it?"

Chapter 66

Wisty

HEATH IS ON the screen, and I guess I shouldn't be surprised.

Whit squeezes my shoulder, and I let out a long slow breath.

It's fine. I'm fine.

And then it starts.

The camera follows him in profile as he roams the City at night, and it's almost like I'm walking with him through those winding streets after a party, the excitement palpable.

But it's not me he's walking toward, not this time—it's a huge man in a dark cloak with a gruesome smile, and a message changes hands.

There are countless scenes like this one. The messages, the cloaks, the alley. Heath.

The men are bigger, sometimes, or hairier, but I learn to recognize them each time.

Because in the next scene, I watch those same thugs

270

kidnapping children, throwing their small bodies into trucks and carting them up the Mountain.

I'm fine, I think. *I'm fine*, but my throat tightens.

Heath was my boyfriend then.

In between wooing me on the dance floor and tumbling through my window, he was prowling the streets with dark plans.

While he was creating flowers for me and stealing tender kisses, he was also taking children for the Wizard King.

And the whole time, while I was falling in love with him, *my boyfriend was The One's son.*

How didn't I see any of that?

I feel my brother's eyes on me, studying my face with concern, and I know what he would say:

I didn't see it because I didn't *want* to see it.

When the lights go up, Bloom looks at me with smug expectation, but if he thinks I'm going to lose it in front of these feeble old goons, he's wrong.

"This isn't news. We already knew Heath was a traitor," I say coldly. I look each Inner Circle representative directly in the eye. "I hope you've caught this criminal and put him behind bars, where he belongs."

"Alas, this particular traitor still eludes us," Bloom says with a pout.

I suppress a small smile. I know I should hate him now, really hate him, but part of me is pleased Heath is too smart for them.

"But the sad truth is that our fair City is teeming with malicious individuals," Bloom continues ominously. "Fortunately, some of this man's collaborators have presented themselves to us!" he reveals with dark delight.

The screen clicks on again, and I watch it with rapt attention. I'm afraid to look, but I need to see, need to know how bad he really is.

What else was he planning that I didn't know about? What other horrible people could Heath be working with?

The reel starts, and my face stares back at me—my freckles, my features, my pores—giant on the screen.

It's like a slap, and I actually lurch backward, stumbling.

"What is this?" I demand angrily. "I'm not a traitor!"

"No?" Bloom raises an eyebrow, and juts his chin back to the screen. "Watch."

I do watch, and it's torture.

It shows the cable I cut, and the van I smashed.

It shows the man on his knees pleading for his life.

I see my hands touching those things, my lips speaking those words. My red hair, brighter than flame.

But I can barely recognize myself in these scenes, and I feel tears spilling down my cheeks.

Sure, the film shows Whit, too—there're a few grainy images of him crouching in an alley, and there's a long, slow pan as he sets off on the path toward the Mountain, Mama May weeping after him.

But mostly it's me and Heath. Shattering windows, scaring children, and burning everything around us.

At the end, the film skips into a hazy slow motion of our passionate kiss inside the fire. It feels excruciatingly hot in the chamber now, too, and I clutch my collar, squirming in the audience as the scene drags on and on....

And then, it cuts, and my eyes fill up the screen.

My eyes... but *not*.

With fire reflected in them, they're wild and red and hungry, consumed with power.

I want to turn away, but I can't.

I'm a terror.

Chapter 67

Wisty

THE PROJECTOR CLICKS OFF, and I can still see the flames, like they're singed inside my brain.

"Where do I start, Ms. Allgood?" Bloom cocks his head. "Illegal use of magical force? Arson?" He leans forward, and the microphone squeals. "*Murder?*"

"I...I..." I mumble, but I can't find my voice, and I shrink in shame.

I don't look at them, though—*won't* look at them. Instead, I study my aching fingers and find them ragged, the nails bitten to the quick, and as I stare at the blood pricking, I feel a rising sense of panic.

How did I let it get so out of control?

"Conspiracy, espionage, kidnapping?" Bloom is already rattling off a list to Whit. "It disappoints us greatly that the magic makers have decided to betray their homeland and collaborate with the evil Wizard King."

"That's insane. I went up to negotiate!" Whit protests. "And to free the kids, not kidnap them."

"And yet you returned without any of our lost children, to tell us we face imminent attack. Hmmm." Bloom knits his eyebrows together as if he's genuinely confused. "What do you make of this situation, Mr. Piper?"

"I would say that perhaps Mr. Allgood's mission failed spectacularly," says ol' Droopy Eyes.

"Or else he had other motives?" another eager, mustachioed man suggests.

"The kids were brainwashed!" Whit explains impatiently. "They refused to leave the Mountain King's side."

"Ah!" Bloom purses his lips as if considering. "Please send out a press release," he calls down to the scribe. "Mr. Allgood wishes the citizens to know that the missing children, ripped from their mothers' arms, actually *want* to be among these savages."

"That's enough!" I command. I feel a spark of hot anger, feeling fiercely protective of my good-hearted brother, but then I see the image of my bloodshot eyes and drop my hands.

That's not me, that's not me, that's not me.

Bloom leans into the mic again and his loud breathing echoes. "Based on the evidence we've seen here today, I believe it's clear to the Inner Circle"—Bloom glances around for confirmation, and the dopey heads nod obediently—"that it is actually the City's treacherous community of magicians who are working for the Mountain King."

Of course he would bring our parents into this, somehow. *This was a trap from the beginning.*

That's what pushes me over the edge, and the heat rushes to my fingers. Out of the corner of my eye, I see Whit reaching toward me.

But before our hands make contact, everything seems to pause, and the fire leaves me cold.

"Seize them!" Bloom booms, shaking his head in disappointment.

Chapter 68

Whit

I CLENCH MY FISTS in fury as Wisty and I struggle against the guards.

They can't do this! But they can. They *are.*

I was the strongest foolball player in the City, undefeated for years and years. I possess a powerful magic that should make escape easy. But against these unimpressive men who are wrenching my arms behind my back, I am almost paralyzed.

How is that possible?

And then... I see.

A man stalks across the chamber floor toward us, and I stare in disbelief, feeling my insides turn to ice. The white-blond hair, the wicked eyes, the snakelike swagger—it's unmistakable.

No.

I glance at Wisty desperately—*am I going crazy?* But all the color has drained from her face and she looks as horrified as I feel, and I know that she's seeing exactly what I'm seeing.

A ghost.

Just like Celia in the forest. And Margo and Sasha. Only this time, it's not a friend. It's not someone I'd ever hoped to see in this world again.

It's *Pearce*!

Pearce, The One Who Is The One's enforcer, high-ranking officer of the former New Order. Pearce, a teen-ager with serious magic power just like us, except he gets a weird kick out of torturing and murdering people.

"Did you miss me?" he asks.

"We . . . we *killed* you," I whisper.

But we didn't, did we? We left him for dead in the bone forest of Shadowland, but we didn't make sure he was dead—I couldn't stomach it.

Pearce shrugs. "Unfortunately, the idea of being dead didn't appeal to me all that much. I like to stay busy, and General Bloom, here, keeps me entertained."

Bloom, who has climbed down from his glorified step stool, puts an arm on Pearce's shoulder in a show of solidarity.

I gape at him. So that's how they did it. We knew Bloom must've had help from someone in the magic community. That's why that fence around the barracks is so strong, and why I can't easily fight these guards.

Pearce is doing it.

"You accuse *us* of being traitors?" I yell furiously at

Bloom. "This *slug* worked by the side of The One Who Is The One. You think *he's* not a traitor?"

"We've pardoned the former New Order affiliates, you'll recall," Bloom says.

An action I never supported, I think bitterly. I look at my sister but bite my tongue—she already feels bad enough about Heath.

"This officer has proven himself to be a loyal ally in our City's time of turmoil. He's been invaluable in securing the cooperation of the magic community, neutralizing difficult situations, as you can see."

I sigh and Wisty rolls her eyes. Ever the politician, Bloom prattles on with his sugarcoated explanation, but this means absolutely nothing to us.

"Pearce, kindly escort the Allgoods to their cells."

I surge forward again, focusing every ounce of energy I have into violently striking out at Pearce and getting out of the guards' grasp. Pearce almost killed me when I fought him in Shadowland, but in the end, I was able to overtake him.

He's stronger now, though, I realize with horror. Instead of building, my magic feels like it's draining out of me. I don't know where he's getting his power from, but it's debilitating.

This is so much worse than we thought.

Chapter 69

Wisty

I WATCH PEARCE carefully as we're bound in chains and taken from the chamber.

My mind is racing, and my head is a fuzz of building heat. With my magic defused, the energy has nowhere to go.

I know we'll get out of this. We've been in prison before, and as livid as I am about so many things gone terribly wrong, what concerns me the most is Pearce, alive. I've seen what he's capable of, and I'm positive he's so much more of a threat to the safety of this City than Bloom or some stupid ice wizard.

What is he plotting?

Seeing me looking at him, Pearce moves closer to me, and I tense, the old fear returning. *I am stronger than this.*

"How great was that movie, by the way?" he asks conversationally. He drops his voice to a whisper. "My favorite part was that last scene."

My face starts to flush.

He means the part when Heath and I were making out on the porch. The thought of Heath is painful already, and having our intimate moment broadcast to a group of dirty old men was humiliating, for sure.

But bile still rises in my mouth when I remember the time Pearce freaking *assaulted* me, shoving his tongue in my mouth. I grind my teeth in disgust but refuse to give Pearce the satisfaction of a response.

"Young lovers embracing, such hungry hands and mouths..." Pearce licks his lips suggestively, and my skin crawls. "A little tongue..."

I totally lose it then, insane with rage.

"I'll destroy you!" I shriek, gnashing my teeth as I try to strike out at him.

I still can't move, though, and Pearce just chuckles as the guards haul us down the chamber steps toward the waiting police vans.

"I always did love your passion, Wisty."

Outside in the Square, citizens are gathering in groups to watch the spectacle.

"Don't worry," I jeer at the onlookers, who look both disgusted and nervous. "He's here to neutralize us...."

I squint at the two police vans, trying to direct the hot fuzz in my head into some sort of release. Pearce's block is powerfully strong, and the pressure in my head is excruciating. Still, I'm putting everything I have into this, and I can feel my magic weakening the barrier, just for a moment.

"...So that something like *this* doesn't happen!" I yell, hurling the energy forward with one final, exhausting push.

It's not much—certainly not anything like the strength of the forest fire—but it's enough.

The vans flip into the air, careening toward the middle of the Square. They smash upside down into the ugly fountain, and their windows shatter satisfyingly. The crowds scatter in terror and I can't help but smirk.

Try to take all my power from me. Just try!

Unfortunately, two new vans pull up almost immediately, and I'm so weak from the ridiculous effort of that last display that I can barely stand as they drag us toward them.

"Why don't you make an example of the evil magicians?" Whit challenges the tubby politician angrily. "Why don't you just kill us now, Bloom?"

"Whit!" I hiss. I'm as guilty of letting my temper get away from me as anyone, but this situation is already bad enough without taunting Bloom into killing us.

"You really think they're just going to *neutralize* us?" He looks at me meaningfully, and with sick realization, I get what he's driving at.

We know what Pearce does, and it doesn't usually end in a cushy cell. I've watched him melt off enough children's faces to know that "neutralize" really means "nuke."

We're no longer beloved by the people, but our deaths might still cause an uproar, and Bloom doesn't want that.

Instead, they're going to cart us off to some dark room and quietly murder us. It won't even make the news. Our parents probably won't even know we're dead.

At least if he did it in the open, we might have a chance of escape, or at least an uprising.

"Yeah, kill us right here in the Square, so these honorable citizens can see what kind of justice your corrupt Council delivers!" I goad.

"That won't be necessary," Bloom answers in a bored tone from the top of the steps as the guards throw us roughly into the back of the police vans. "If we killed all the magicians, who would we sacrifice on the front lines of the war?"

Chapter 70

Whit

"ISN'T THERE ANYTHING TO EAT?" I plead at the door of our dank underground cell.

"Get back from the bars!" a guard orders. He smashes my fingers with a long, metal pole, and the crack of pain is so sharp I see black spots.

I'm still weak from the Mountain journey, with wounds half-healed and magic zapped, but mostly it's the ache in my stomach that is keeping me up.

"And can you please turn on the heat, already, for the last time?!" Wisty bellows at the dim-witted oafs.

Oh, yeah, and I'm also really, really cold.

"Why don't you heat up the room yourself, witch?" comes the consistently clever reply.

Wisty keeps taking the bait, though, because she just can't believe her power really isn't working.

She scowls, pressing her fingertips together for the hundredth time since we were thrown into this tiny prison.

When, for the hundredth time, nothing happens, she shakes out her hand and goes back to pacing feverishly.

Can I *tell* you how much we are both regretting the power she wasted on those vans?

"Whatsa matter? Lost your spark?" the second guard cackles and flings a cup of ice water through the bars.

The glass doesn't soak Wisty—it just smashes all over the floor where we'll have to sleep—but it does make both of us erupt in anger, which then makes the guards almost pee themselves with enjoyment.

It's a regular party in here—we always seem to attract really high-quality professionals during our jail stays.

"This feels familiar, eh?" I say, trying to get Wisty to talk. She's been pacing for hours, and I can tell she's getting more and more anxious.

"Of course it feels familiar. What goes around comes around, and every single government is the same," she answers in a flat tone.

"Come on, Wisty. You don't believe that." I laugh, because the pessimism is so totally unlike her, but I see right away that was the wrong call.

"Don't I?" she says hopelessly.

"Hey," I say, rubbing her back. "We're going to get out of this, okay?"

But it's not the prison cell she's obsessing about.

"Did you *see* me in the video, Whit? Did you see my eyes?"

I knew this was going to come up, but I nod, keeping my cool. "I saw."

The panic heightens in her voice. "And what did you see?"

I know I have to be careful here. Avoid saying *Glowing red orbs of need*, for example.

"I saw someone who I know is a good person and a brilliant witch get a little...carried away," I tell my sister, which is also the truth.

Wisty stops pacing and hugs her arms around herself. "I saw The One," she says, and suddenly I feel even colder. "Or a glimpse of him. I saw his lust for power. I saw that it could grow. That it could take me over. That it could be something to live for."

"So don't let it!" I blurt out, and she looks away.

This might be the first time my sister has scared me—I mean *really* scared me—in my life.

"Wisty." I squeeze her shoulders and look into her eyes, making sure she knows how serious I am. "Don't. Let. It," I repeat.

"It's not that easy," Wisty says, and slides down the wall of the cell to the concrete floor. "It's Heath. You have *no idea*, Whit. When we combine our power, a part of it just... takes over my brain. It feels like nothing else in the world to be with him."

"But if the magic you make with him is toxic..."

"I don't know how to stop," Wisty says in despair. "But Bloom's video..." She meets my eyes, and I know what she's thinking.

All those awful scenes are imprinted on my memory,

too, and my stomach starts to twist. I shake my head slowly.

"I need to stop," she agrees.

"Just give yourself a break. Remember how it first felt to use the magic? How it was better than anything, but you could feel the goodness, too?"

Wisty looks a little skeptical, but she nods.

"Maybe you just need to start over, to get it back to good. We can try tomorrow."

Wisty kicks away the shards of glass and lies down on the floor.

"No, tomorrow we need to get out of this prison," she says, yawning. "And then we need to deal with Bloom, and the Mountain King, and especially Pearce. Tomorrow's booked."

I ball my jacket up into a pillow and lie down next to her on the crude floor.

"And find food," I add as my stomach growls. "Okay, so maybe we'll work on good, happy magic the day after tomorrow."

"Deal."

Chapter 71

Wisty

WORST NIGHT OF SLEEP *EVER*.

I'm already having a seriously rough time on the hard floor of our prison cell when I groggily make out the hollow sound of something tapping against metal. Then a tug on the chain at my foot jerks me fully awake, and I open my eyes, annoyed now.

I look around for whoever thought it would be hilarious to make life just a little worse by depriving me of sleep, but I don't see any guards outside our cell.

No. I see someone else. Someone I wasn't expecting at all.

I see Heath.

"What are you doing here?" I gasp, too loud, and Whit shifts in his sleep.

I step carefully over my brother and face Heath on the other side of the bars. He looks as haggard as I feel—like he hasn't slept in days. *Good.*

"Heard you got some fancy new digs, and I wanted to check it out," Heath answers, peering in. When I don't laugh at the lame joke, he runs a hand nervously through his lush hair. "And I just wanted to see you. I *had* to see you."

A tiny, pathetic part of my heart sings when he says that.... Fortunately, the rest of me remembers that I should hate him.

"I told you," I whisper coldly. "I have no desire to talk to the spawn of evil."

Heath rolls his eyes. "Come on, Wisty. You don't really believe that. You think I'm evil? After everything we've been through together?"

I shift uncomfortably and he must see me falter, because he gives me one of those looks that, even in the dark, is bright and intense.

"After all the sparks? The flames?" he purrs in his sexy voice, and puts his hand on top of mine.

"Don't!" I snatch it away and cross my arms. "You betrayed me," I hiss. "Please just go."

"Will you at least let me explain?"

I groan, but I can't deny that it's been killing me, not being able to understand his story. I deserve that much, right?

I'm looking at him, debating, when Whit sits up. When he sees Heath, he throws himself at the door, more ferocious-looking than I've ever seen him. "Get away from my sister!" he shouts angrily. "Guards!"

"Shhh!" I hiss, trying to cover Whit's mouth. "We're just talking."

Whit furrows his brow, and I can tell he's hurt. "What about everything you said last night?"

I sigh. "I know. I just... just give me a minute, okay?"

Whit nods curtly and stalks to the other side of the cell, opening and closing his fists in frustration. "He's a *liar*, Wisty," he warns over his shoulder. "Just remember that."

I turn back to Heath and narrow my eyes. "Talk fast."

"Okay..." Heath says. "Well, my mom is a witch, and I guess years ago, she and The One had something like what we have—"

"Had," I interrupt, and he winces, but continues.

"Long story short, she rejected him—for reasons I won't get into right now—and he went really crazy, fell in love with his own power instead, took over the City, and... you know the rest."

Boy, do I ever.

"Uh-huh. And where were you in all this?" I ask.

"My mom kept me on the Mountain with my grandfather, but the old man was just as terrible. Controlling, maniacal. My mother tried to protect me from him, but I still have the scars."

Harden your emotions, I think, but still inch my hand a bit closer to his on the bars.

"Life on the Mountain was stifling," he continues, "so I

ran away to be with my father. I thought I could win his love, but..."

He clenches his jaw, and I can see the pain there, the rejection, still so raw, and my heart breaks for him. I just want to hug him, to hold him and protect him and...forgive him.

"When he died I just wanted a fresh start," Heath says. "You know?"

"I've heard *that* before," Whit huffs.

I shoot my brother an annoyed look, and he holds his hands up and walks to the far end of the cell, pacing angrily.

"But how could you not tell me that your dad was The One?" I ask. "I mean, come on! That's a pretty big deal!"

Heath shrugs dejectedly. "Because I didn't want to lose you." He looks up at me, his brilliant eyes shining. "Because I was in love with you."

My resolve softens at the sound of those words. We never said them aloud, but I know both of us felt them. It echoes in my thoughts: *I was in love with you*. Why, oh *why* do I only have to hear that in the past tense?

"Were," I murmur, but in my head, it's a question.

"I'm *still* in love with you, Wisty. Whether you like it or not."

He reaches his hand through the cell bars, and I let him touch my face. Even though I shouldn't, I reach up and put my hand over his.

"Don't *touch* her!" my brother growls from a few paces away. "You have some nerve, creep," he adds.

"As you command, Wizard." Heath surprises me by gracefully slipping his hand out from mine and withdrawing it from the cell. Ever the gentleman.

I chew my lip anxiously. Can I forgive him? I don't know if I'm ready to let Heath back into my heart completely right away, but maybe we can start over, try again. . . .

Then I remember something that Heath still hasn't explained.

"I just have one more question. . . ." I say, and Heath looks at me expectantly. "Why were you working with the Mountain King?"

"What?"

"I saw you, on Bloom's film. Why were you working for your grandfather if you believe he's an abusive maniac?"

Heath blinks and lets out a slow breath. "I . . ." He taps the bars, stalling, and I glare at him impatiently. "I can't talk about that right now. But I promise, if you just trust me, everything will make sense, soon. Very soon."

"Trust you?" I repeat, and he nods. "We're going to war," I say angrily. "Bloom is going to shove us onto the battlefield and let us be slaughtered by the Wizard King's army, and you're *working for him*. How can I trust you when you're still lying to me?"

Heath sighs heavily. "Then this is good-bye, I'm afraid," he says, pulling back from the bars.

Seriously? I scowl at him. I can't believe I almost forgave this creep.

"Next time we meet, you'll change your mind about me, though, I know it. I'm going to make all of this right."

"See you on the battlefield," I mutter.

Chapter 72

Whit

A BUCKET OF ice water hits me full in the face and I shoot up out of sleep, gasping.

"You'll regret that!" I sputter angrily, but a kick to the gut with a steel-toed boot makes me double back over.

Two guards grip me under the arms and haul me to my feet. As they start to hustle me out of the cell, I whip my head around, more shocked than when the water hit me, not comprehending what I'm seeing. Or *not* seeing.

Wisty is gone.

"What did you do to her?" I yell, wrestling against their grip.

But my body's weak from the beating it took on the Mountain, and my magic's weaker. The guards ignore my protests as they drag me down the dark prison hallway, my clothes still dripping.

The prison van they throw me into is packed, and the air stinks with the sour smell of sweat and unwashed bodies. Something else, too. The small space, the hunger, the heat...it starts to mix up inside you, and when it comes out your pores, it smells like fear—mine along with everyone else's.

Let me repeat: My little sister is *missing*.

"Wisty?" I call out desperately. "Are you in here?"

No answer. My heart wilts.

She could be scheduled for execution. She could be suffering through torture.

She could be with Heath.

The door's closing on me now—closing on my chance to find Wisty.

"No!" I lunge, and it smashes into my nose with a sickening crunch. Tears spring to my eyes, and a bright-white pain seems to explode behind them. I stumble backward blindly, but the space is so dim and packed with bodies that I instantly run into elbows and step on feet.

"Watch it!" someone sneers, shoving me. I slam into someone else, and in an already tense situation, it doesn't take long before everyone's pushing and shouting.

"Keep it down in there!" A guard's greasy face leers at us through a mesh screen.

I pinch my nose and feel the blood pooling between my fingers.

"Tell me where my sister is!" I demand, trying to inch closer to the single window.

"In a dark, dark place, with nobody to help her, where nobody can save her." I can smell the booze on his breath.

"But don't worry," he says with a grin. "You'll see her in Shadowland soon enough."

Then he hits the side of the van twice, and we pitch forward.

From what I can see through the small slit of window, it's madness in the streets. A group of frantic citizens surrounds the van. We can hear them pleading for help and protection, and when the driver lays on the horn instead, their voices get more threatening.

The van starts to rock, and we bump against the sides and into one another. Then the engine revs and the van surges, and I cover my ears at the terrible sound of what I fear could only be bodies underneath the wheels. And then our tires squeal along the road away from the City.

The van goes absolutely silent, except for the sound of a few people retching. It reminds me of how Mrs. Highsmith described the buses that took my parents to the ghetto.

I look at the bowed heads and slumped shoulders as the van sways. "I'm looking for my sister, Wisty," I call out into the darkness. "Did they take your families, too? Are they moving us to the barracks to join the other magicians?" But expressions are hard to distinguish in this light, and each prisoner huddles into himself. "Does *anyone* know what's going on?" I plead.

"I'm no magician." A kid sitting on the floor with his knees pulled up to his chin scowls at me. "The magicians took my little brother. I'm not going to let some demon King take everything I have left."

He can't mean...

"Where are we going, then?" I press.

The light from the window illuminates the boy for just a moment. His fingers tighten around a clublike piece of wood—a rolling pin, I think—and his eyes seem to jump from their sockets.

"To the Mountain," a gruff, older voice answers from the darkness. "To war. Where else?"

And a crude little kitchen tool is this kid's only weapon.

Chapter 73

Whit

THE FIRST THING that hits me when the truck door opens is the bracing wind raging down from the Mountain. It brings back some seriously bad memories. The guard shoves me out of the truck in chains and I immediately start scanning the swollen crowd in front of me for a flash of Wisty's red hair.

Hundreds of terrified people are sprawled across the muddy field that faces the Mountain. Up on the front line, the magicians stand chained in snaking rows with stoic expressions. And behind them, the volunteer soldiers from the Gutter toy with their pathetic weapons—lengths of pipe and hunks of brick.

No one is dressed for the icy cold. No one is dressed for battle. This is a disaster already.

"Have you seen Wisty Allgood?" I tug at arms as the guard pushes me forward, my voice rising. "My sister, Wisty? The famous witch?"

People shrug me off or scowl or stare blankly ahead. Their silence can't mean anything good, and my mind jumps to the worst. *What are you hiding? Is it so bad you won't say?* I want to shake them, to scream in their faces, but the guard keeps shoving me forward.

He locks me into one of the back rows of magicians—with the so-called traitors. Like everyone else, I keep stealing nervous glances up the Mountain.

Where's the man who dragged us here?

I spot Bloom's sour-faced cronies first. They're the only ones who are really armed. Still in their suits, they hold salvaged guns from the old arsenal in a delicate two-handed grip, at least a foot away from their bodies. Every time one of them turns, the row of people behind them duck for cover.

There's Bloom. He's actually near the back of the army with the stragglers, the coward. I can just see the gray blob of his toupee floating back and forth as he paces. Finally, our fearless leader faces his ragged army and clears his throat directly into an oversize microphone.

"Good citizens! The Mountain Wizard rides today, but not to fear! The magic makers swear their dark power can be used for good."

There are a few crass protests from the hoodlums in the back. Bloom holds up his hands for order, but at the same time, he nods.

"I know, I know. But they claim to love our fair City, and I say let them prove it! Let them stand on our front lines and protect our honest citizens! And if any traitors have been aiding this villain, let them suffer at his hands!"

They're really going to sacrifice us all? *That's* Bloom's war strategy?

I feel the panic building all around me, in the soft tinkling of chains as foot shifts to nervous foot. In the twitching muscles of almost still faces. I feel it in my bones before I can even hear the sound of horses' hooves.

Panic. Echoing closer. And closer. And closer.

I clench my fists together furiously, and flex every muscle against the chains. I want to fight, but not in the Wizard King's war; I want to fight back *now*. I want to start a riot right here, to lock our arms and rush the stage and strangle Bloom with these chains until his nose bleeds and his cheeks turn blue.

But I look around and see that the other magicians Bloom's holding hostage are teachers and salesmen, artists and doctors. Grandmothers and little brothers. I see faces numb with shock and eyes wet with grief. They're leaning on each other, propping one another up. Sure, some of them have enough power to levitate a little or read your palm, but they're not soldiers. Not *killers*.

And their chains won't budge.

Then, in the row behind me, a sweet whistling sound reaches through the devastation like arms cradling me— it's pure, so comforting, so *familiar*. I turn around.

"Dad?"

The whistling stops, and my father blinks at me through swollen eyelids.

"Dad! Are you okay?" Before he can even respond, I lunge toward him to give him a hug. I'm jerked back by the shackles, but it doesn't matter. If my dad's here, we can figure this out together.

"They took Wisty," I report breathlessly. "I don't know who did it, but she's gone, and my powers are suppressed by the chains, and..." I swallow and collect myself. I shouldn't make Dad feel worse. He doesn't look well. "It's just really good to see you, Dad," I tell him anyway. "Where's Mom?" I look around us. "Did you guys get separated—"

"Your face," my dad interrupts in a sad, bewildered voice. I'd forgotten—my nose must be a mess of bruises and dried blood. As Dad reaches a hand toward me, he lurches to the right, and I hold his forearm to steady him. He looks a lot worse than before, I realize. The sunburn has turned to oozing blisters, and he seems a lot older. So thin and so frail. He hasn't shaven, and his stubble is coming in patches of white.

"Dad, what's going on? Are you sick?"

He smiles, cracking the scabs on his lips. For a second, that smile, shocking as it is, reassures me. Then he looks up at the shifting clouds and says, as casual as anything, "Nice day for a war, isn't it?"

Okay, I'm no longer reassured.

That isn't something my dad would ever say. I blink at him and look closer. His eyes are unfocused and his breathing sounds ragged. *He's delirious.*

"What did they do to you?" I murmur.

"Oh, look," Dad says brightly as he nods over my shoulder. "Here they come!"

Dizzy with dread, I turn and see a mass of black dots in the distance, spilling out of the forest and swarming over the few rolling hills that separate us.

The Wizard King is almost here.

Chapter 74

Wisty

"LET ME OUT OF HERE!" I shriek as I feel the ground shift under my feet.

The goons are hauling me—and the cage I've been in all morning—out of the vehicle, and I inhale sharply as I squint through the sudden flood of light.

The vast Mountain army fans out across the snowy hills as far as the eye can see, its white banners whipping in the wind. Leopards prowl along the front lines, and behind them are foot soldiers and horsemen and archers— thousands and thousands and thousands of them.

I resist the temptation to retch at the sight.

My cage sways as they carry me across the field between the two armies—if you can even call them that. Anyone can see Bloom's "army" is a cruel joke compared to the masses we're facing.

This isn't going to be a war. *It's going to be a massacre.*

My stomach drops and my mouth goes dry at the

hopelessness of the situation. But what finally breaks my heart is this:

Heath is sitting on top of a horse, right in the middle of our enemies.

He winks, and I scowl. The last thing I want to see before I die is Heath's traitorous face, but the spikes around my head won't even let me turn away.

"Wisty!" My brother's hoarse voice rings out, shaking my attention from Heath. Despite the fact that I can't see him, relief floods through me. *He's alive.*

"Whit!" I yell back. "Where are you?" I grip the bars and strain against my binds.

"With the magicians. With Dad. We thought you were..." He breaks off, trying to hide his emotion, but then I hear him call out with new resolve. "I'm going to get us out of this, Wisty, I swear!"

The war hasn't started yet, but at the mention of my name, objects start to fly at my cage—rocks and sticks and clumps of grass. The worst part is I don't know which side they're coming from. Which people hate me more?

"Stop it!" Whit is screaming.

"I'm okay! It's going to be okay," I reassure him, but my eyes are welling with tears.

Inside my cage, handcuffs chafe my wrists, chains weight my feet, and there are sharp points inches from my body in all directions. To top it off, my magic is still all screwy. *Nothing is remotely okay.*

A splintered piece of wood lands in my metal cage. I

kick at it angrily, but then I realize what it is: a broken drumstick, just like the one my mom gave me when I first discovered my power. A sort of wand.

Mom? I look through the bars at the terrified and devastated faces below, and know she's among them. The citizens may have turned on me, but *these* are still my people. The tired and the broken. The unlucky and the abused. My family.

"*Lead*," my mom's voice echoes in my head. It could be my imagination, but I swear, the drumstick *twitches*.

I swallow. Pearce isn't anywhere in sight, and despite the binds, I can still feel a hint of my own magic in me, strong, just below the surface.

Maybe...just maybe...?

My eyes bore into the scrap of wood. I feel another power wrapping tighter around mine, trying to choke it off, and the chains singe my skin. I grit my teeth and focus so hard my head feels like it might explode, and somehow, the drumstick starts to rise. Up and out of my cage, higher and higher, until I'm sure everyone can see it.

"Listen to me!" I shout as the men parade me in front of the ranks. "I know it seems like there's no hope for this fight...."

Like it's all over.

My voice wavers for a moment as I think of Heath fighting for the other side. Nervous eyes in the crowd are looking toward me now, though, looking for hope, and I push my own pain down into the pit of my stomach.

"But...think of all you've been through!" I remind them. "The New Order sanctions! The bombs and the prisons! The ghetto!"

The tip of the drumstick starts to smoke as my magic pushes through the unseen barrier a bit more, and a tiny flame flickers to life. That strange other power working against me now flexes inside my guts, trying to extinguish the faint flicker, and I wince from the pain—but still, my fire glows. It gives me the strength to continue.

"What makes you special is not just your magic! You may not be trained soldiers, but if you're here right now, it's because you're a *survivor*!"

The City people are silent now, focusing on my drumstick vigil, hovering above them.

"We've all lit a candle for someone we love," I continue, sweating from the continuous effort. "Well, I've lit this one for you, my fellow citizens! We'll survive this, because we're fighting for our homes and our families! We'll attack the Mountain soldiers with everything we've got!"

And with the light in their eyes, I see hope reflected, and anything seems possible. It's just for a second, though, and then the moment's gone.

It's not just because thousands of people are calling for our blood, either.

It's because across the narrow field—even behind the thick fur wraps and full helmets—we can see the Mountain soldiers' faces.

I can see the stony gray eyes from one small figure

staring coldly at me from under dark fringe. And though that look says I'm less than nothing, and the young warrior with those eyes wouldn't hesitate to swing a gleaming axe at my throat, I realize I can never fight against these soldiers, or ask my people to.

I let the smoking piece of drumstick *thunk* to the ground.

Because those eyes belong to Pearl Marie Neederman.

The Wizard King's army is led by the City's own kidnapped kids.

Chapter 75

Whit

CALM. JUST STAY CALM, I keep telling myself. But when the Wizard King's black horse stalks past me and my dad, past Heath and Izbella, and stops in front of the metal cage where my sister is penned like bait . . . the idea of *calm* stops making sense.

"Is this for me?" the Wizard King asks, staring down at Wisty.

With his face striped in war paint, his head crowned in a circle of curving teeth, and his shoulders draped in layers of spotted fur, the King looks more like a monster than a man. I clench my fists and try to breathe.

"The witch is yours if you turn around now and return to the Mountain," Bloom answers through the megaphone from his place at the back of the crowd.

My heart throbs inside my chest like a bird slamming into a window. "Don't you *touch* her!" I yell.

The King's milky-pale eyes flash threateningly. Those

colorless orbs make a thousand men tremble, and could make another thousand die.

I should be up there, protecting my sister, but instead I breathe out through my nose, holding in the scream. I try to channel the intense energy into magic that could fight and release these chains, but...

Nothing. I'm *powerless*.

"My Kingdom is getting crowded with witches," the King says. I glance at Izbella, but her expression doesn't change. "How about we just accept your full surrender?"

"Why should we surrender?" Bloom challenges. He sounds a little too confident, even for him. "To live as slaves?"

The King grins, and his rotting teeth make his painted mask seem even more horrible. "Because if you don't, you'll all die within the hour, butchered where you stand."

An anxious murmur ripples through the crowd. The people around me huddle closer, bracing for the attack, and I inch in front of my dad, trying to shield him.

Bloom is the only one who doesn't seem rankled. "We know your secret," he says smugly. "We've closed all the portals, and therefore the source of your magic is gone. You're becoming weaker every moment!"

The King bursts into maniacal laughter. "Is *that* what you think? That my power comes from some other dimension? From the sky? Through holes in the ground?" Bloom looks around uncomfortably. "You of all people should know, Mr. Bloom: power comes from people."

The Wizard King turns his horse and walks it back across the narrow strip of meadow in front of our front lines, his eyes cutting through the crowd.

"People of the City, listen to me. You can die today . . . or surrender and live happy lives in a beautiful Kingdom under a benevolent ruler!"

I can't keep quiet any longer. Fighting the Wizard King's child army is a horrible thought, but surrendering is even worse.

"He's lying!" I shout to the City's army, pointing across the field. "Look at the children—*your* children! He's turned them into killers. Into soldiers and slaves!"

"Slavery doesn't mean misery," a boy soldier around ten says cheerfully. "Everyone has a role."

"Each pair of hands makes us stronger!" a young girl adds, raising her club up over her head.

"The Mountain is the shiniest place in the world," an earnest girl's voice swears from the very front row, and my heart aches as I recognize it as Pearl Neederman's. She had always loved sparkly things.

"It has a dark underworld," I call to her. "Their armor hides festering cuts and terrible burns! The King is a monster!"

"No." It's Bloom's voice, echoing through the megaphone. He's surrounded by the Inner Circle members, a small mass of bodies elbowing its way forward through our rows. "The Wizard King tells the truth!"

I'm speechless. *What is Bloom doing?*

310

When they reach the front, the King scowls down on the group from atop his dark horse, and the Councilmen fall to their knees.

"The Inner Circle, acting in the best interests of all citizens, has chosen to accept these generous terms. We surrender our City to the Mountain." It's Bloom's voice, but it's not. It's too . . . *humble*. The condescension is gone, and the arrogance. He's not even clearing his throat.

This doesn't make any sense.

It's stunning enough to see Bloom bowing in complete deference. It's maddening enough to see the Wizard King salivate at the anticipation of his quick and easy victory. But it's completely enraging to then see Bloom do the unthinkable: he offers up *The Book of Truths*. Our sacred book. Our one guide toward our ultimate future.

And Bloom is supposed to protect it!

Some of the volunteer soldiers behind me start to shout, "Hail to the King!"

These are the same idiots who were insulting Wisty and me earlier. "What about hating magic?" I gape at them. "What about magicians being baby-stealing demons?"

But then the *magicians* start to surrender. My stomach plummets as I hear my very own father's voice ring out through the crowd: "The Wizard King saves!"

No. It wasn't supposed to happen like this. A spineless surrender? The magicians in chains? We were supposed to lead our people to freedom!

"What's going on?" Wisty screams as the rows of

people start to push past her cage to merge with the Mountain army.

"I don't know!" I dig my heels into the mud, but they're shoving me from behind, and I'm dragged forward by my chains. "The whole world's gone crazy!"

I stare at the kid soldiers' dead eyes, and look around me with a growing realization. *Not crazy. Brainwashed.*

The King's face paint, the leopard fur, the crown of teeth. It's all for show. To attract attention.

To his eyes. Those terrifying eyes.

It's more than brainwashing. *He's controlling their thoughts.*

"Don't look at the King!" I start yelling, but no one's listening to me. It's too late.

"We will be cleansed!" the masses shout in unison as the Wizard King cackles.

No. It can't happen like this. *No, no, no.*

Then I remember: my sister knows how to control minds. It was part of how we defeated The One.

"He's inside their heads, Wisty!" I yell. "Use your power!"

Chapter 76

Wisty

"ARE YOU *INSANE*?" I shout at Whit.

I broke inside The One's thoughts, like, *twice*.

I barely knew what I was doing then, accessing a single mind that already *wanted* to connect with me. Now we're talking about thousands of people already in the grip of a maniac I've never even met, and my power is weak—to say the least.

Bodies slam against the metal bars of my cage as the tide of people surges toward the King, and I flinch.

"Remember...the...candle!" my brother chokes out, just before he's swept into the mass of crushing bodies.

I start to hyperventilate. It took almost everything I had to light that stupid drumstick, and for what? The Wizard King is taking over my entire City. He's enslaving my parents, and his stampeding zombies are about to kill my brother.

How is this possible? In my wildest dreams, I never

imagined our ultimate defeat being so pathetic. So inexplicable. We expected a noble death. Fire and brimstone, or bloody massacre, even some kind of spectacular magic horror show that only The One—or his father—could have dreamed up. Not this.

But what was the point of my drumstick vigil, anyway? Not to give up, even when it was hopeless—*right, Wisty?*

What else do I have to lose?

Just beyond my cage, the black stallion is flaring its nostrils and stamping its feet as the crowds swarm around it, but above it all, its cloaked rider is beaming.

I study the Wizard King intently. The thick furs hiding a small frame, the wrinkled fingers yanking the horse's reins, the sinister smile quivering with greed...I try to understand it all, to connect to it and channel my fear and panic into a hot ball of hate.

Then his milky eyes flick over me—*now!*—and I bore deep into that emptiness, tapping into the screwed-up messages he's pushing into the spellbound citizens: *I am nothing. I am no one. I want to be clean.*

I try to grasp at the thoughts, turn them around inside my head to set them free. But there are too many. I'm too out of practice, and the power keeps slipping away, just out of my reach.

"Very good, Wisteria," the Wizard King snarls suddenly. "Eye contact is key. Unfortunately for you, I've had a little more practice at this."

His strange, pale eyes seem to glow inside their sockets, almost floating in the garishly painted face. He's right—though I'm aware of his hypnotic power, I still can't look away.

"I warned you to stay away from my son." It's Izbella now. She's all the way on the other side of the field, but I hear her voice. Inside my head.

She's helping him.

I realize it a second too late, though—I'm already gripped in their combined power.

"I haven't done anything!" I protest out loud. "I never wanted to see Heath again!"

"Well, he can't seem to stay away from you," a warped voice hisses as the eyes flash. *"And I'm afraid that's too much of a liability."*

A terrible, high-pitched sound fills the world then, and my head is being crushed by a vise of pain. I try to bring my hands up to my ears in the narrow cage, but the ringing is inside my brain anyway, probing into me like a needle.

I smash my head to the side, over and over, trying to kill the wail. Blood bursts out of my ear as it connects with one of the spikes, but all I can think is that I want the awful noise to stop.

Then I stop thinking completely. I can't. I'm just screaming. Wordless, thoughtless, raw.

"Stop it!" a voice is yelling, and though it sounds a

million miles away from the scream in my brain, I know one thing immediately. *It's Heath's voice.* "Mother! You said she wouldn't be harmed!"

More distant shouting, a female voice. But the only sound that cuts through the pain is his. Heath's.

"Mother! I command you! If you kill her, you kill me!"

And then...it stops.

I hear the clang of metal as the chains fall from my wrists and the walls of the cage collapse. It's like a dam breaking, and my magic surges full force through my entire being. The black horse rears as my fingers spark, and for a moment the Wizard King and Izbella lose their connection.

I rub the raw skin of my wrists and look up at the icy old clown and the frosty feathered witch who almost killed me.

I'll destroy them both.

"Wisty, no!"

I whirl around on Heath. *I knew it.* I narrow my eyes, ready to blow him away with the rest.

"They're too strong together," he explains, holding up his hands. "You'll never beat them alone, Wisty. Let me help you—please!"

My head is still swimming as I struggle to understand what's going on. Heath came here to fight on the side of the Mountain....

So why is he saving me?

Panicked and confused, I look around for my brother.

But he's lost in the chained crowd—a crowd that's already closing in on us at the King's command.

"You need me!" Heath insists. "Together, we're the only thing that can stop them!"

Izbella said we're a liability, I think. *I like that.*

I reach for Heath's hand.

Chapter 77

Wisty

THE MOMENT OUR fingertips meet, it's electric.

Forget the portals—we're pulling energy from everywhere. From the people. From the ground. From the air all around us.

It builds, hotter and hotter, and then our power bursts out of us. There's a loud clap as it clashes with whatever toxic vibes the King's putting out, and the midday sky flashes to a white so bright you have to shield your eyes.

The horses pace in wild-eyed terror, and the leopards' fur stands on end. Axes and swords are clattering to the ground.

The King is already starting to lose control!

I'm pulling, pulling, pulling at the enslaved thoughts of the Mountain soldiers, and it's the strangest sensation of double vision. As I watch one kid's eyes roll back into his head, my inner eye sees the circuits inside his gray brain starting to light and fire. And when the boy's eyes snap back to me, they're clearer somehow—*conscious*.

The Wizard King's face is so twisted with concentration now that his war paint is starting to crack, but he's getting weaker.

And we're getting stronger. *Power comes from the people.*

My heart thuds, my body shakes, and the heat generating between me and Heath is pure, liquid lava flowing through my veins.

I'm light-headed with lust.

I'm drunk with strength.

Superhuman.

How did I ever think I could give this up?

Our influence moves through the ranks, rolling outward in waves on both sides of the field now. As the magicians' chains snap open and snake away from them, I squeeze Heath's hand.

We're actually freeing them!

All around us, people push and stumble and cover their heads, gasping in blind confusion as they wake up from the trance, lost in the middle of what must seem like all-out war.

Then there's a crackle, and the sky goes dim, like the whole world's shorting out. I hear the voices start to buzz all around me. Inside me. Louder and louder: *Kill the King*.

What's going on?

The kid in the front row locks eyes with me. I see the

deadness there again and I know: he's not really free. *We're* controlling him now.

No—*Heath* is controlling them. Using *my* power.

I just wanted to free *them!*

"No!" I plead. "Not like this."

But Heath grips my hand tighter, and my head hums louder and louder with the murderous thoughts of an entire, brainwashed army.

Kill him, kill him. Kill the Wizard King.

My neck's straining, my toes are clenching, and the veins in my arms are standing out as I struggle to rein in Heath's murderous energy.

But it's taking over.

The King's scream pierces through the cacophony of noise. Heath's soldiers pull him off his horse, and I can see how thin and wrinkled he really is as the furs fall away from his shoulders. How old. His bony arms clutch at his ears, and his long, yellowed beard drags in the dirt.

The King is convulsing on the ground as our dutiful citizens beat him.

This isn't what I want. *Not at all!* I feel like there's a train barreling right through the center of me, and half of it has jumped the track. If I don't stop this now, we'll all go up in flames.

"I said *no!*" I shriek, finally leaping back and ripping my arm away from Heath. When the connection breaks, there's an explosion of sparks, and unbelievably, it singes my hand.

I don't even know what to say. I scowl at Heath, clenching my fingers against the swell of pain, and he glowers right back.

"What's the matter, can't finish the job?" the Wizard King sneers up at Heath. "For a moment there, I almost respected you, but I should've known better. You always were such a disappointment, a disgustingly oversensitive and pathetic little child, sniveling to your mother and wetting the bed."

"You *tortured* me!" Heath shouts, and I'm shocked to see his eyes welling with tears. "You made me feed my friends to the leopards!"

"I see it didn't toughen up your delicate sensibilities." The King is still kneeling in the dirt, but from the tight look on Heath's face, he could be towering above us.

Heath presses his lips together and shakes his head. "Wisty and I are in love. Do you even know what that means, Grandfather?"

Do I *love him*? I thought I did, once. I wanted to believe it again when he freed me and took my hand. But that hand is blistering right now.

"Our love means you can't touch me anymore!" Heath says to the King defiantly. "It means I'm stronger than you'll ever be. It means this is my army now. My *City*!"

"Yours?" the Wizard King echoes, and spit flies into his beard. "Don't you mean *hers*?" He points a bony finger up at me, then smirks back at Heath. "You really think *you* have any power at all? Even your idiot father saw how worthless you were." The old man's eyes flash with glee. "Tell me, what did it feel like?" he taunts.

My connection with Heath must still be strong, because at the mention of The One, I feel the hurt blooming huge and raw inside me—a small echo of what Heath is feeling. *His father always hated him. The One couldn't love.*

I squeeze Heath's arm supportively, and even through the leather jacket, I can feel him trembling. His sanity is stretched like a rubber band, his anger winding tighter and tighter, ready to snap.

"Enough!" I warn.

But the Wizard King won't let it rest. "What's it like to be such a sad, weak little nothing that The One Who Is The One chose some City witch over you, his own son?"

That does it. Heath lets out an enraged scream and leaps at his grandfather, seizing the old man's head with two hands. Crushing the temples, trembling with the pressure he's driving through the King's skull.

I've seen this before. I know what's coming next. And it terrifies me, for more than one reason.

A scream escapes uncontrollably from my lips as it begins: the disintegration of the Wizard King's face. The peeling away of the tissue.

And…it melts.

Right. Off.

The wrinkled skin with its greasy face paint oozes into a puddle. I stare at the Wizard King's empty, unblinking eyes. At the raw muscle, red and stringy over his cheeks.

At his fleshless mouth, frozen into a perfect round O—a shocked, final gasp.

The King is dead.

Heath shakes the gruesome remains off his hand in disgust, and when one of the prowling leopards laps at his fingers, he *smiles*.

"Is it—*you* . . . ?" I blurt out, because I still can't form coherent thoughts.

Heath looks up from the wild cat, finally noticing that, along with the thousands of other people gathered here, I'm gaping at him in openmouthed shock.

There's only one person I know of who can melt the face off a skull.

Heath shrugs sheepishly and looks at me from under his eyelashes—like a guilty little kid who really isn't feeling very sorry.

And then Heath, as I knew him, starts to disappear.

Chapter 78

Wisty

IT HAPPENS IN SECONDS, but it feels like an eternity.

Heath's dark mop of wild hair gives way to a slick white-blond helmet. His mesmerizing turquoise eyes pale to a flat, icy stare. And his kissable lips melt into a nasty pout.

No no no no no. My mind hums with Whit's doubts and Byron's protests, all the warnings I ignored and resented: *Heath's New Order,* they said. *He's up to something. He's bad news. Why aren't you listening? Just listen to us, Wisty, LISTEN!*

I didn't want to listen. I refused to see. But when I open my eyes now, the stark truth stands there before me.

The last of the boy I once loved has faded away, and all that's left is a two-faced, double-crossing double agent.

"*Pearce.*" The word tastes sour in my mouth.

"That would be me," answers the villain in the black leather jacket that's now way too big.

Heath said I'd change my mind about him. *Oh, have I ever.*

On either side of me, thousands of people holding weapons wait for the signal to kill each other. I don't see them anymore, though—my world has shrunk to a small, surreal bubble.

It's just me and a boy in the middle of a field. Having the worst conversation of my life.

"Congratulations. You fooled everyone." I shake my head bitterly. "And I'm the biggest fool of all."

"Don't say that." Pearce's forehead wrinkles with concern and his mouth purses. "I'm so sorry I had to deceive you, my little firecracker," he says, stepping toward me, arms outstretched.

My stomach churns into a sickened knot. "Never call me that again!" I snap as I scramble backward, away from those murderous hands.

"It took me a long time to get all the puzzle pieces in place," Pearce continues. "But it was the only way. We were *meant* to rule, you see. The prophecy says that a witch and a wizard..."

"Can never be together," I finish, remembering Izbella's warning on the Mountain. She was right about Heath and me. *She was right all along.*

"According to some stupid curse." Pearce laughs, and

his teeth look too white, too pointy, too merciless. "Together, we're the most powerful force in the Overworld! Who will fight us now?"

I narrow my eyes. There *is* no *us*, no matter how many times we've merged our power.

"*I'll* fight you, Pearce!" I scream, and hurl a fireball at his head.

Chapter 79

Wisty

PEARCE DUCKS AS the fiery tail of flame whizzes past his ear, but I'm already heating up even more, fueled with fury.

Now that the magicians are out of the chains, Whit's sprinting across the meadow while the rest of them are just trying to regain their strength. "He'll have to fight us both!" Whit calls out.

I can't let that happen. Pearce almost killed Whit once, and there's no way I'm letting this madman near my family again. Especially when this is all my fault.

Whit's legs suddenly lock up, midstride. "What are you *doing*?" he shouts. The veins in his forearms strain against my magic, and his face is purple with frustration. I've frozen him in place. "Wisty, let me go! We swore we'd stick together!"

I turn away from my brother. This is *my* fight, and I need to see it through.

"Don't you think you're overreacting a little?" Pearce asks, as smarmy as ever.

I gape at him. "Overreacting?"

With a flick of my wrist, I send another explosion careening toward him. It just misses his feet, but the impact blasts a huge crater into the hillside.

Pearce stumbles backward, the mud sucking at his boots.

"You kidnapped little kids! You committed crimes under the N.O. that I don't even want to think about. You put my parents in the ghetto, and you locked me up in a cell! *Overreacting?*" I repeat, my voice quivering. "No, I don't think so!"

Pearce grins, giving me that secret look Heath used to give me—like my rage actually *turns him on*.

I want to puke.

"Don't you see, Wisty?" Pearce says. "You broke through all that *because* of our connection. When I saw that candle flame, I knew for sure."

"Knew what?" I ask.

"That you loved me. You couldn't resist the power that is our love. And yes—love sometimes has a somewhat nasty, enraged side. But it's still *power*. It's still *love*."

So the chains, the prisons, the war…it was all some sort of test?

"Remember this?" A flower grows up out of the palm of Pearce's hand. It's the beautiful Mountain flower Heath gave me when we first met—when I actually thought the danger was sexy. Pearce holds it out to me like a peace offering.

I scowl. The petals start to smoke, and the stem turns to ash. I'm done with peace.

Pearce pouts in mock offense, and a field of those evil flowers sprouts up around me. They lash around my ankles and ugly red welts bloom on my skin from their toxic petals. They sting like a hundred hives of wasps.

I flame out to get the suckers off me and burn up half the hillside.

"Romantic," I say dryly. "Almost as romantic as the mass genocide you had planned for today."

Pearce lets out a groan of frustration.

"We're *better* than they are! Don't you see that?" He arcs his arm over the field. "They're vermin. But our passion, our *power* can make them an army larger than any our world has ever known. A blank slate on which to build our empire."

I gaze out over the thousands of slaves, their lips upturned slightly, their brains turned on a dimmer.

A Kingdom built on nothingness.

"You said you hated The One Who Is The One." I shake my head in disgust. "But you sound just like your father."

He's so fast I don't see his blow coming. It's not lethal, or even magic—just pure cruelty. A fist to my face. I writhe backward in pain, stunned by his savagery.

Pearce has been holding back, I realize. Our power

might be equal—mine might even be stronger—but against his sheer physical strength, I'm useless.

But I won't give up. I can't. I have to stop him. Even if it kills me.

A bolt of lightning cracks out of my hand like a whip, searing the earth inches from where Pearce stands.

A second later, pain shoots up my left forearm as Pearce snaps the bone. The agony is so intense I bite my tongue and taste the iron tang of blood.

"Why are you making me do this?" he asks, looking all sorry.

Like every other time he hurt me.

"Because you're a liar!" I yell, flinging sparks.

Something ruptures inside me, and suddenly I'm wheezing to get air.

"A murderer!" I rasp.

"Why can't you just say you'll be with me?" Pearce pleads.

I start to cough up blood.

"Because I. Don't. Love. You!"

A crushing strike flips me onto my back with a sickening crack. Pearce lands on top of me and pins my wrists to the ground. I look up at him dizzily.

"This was all for *you*!" Pearce shouts in my face. "For *us*."

He grabs me under the chin and shakes my head violently to make me look at him. His fingers are pressing into the hollows of my cheeks so hard I can already feel the bruises starting.

"Don't you get it?" he says softly. "You could be my queen."

He stops squeezing and traces his hand lightly down the side of my face. His tenderness is what makes me truly terrified for the first time, and my skin crawls, waiting for the burn to begin.

"Wisty!" I hear my brother's voice cracking with grief and terror. He knows where this is going as well as I do.

I squeeze my eyes shut tight. I refuse to watch Pearce's satisfied face in the moment of my death—I'll never give him that satisfaction.

But my face isn't melting. Instead, I feel his slimy lips, pressing against mine. My eyes fly open.

He's kissing me? Now?!

I spit in revulsion, and a stream of fire shoots out. I don't know if I've morphed into a dragon or I'm half dead or what, but in that moment, I'm so crazed with rage it doesn't matter.

"I will—*never*—be your *anything*!" I shriek into Pearce's burned face. "Not as long as I'm breathing."

"Your wish is my command," Pearce says, and slams the back of my head into the ground.

Just before I lose consciousness, I swear I see a bear running toward us.

Then everything goes dark.

Chapter 80

Wisty

THE ROAR OF the crowd is a painful vibration in my temples.

I have to get up.

My brother is fighting for me. My power had been so drained by fighting Pearce that I couldn't restrain Whit anymore. By now, he could be *dying* for me. And I'm just lying here sprawled on my back, with the wetness from the ground—a mix of icy puddles and blood—seeping through my clothes.

I roll over and rake my hands through the dead grass, pulling myself to my knees. My whole head feels bruised and swollen, too heavy on my neck, and I have to squint through the soldiers' legs to see across the field.

The world around me has gone mad, cheering and howling and rooting for their favorite wizard. It's like they've all become barbarians, lusting for blood.

My vision may still be blurry, but I can see Whit's in

trouble. He's midmorph—his head is a terrifying, roaring grizzly, but the rest of his body is human, and his chest and arms are a mess of bloody gashes, some of them scary deep.

He's losing power. He couldn't keep up the morph. *I have to help him*.

I must've been out for a long time for it to get this bad. And it's about to get worse. A giant snake—Pearce's true form, you could say—slithers after him, its hooded head lashing out.

Despite the searing cold of the Mountain winds, Whit's spraying sweat as he keeps dodging the venomous strikes. I can tell he's wearing out as he stumbles backward, and his growls are starting to sound more like wails.

Move, Wisty! I lurch to my feet, cradling my injured arm against my chest as I race across the field toward my brother.

"Together!" I remind him as the snake hisses, its ugly head swaying and darting toward its prey. "No matter what!"

Whit's face morphs back. His eyes show that he's exhausted, but they're glistening with love and gratitude. "No matter what," he echoes.

The second he grips my palm, I feel his healing energy flash through me. I stand up straighter on steadier legs, and our power starts to build.

Then all air suddenly leaves my lungs as my ribs crush inward. My organs feel like fruit pulp. The snake is wrapped around me and Whit, and it's squeezing the very life out of us!

But Whit's still squeezing my hand, and his magic starts sewing up my broken bones. I start hacking as air rushes into my lungs, and the sudden surge of our combined power flings the overgrown slug off us.

The snake's tail shrinks, its body thickens, and Pearce is standing there, glaring at us.

"Last chance, Wisty," he says. "You can still choose to be with me."

I shake my head. "No more chances. We end this now."

"Whatever you say." Then there's a cracking sound, and I cry out as he shatters my left kneecap. I narrow my eyes.

No more holding back. *It's on.*

Chapter 81

Wisty

THE MASSES AROUND us are yelling and heckling, shrieking and clapping. It's like it used to be at Whit's foolball games, only the stakes are much higher. Much. Higher.

"Slay the demon!"

"Avenge the King! The Allgoods must die!"

I'm quickly able to block it all out as we focus on taking Pearce down. Whit and I stalk Pearce across the frozen field, hitting him with a higher and higher voltage, shocking him again and again as the mobs scream on.

There's no fire raging wildly, no fancy smoke-and-mirrors morphing. Our magic is pure, united, and consistent, and because I can trust it, I know how to control it. My power joined with my brother is the opposite of what I felt with Heath.

The intoxication of that was nothing but illusion.

Pearce's face suddenly twists into a demonic rage—but not from pain, I don't think. It's more like he just heard

335

every word in my head. "A magician's life force is illusion!" he yells. "And love is an illusion, too, Wisty—isn't it?"

"Don't listen to him," Whit encourages me. "Focus."

Whit and I are holding strong, but Pearce isn't even down on the ground yet. Some of my old magic lingers in him, passionate and unpredictable, and it lashes out at us with scratches and gouges and ringing ears.

A sudden massive shower of razor-sharp icicles seems to come from nowhere and rakes us bloody. One almost takes out my eye.

"A disappointment," Pearce declares bitterly. "I'd hoped it would take out your heart."

This feels personal. As much as I hate the thought, I know that Pearce and I are connected. Every time we hit him with the voltage, I feel a zap of pain echoing in my heart and shuddering through my veins. I don't know if it's that shadow of our magic together or something else....

Love?

Whatever it is, it *hurts*.

"Wisty!" Whit says, catching me as I fall back. "You okay?" My brother sends waves of powerful healing energy through me and I nod gratefully.

But the next jolt we direct at Pearce's spine makes my back twist in agony.

"Just keep going. We can't stop," I cry, writhing. "Ah!"

"You *feel* it, don't you?" Pearce asks, smiling through a mouthful of blood.

"I don't feel anything," I say coldly, and send another shower of bolts slamming through him.

The surge makes his muscles turn to jelly. The next makes his whole body seize until I think he's going to start sparking.

"Time to get serious, Whit." He knows what I mean. We're now focusing all our energy right inside Pearce's brain.

His head flies backward.

His teeth rattle.

His arms shoot out in protest. It's then that I start to cry.

We fling him across the field. We zap him so hard the trees around him catch fire.

And with each blow, my tears fall more freely.

We finally drive him to his knees. There is so much power flowing through him now, the current holds him up straight as a board. His eyes roll back into his head.

One more volt of our magic is all it would take.

The crowd is in a frenzy, banging weapons together and pushing closer.

I look down at the boy I once loved. *The snake*, I remind myself. *The murderer*. He's still dressed like Heath, though— the black leather jacket and the motorcycle boots. Only now they're covered in dirt and blood.

Something in me shatters. I don't know if I can do this.

Even in this weakened state, Pearce seems to read my hesitation. "Do it," he chokes as foam bubbles around his lips.

I know he's right. If it doesn't end now, it'll never end.

"Finish it!" Pearce commands, gritting his teeth.

I raise my arms overhead.

Go! I think.

But just as I'm about to squeeze Whit's hand, a voice rings out over the field: "Enough!"

A woman rides forward from the Mountain People on a white horse, her feathered cloak rustling in the breeze.

It's Izbella.

Chapter 82

Whit

"*PLEASE!*" IZBELLA SHOUTS as she climbs off the horse. "Spare him!"

I glance at my sister, and though we don't release Pearce completely, we stop the surge just before it explodes into his brain.

The effort that takes is incredible.

I'm shaking violently, and my hands are balled into fists. My stomach aches from the stress of holding the magic in, like it's an actual mass in there, growing larger and pushing against my insides.

"Just kill me," Pearce demands. "I don't want to live without her."

It almost impresses me. Maybe even *moves* me, just a little. He's not whining, or crying, or begging. It's like the last shreds of energy he has left in his being are all channeled into making this one certain declaration about my sister.

339

His last word on the battlefield is "her."

Wisty winces like she's been hit, and her shoulders slump inward. Still, she raises her arms up higher, her eyes determined.

"*Don't!*" Izbella screeches. She lunges forward, clawing at us, and we instinctively push back. The surge is stronger than we expect, though, and sends her reeling backward more than twenty feet into an icy puddle of mud.

Wisty's arms are striped with raised welts, and a scratch on my face is dripping blood, but it's impossible not to feel guilty looking at the wailing woman rocking on her knees, folding into herself.

My throat is dry, and I can feel my own parents' eyes following us. *How did it come to this?*

"As a mother, I'm begging you," she cries. "Have mercy."

Mercy.

I clench my teeth at that word, thinking about all the people Pearce has killed, all the sympathy he's lacked. I hold my power strong.

"Can't we work for peace?" Izbella searches our faces despairingly.

"That's a joke," Wisty scoffs. "How can there ever be peace when there are men like your son in the world? Men like The One? Like the Wizard King?"

"Yes." Izbella narrows her eyes. "It's a dangerous madness that overtakes the powerful. I'm sure you, of all people, would agree."

"I'm not a murderer," Wisty spits. Though her face looks full of fury, I can hear the hurt in her voice.

"Neither am I. The King is dead. I am the Mountain Witch and these are my people." She gestures behind her. "From this day forward, the threats will end, the water will flow, and we will walk away from this war. I swear it on my son's life."

"What about the lives of all the other children? The ones he helped abduct?"

Izbella closes her eyes and sighs softly, and the child soldiers lower their weapons, one by one. They blink with confusion as she releases them from her control. When Pearl looks up at me with understanding and devastation and shame on her face, I can barely hold myself together.

"The children are free to go."

Except for all the ones who didn't make it. Except for the ones they left to freeze in the yard, or killed without mercy.

Mercy.

But that's the difference between us and Pearce, isn't it? We couldn't stomach watching people die.

"This isn't right," I say suddenly, turning to my sister. "We can't do this."

Wisty bites her bottom lip. "But... he tried to enslave the whole City! What if he comes back even more powerful and more dangerous next time?" The tears well in her eyes and she looks down, ashamed. "I fell for all his lies once...."

I smile sadly at my sister. "I hear you. He's sick and wrong and utterly psychopathic. But..." I swallow before I let these strange words tumble out of my mouth. "I never thought I'd say this, Wist, but the way he looked at you on that battlefield, I saw a shadow of something else there. Something like the way I used to look at Celia. Something like what I feel now when I'm with Janine. And if, somewhere in Pearce's twisted mind, he did all this because he cares about you...that makes him human. Not like The One. And that's *something*, right?"

"Yeah." Wisty takes a deep breath and nods. "I guess it's something."

I squeeze her hand one more time, and then we both let go.

Chapter 83

Whit

PEARCE, RIGIDLY SEIZING with our power just moments ago, looks boneless as he collapses in an unconscious heap. Curled up like that, he really does just look like a helpless little kid, and I know immediately that we did the right thing.

An hour ago, thousands of soldiers were preparing for a bloodbath. Now, two armies look on as a mother gathers up her son's limp body with incredible tenderness, and as she struggles to her feet with his long limbs dangling from her arms, and plods slowly toward the Mountain.

Just before she reaches the edge of the forest, Izbella turns. "Remember, Allgoods," she warns. "There is nothing more dangerous than the combined magic of a witch and a wizard. Be careful how you use it."

As she vanishes with Pearce through the trees and the mist, I turn to my sister with shining eyes. "Looks like you kept your promise, Wist." She looks at me questioningly,

343

and I hand her the broken, ashy drumstick. "We all survived."

I'm pretty sure everyone is just happy with that at this point—we're a grubby mess of tears and sappy, swaying hugs, and a few overjoyed survivors are even kissing the scraggly patches of brown grass.

But without the protection of their King or Queen, the Mountain men look across the field at us in sudden terror, and waste no time hightailing their horses toward the hills. Even Larsht gallops away, a white flag of surrender flying in his meaty hand.

I watch that flag, waving its way up the path, and suddenly, it bursts into flames.

My troublemaking sister's at it again.

Larsht curses and drops the roaring fabric, but seeing the fire, his horse pulls its lips back from its teeth, flares its nostrils, and rears. Larsht falls to the side and grips the mane as the bucking animal drags him along. When he finally gets control, Larsht looks back for a long, resentful glare out of that intimidating glass eye of his.

Wisty's giggling hysterically by now.

"Back to the good?" I ask, raising a mildly disapproving eyebrow.

She shrugs and rolls her eyes. "A witch has gotta have *some* fun, right?"

EPILOGUE

DESTINY'S REWARD

Chapter 84

Whit

I'M RUNNING THROUGH the City, winding down alley-ways and sprinting across intersections, my feet pounding along the cobblestones.

It's not like other times I've run through these streets, though. I'm not being chased by soldiers or wolves; I'm not trying frantically to escape or save anyone's life.

I'm not afraid.

"Come on!" I call out to Pearl Neederman, barely slow-ing as I pass her house. "We're going to be late!"

"Speak for yourself, Wizard," Pearl scoffs. She shoots past me in her new sneakers. "Try to keep up!"

I shake my head and smile, happy to see this sarcastic little pipsqueak is back to normal. "See you in the square!" I call after her.

The streets look different, too. We're fixing up the houses and picking up the garbage. People are outside, walking their dogs and helping their neighbors. Underneath all the old red banners and the smog and the ash and the rubble, this really is a beautiful place.

We still have one more thing to wrap up to put the past behind us, though—one final piece of unfinished business.

"Citizens, it's time to decide: what should we do about Mr. Bloom?"

When I hear the echo of Janine's voice as I turn the corner to enter the city square, I feel a quick shiver of admiration. She has no idea how sexy her confidence is, and I think the crooked scar running down her neck just makes her more beautiful.

The square's packed, like always, and even more people are trickling in behind me. They sit on benches or stoops to watch the proceedings, and when there's no more room, they stand. They want to be a part of this.

And they can.

That's why we're holding the Council meetings in the square now. So while the Council members sit on the marble steps to debate, anyone can come, and every single citizen owns a copy of *The Book of Truths*.

Janine's running the meeting today, and she's a natural at it, but someone else will be in charge tomorrow, and there'll be a whole new Council next month.

No more secrets. No more lies. Power to the people.

Only kids can vote at the meeting, though. Adults can give their input, but let's face it—when they try to lead, their big, fat egos get in the way.

"I am an elected official!" Bloom glares around him

from the center of the square, where he's standing next to the fountain. His toupee is all askew, and now he's the one in handcuffs. "Do you know who you're dealing with?"

Case in point.

"Unfortunately for you, Mr. Bloom, we know exactly who we're dealing with." Janine stares at Bloom coldly from the steps above. "The collected citizens have found you guilty of hijacking the Council, imprisoning innocent people, and dragging the City into a war it had no chance of winning."

"I was merely trying to do what was best for the citizens," Bloom protests stubbornly. "They chose me to lead!"

The crowd doesn't like this at all, and starts to push in.

"You tried to lead us to our deaths!" someone shouts.

"You manipulated us!"

"You acted like a power-hungry sociopath, and your stupid wig isn't fooling anyone!" Wisty chimes in, grinning at Bloom from the sidelines.

Seeing my sister in the middle of this hostile group, Bloom's face blanches. "Please," he sputters, wringing his chained hands. "Please don't kill me."

"Don't worry, General—you'll live," Janine announces, and the square quiets down. "Believe it or not, we actually want you to be happy."

"And we know how much you like bossing people around!" a little girl on the Council adds.

"Since you're a natural leader," Janine continues, "we

thought it would be fitting if you were given your own personal Council to rule as you see fit."

The monkeys pour through the doors of the old Capitol building. They scurry down the marble steps, shrieking, and race toward Bloom en masse.

"This isn't funny!" he bellows as they leap at him, crawling up his legs and hanging from his arms. As he dances around, trying to shake them off, the square erupts in laughter, and Bloom's face reddens. "There isn't anything funny about this, I said! I'm a decorated general!"

"Your new soldiers await your every command," Janine agrees, trying to hide her smile as a monkey snatches Bloom's toupee. "And don't worry. They'll be accompanying you to your new home in the desert."

That's our cue. I push through the crowd, and Wisty and I link arms.

"I'm being *exiled*?" Bloom says angrily.

"Oh, I hear the desert's not so bad," I say, squeezing my sister's hand. "If you don't worry too much about the Lizard People and the giant scorpions..."

Wisty and I unite our power and Bloom and his monkeys start to spin. Faster and faster. A blur of fur and shrieks, until they're sucked right into the vortex. "Hey— this really isn't funny...."

Bloom's voice echoes until there's nothing left in the middle of the square but a rusty pair of handcuffs.

Chapter 85

Wisty

THE WHOLE COMMUNITY is here, gathered at the foot of the Mountain, and something incredible is happening: the water is flowing again.

As we watch the white-blue line trickle down between the rocks, I know I'm not the only one holding my breath. It means life for so many families, and when it finally gushes over the cliff in a waterfall, every one of us cheers.

I swear, it's the most beautiful thing I've ever seen, and the challenges ahead of us feel a bit more surmountable.

I know it wasn't that long ago that we were celebrating in the square after The One's fall, and I get that it's not all fireworks this time—that we have to rebuild things like wells, and portals...and trust.

But watching the kids splashing in the collecting pool and families filling jugs of fresh Mountain water, it's impossible not to feel dizzy with simple gratitude: today's a day for celebrating what we have.

So why, in the shadow of that Mountain, am I standing away from my friends and family, still so painfully aware of what's missing?

A certain sly smile; a certain intense look; a certain spark lighting up my whole being.

Now, just a blank space.

He's alive, I know it. I can feel him. The connection lingers like a phantom limb, surprising me with a flutter in my stomach, or a tingle in my fingers.

The anger's stronger than that, though. It's *fury*, every time I think of his betrayal. More than anything, I wish I could erase the memory of him altogether.

Instead, the Mountain looming above is a constant reminder. I can't help tracing the steep slope with my eyes—to the white-tipped peak, where the fog swirls. I can almost feel the cold up there, reaching for me with its icy fingers, and I hug myself, shivering.

Someone drapes a wool jacket around my shoulders.

"You looked a little chilly," Byron explains, and carefully adjusts the collar up around my chin. Of course. Only Byron Swain would wear a full suit to a picnic in a field.

I blink at him, surprised by the simple kindness, though I guess I shouldn't be. I treated him so badly, and here he is giving me his coat. Who else would do that for me? *Certainly not Heath . . .*

"Thank you," I say, and burst into tears.

"Hey, there. No need to cry." He rubs my back somewhat awkwardly. "If my face offends you that much, you can always turn me into a rodent. I don't even mind that much anymore, really. I'm happy to run around in a hamster wheel if it'll cheer you up."

I snort with laughter and wipe my eyes. "Really, Byron? You'd do that for me?"

"You know I'd do anything for you, Wisty," Byron says a little too solemnly.

"Anything?" I challenge with a smirk.

He grins and reconsiders. "Well, maybe I wouldn't melt off my grandfather's face," he answers, nudging me playfully. "But then again, I'm not that close to my grandpa, so if you promised me a kiss, maybe..."

I shake my head, but I can't help but smile. The hurt is raw right now, but I know it'll get easier, and this stupid heart will stop short-circuiting.

"You're a great friend, Byron, you know that?"

"Just a friend?" he asks, wiggling his eyebrows comically.

"You never give up, do you?"

"How could I?" Byron shrugs. "What can I say? You definitely make an impression, Wisty Allgood."

Chapter 86

Wisty

"MISSUS FIRE WITCH?"

The tiny girl beaming up at me is one of the kids we saved from the van—*Bettina Alexandra Gannon*. She was right: I didn't forget her.

"What's up, munchkin?"

"Well…" Bettina twists her pink dress in her hands. "Since you're the most famous person I ever met and you saved me and my friends and the whole world, can you make me a souvenir?" She says all this in one excited breath that grows in volume until she's shouting in my face.

I grin. "Sure. I guess I could do that."

"Thankyouthankyouthankyou!" Bettina squeaks.

Thing is, I have no idea what to give her. What does a famous witch known for her firepower get a kid? Matches?

I hide a smirk. *I'm sure her parents would love me for that.*

"Bettina!" her mom calls, as if reading my mind. "It's time to go home—it's getting dark."

"Just a minute, Mom!" Bettina looks at me expectantly.

Bettina's mother isn't the only one concerned with the twilight, I notice. Families are packing up food and hurrying their kids out of the pool. I wish I could give them back their innocence; I wish they didn't have to be afraid. But even though the City feels safe again, we don't always know what can happen after dark.

I feel a tug on my pant leg. Bettina's still looking at me expectantly, waiting for her souvenir.

I crouch down so I'm at eye level with her. "Okay, what kind of stuff do you like?" I ask.

"I like magic!" She beams. "And dancing! And sparkles!"

Something sparkly. Hmm.

The first star of evening catches my eye, twinkling brightly. It reminds me of Pearl's chandelier, and how the colors shimmered in the Needermans' dim basement. With broken, discarded glass, Pearl gave us hope.

Everyone should have a light like that.

"Ready?" I raise an eyebrow at Bettina.

She nods eagerly, and I concentrate on the darkening sky. That hum of energy that I know so well—the thrilling heat—starts to make me flush. I swallow hard.

You can do this.

The truth is, I've been avoiding this feeling since my battle with Pearce. Whit and I used magic at Bloom's trial, but not fire. The memories of Heath are still raw, and the

355

thought of that warmth felt so negative, so destructive, I wasn't sure I could ever face it again.

But this feels different—not tainted by lies or vengeance. It feels *good*.

I can't protect this City from everything—I realize that now. But this is something that I *can* do. A gift, not just for Bettina, but for all the City's children.

The power builds slowly, a low, simmering burn that moves up from my toes and through my veins. I take a deep, shaky breath, clenching and unclenching my fingers, making sure I'm in control.

I let all my hopes for these kids, all my pride from the incredible things we've accomplished, all my joy, all my love, swell inside me. That energy makes me shudder with its force; it's as strong as anything I had with Heath.

Stronger.

When I can't hold it in anymore, I fling my fingers out and release a massive fireball. It blazes into the sky and settles above us, an awesome sphere of color and light, glittering like a second sun for all the children of the City.

It's for anyone who needs a blast of color on a gray day, too, and for others lost in darkness who need to find their way home. And it's a reminder that things are going to be all right—for all of us.

Bettina claps her hands joyfully as she looks at the sky, and I spot Pearl and the other Needermans across the open field, gazing up, too. There's Mrs. Highsmith and my parents, a few other magicians, and an old former

Councilman, all of their eyes shining. More and more people stop to look.

It took the trauma of war to make our community strong again, to trust one another, but here we are. Young and old, from the suburbs or the Gutter, all the citizens are smiling under the same sky, faces illuminated by my gift.

"Not bad." Whit steps from behind me, arms crossed over his chest.

I turn to him, screwing up my face. "Not bad?"

"Yeah, yeah." Whit breaks into a smile and drapes his arm around my neck, hugging me to him as we walk across the meadow to join our family. "It's pretty much perfect."

OUT NOW IN PAPERBACK

ANGEL
A MAXIMUM RIDE NOVEL

James Patterson

**HOW DO YOU SAVE EVERYTHING AND
EVERYONE YOU LOVE . . .**

Max Ride and her best friends have always had one another's
backs. No matter what. Living on the edge as fugitives, they never
had a choice. But now they're up against a mysterious and deadly
force that's racing across the globe – and just when they need one
another the most, Fang is gone. He's creating his own gang that
will replace everyone – including Max.

WHEN YOU CAN'T BE TOGETHER . . .

Max is heartbroken over losing Fang, her soulmate, her closest
friend. But with Dylan ready and willing to fight by her side, she can
no longer deny that his incredible intensity draws her in.

BUT YOU CAN'T STAY APART?

Max, Dylan, and the rest of their friends must soon join with Fang
and his new gang for an explosive showdown in Paris. It's unlike
anything you've ever imagined . . . or read.

JAMES
PATTERSON

**To find out more about James Patterson
and his bestselling books, go to
www.jamespatterson.co.uk**